THE

BLUE

TO CINDY & BRIAN —
GREAT FRIENDS, NEIGHBORS &
COMPATRIOTS IN THE APTOS HILLS.
ALWAYS GREAT TO HANG WITH YOU,
TALK STORY, AND GET DOWNRIGHT
PHILSOPHICAL!

BEST ALWAYS

Webig Sun
aka
Wm Sut 9/1/14

THE
BLUE

William Sun

River Sanctuary
PUBLISHING

Cover image by Alana Zussman

Author photo by Ray Madrigal

ISBN 978-1-935914-31-0

Printed in the United States of America

Additional copies are available from:

www.riversanctuarypublishing.com

"Love is All Around," written by Reg Presley.
Universal Songs of Polygram International Inc.
Permission applied for.

"Blue Jack of Diamonds," written by Jeffrey A. Boyan.
Phillips Records, 1968 (on the album *H.P. Lovecraft II*).
Permission applied for.

RIVER SANCTUARY PUBLISHING
P.O Box 1561
Felton, CA 95018
www.riversanctuarypublishing.com
Dedicated to the awakening of the New Earth

Acknowledgements

Though its conception was a glimpse of a cove on a remote Greek island, the actual writing of this book was born before the end of the 20th century at the final incarnation of The Santa Cruz Writer's Workshop in Happy Valley, California. I owe this birth to a short-story writing prompt from my friend James D. (Jim) Houston. May he be at peace in the bosom of his beloved Pacific Basin.

The flavor of Greek culture throughout the story was enriched and authenticated by Zafiri Souyoultzis, a native of Lesbos, and one of the most big-hearted individuals to grace the planet. May his *joie de vivre* spread to the multitudes.

I'm indebted to Lezanne Jeffs for her positivity and encouragement. Heartfelt thanks go to the tough-love critiques of Mark Dahlby and my near centenarian mother-in-law, Dr. Shirley Zussman. May they be unattached to how I have chosen to apply their suggestions.

Katherine Ziegler is to be commended for her skilled guidance via "soul collage" which imparted a welcome dose of cosmic wisdom to the choice of the climax. David Carr also left his indelible brushstroke on the zeitgeist inhabiting the spaces between letters and lines. May they both be blessed for their profound generosity.

Key advice regarding character descriptions was gracefully contributed by my nomadic daughter Christy who also sketched out the preliminary cover design. May her heart's desires be realized.

This labor of love was greatly enhanced by the meticulous editing of poet Dyana Basist whose gentle but firm insistence on more conscious development of key elements and characters was the catalyst for a more illumined manuscript. May her talents be appreciated by an ever-widening circle.

My deep and permanent gratitude extends to Leonard Jacobson for instilling in me the ability to access and awaken into the state of presence—however fleetingly. May his teaching continue to inspire countless souls.

Most importantly, my wife Carol deserves the highest praise for enduring an extended writing season which resulted in the following pages—an epic effort of nearly fourteen years. At times the process intruded pesteringly into our leisure and family time. The psychic underpinnings of the story were poignantly enhanced by her expert, no-nonsense, psychological counsel. May she be forgiving of my indulgence.

W.S. March 30, 2013

For all Children of *The Blue*

Prologue

Another World

Sheryl Jansen has no idea how long she's been underwater. In truth, the "she" she knows herself to be dwells suspended in a state beyond ideas. Beyond dreams. Beyond any semblance of normalcy.

Her refuge is Indigo Lake, a half-mile-long by two-hundred-foot-wide, kidney-shaped, spring-fed body of water in south-central Florida, privately co-owned by a group of twelve fortunate families. The neighbors have all gotten used to this tan, gangly girl frolicking in the lake so constantly it has begun to seem incomplete without her in it. Sheryl, a classic, shoulder-length brunette, is out in the sun and water so much her long locks have become nearly blonde.

On this radiant June afternoon, Sheryl has bee-lined to her liquid haven after going through the motions of Junior High graduation. Mother's parting words still throb in her ears.

"Sheryl hon, you gotta work harder. Your grades are lagging. We had a deal. Mr. Jacobs says you seem to have lost interest in the violin…God knows those lessons cost…And this fascination with Aye-key-doe…or whatever they call that durn contortionism…That hogwash won't earn you any points with college admissions. I'm tryin' but I can't fathom why you're not on the train to Harvard. You can be a lawyer. God knows we need to counteract the way they're ruinin' the 'Glades. Hell, the whole damn region."

Some could call it grace or some destiny, but as Sheryl pretends she's a member of the school of small silver fish dancing among the emerald-colored plant life, her immediate underwater world floods into the depths of her. Saturates her very spirit. Dissolves it. Diffuses it. Into the water. Into the plants, the fish, the sand bottom, the light shafts, the specter of sky above.

Without noticing, Sheryl has become not just another fish in the school, but the lake that contains them. And the sky above the lake. And the shafts of sun penetrating the lake. And the lucid hues of the underwater plants. It's as if Sheryl's essence is infinite. Yet her body continues to swim along the bottom, its movements little more than a reflex.

When Sheryl "comes to" she's unaware that she has stayed underwater many more earth seconds than would have been humanly possible had she simply held her breath.

"Holy Moses!" she yells upon breaking the surface—an expression genetically inherited from her father Sam Jansen, rising star in the U.S. Department of State.

"What was that?"

Sheryl pats herself all over to make sure she's alive. She spots her house at the far end of the lake perched normally adjacent to the Thompson's as if nothing significant has happened. The sight of it ought to be comforting. But Sheryl is affected and afflicted by an ominous impression that she has passed through some sort of gate which only swings one way.

1

Andre's Swim

Though he does not know the place summoned him, as far as Andre knows, he has found one hell of a paradise. A narrow lip of coarse amber beach kissing the sea. A seductive drop-off into a blue so beckoning Andre is almost giddy as he swims over it. Suspended above the abyss like an old ship with new sails, the pressures of his life are akin to weak barnacles detaching from his underbelly and dissolving on the unseen bottom.

Kapetan Yanni's is about as far from a destination resort as it is possible to get without a guide. Nine rustic bungalows embedded above a cove at the foot of volcanic cliffs in the sheltered lee of the Cycladic winds. The same legendary winds that buoyed the sails of Jason and the Argonauts. Winds born of the clockwise turning of currents in the Atlantic, sucked past the fabled lips of Gibraltar, across the larynx of Italy and pulled yet further east into the open throat that is the Aegean Sea.

As often as not, Mother Africa hurls her own desert-crazed breath north- ward. Occasional breezes from the Baltics, sprinkled with the faint scent of northern fjords, induce locals and visitors alike to re-imagine their futures. Enchanted winds all, meant in some divine poet's dream to soothe the inflamed, rock-studded lung that is the Greek Isles.

After knifing through the calm, crystalline waters of the welcoming cove, lean and fair-haired Andre freestyles assuredly out to open sea where sev- eral winds have converged to stir up erratic whitecaps.

Andre smiles into the salt water remembering his host, Kapetan Yanni, warning all his guests with great solemnity at dinner: "Bad currents. Waves push you against rocks."

But Andre relishes this zone of danger on the outer edge of heaven. In fact, he needs it.

In San Francisco, his current project has managed to sap his life force. He had tracked down a rare pre-Columbian jade statuette of a quetzal in a village in Nicaragua. Got it through customs as a common tourist knick-knack. Then he designed a gorgeous gallery in his clients' home to display it as a centerpiece along with some other treasures they had collected, only to have them reject his detailed rendering.

The couple could never verbalize what they wanted—but they knew that what he proposed isn't it. Even before he proposed it. He talks himself into knowing it will work out though. It always does. But the process is grating.

"You gotta have a doctorate in psychology in this business," he remembers mumbling to himself for the hundredth time.

Weeks ago Andre saw this coming and casually suggested another solution. He cunningly and parenthetically crammed a simple, elegant idea into an unrelated issue about wall finishes. He knew his rendering—any rendering—would be rejected by this self-absorbed couple. So he pirated a design from one of his other projects as an opening salvo so as not to burn up his time.

He suggested a two-week period to let the air clear, knowing full well they will come up with the idea he casually suggested earlier as their own. He'll praise their brilliance and humbly produce it for them. In fact, he's eighty percent there. Despite his positivity, the angst of knowing it could all backfire—the psychological warfare of it—does raise his stress level. And Kapetan Yanni's cove nearly half way across the globe is the perfect equalizer.

Frequent travels to evaluate and collect these art treasures afford Andre the chance to exert himself in watery nature—his ultimate antidote to stress— and these "timeouts" from the workaday world double the beneficial effect.

He senses it is nearing 8:15 and wants to complete his morning exercise and shower before breakfast at nine. He swims rhythmically, grateful for each buoyant breath in this edgy environment.

A beyond-blue world shimmers below him incited by slanting shafts of morning sun. All traces of the sand-and-rock bottom have disappeared. He's well beyond the cove, paralleling the shear cliff forty yards off. Each morning he's pushed a bit further into the rough water.

At a half mile from Kapetan Yanni's beach, a twinge of hunger begins to turn Andre in a wide circle back toward the cove. He closes his eyes to feel the bearing of the turn. Three hard strokes into this private space, he smashes like a slow bullet into a hard, smooth object. The impact causes a shooting pain in his right shoulder.

A submerged rock? Shark or dolphin, perhaps a tuna? I've seen them in the markets...

"Ahuh, ahuh. " It is a coughing, a gasping for air. And it is not him.

He winces at the sight of the recoiling body of a brown-haired woman, dizzy from the collision. Andre moves toward her cautiously lest she grab his arms and they both drown.

"Ahuh...Ach." She spasms trying to exhume the water from her lungs. He knows they are in trouble if she swallows any more Mediterranean. The swells are crested with white caps and looming at close intervals.

"I've got you, I've got you!" Andre eases his right arm under her neck. "I've got you." Supporting her back with his left hand, he ignores the stinger in his shoulder. He notices she is muscular, though not bulky. Rather dolphin-like. From the side, he concludes she is alluring. In a rugged sort of way.

The little voice in his head laughs its vengeful laugh, then speaks. *Damn it! Sorry pal!* It mocks him.

The voice calls forth that familiar, sad pattern which has come to define Andre: a long-scheduled trip to some warm hideaway with a few good books, a bathing suit, his work-induced exhaustion, and little else. Andre's only intention is to unwind and blend like a chameleon into the background.

But he never does. His search for the *Beloved Other*—his counterpart—takes him over, displacing his plan for anonymity.

Inevitably, some intriguing female rivets his eye, becoming the object of his vacation. He hopes he might meet her by chance somewhere on the grounds or in the street. In some uncontrived fashion. But this never quite happens. It's as if he's constructed a bubble around him which is impenetrable from either side. If the opportunity were to arise, he knows he'd be too intimidated to approach her. Something almost genetic in him dictates that he avoid coming on to her. Dictates it religiously.

While images of this tired pattern distract him, the real woman seems to erupt out of her trauma, breaks his grasp, twists around and viciously karate-chops him on the temple, then the base of the neck. With machine-like precision, she repeats the assault with her other hand.

Instinctively he releases his hold. The blows are skilled and vicious. Disabling. Andre is unaware of taking a reflex-induced, sharp, deep breath before his vision shuts down and his body goes limp beneath the vibrant Mediterranean.

2

Sheryl's Swim

Sheryl is swimming as hard as she has ever swum in her life.

She can't stop the tape of this morning's earlier events from replaying in her mind. Repeatedly. Cruelly. Complete with scratchy, grating soundtrack. The gut-churning argument with Kostas, her Greek boyfriend. The panicked knowing, the way only women know—that deep-in-an-empty-crevice-of-the-heart knowing—that his "business" deal in Athens is a ruse for a rendezvous. With whom she does not know. Nor would he say. Nor give her the courtesy—the twisted mercy—of the truth. She who's caged for three more days on a tiny Greek island in his villa. Hating him, hating her connection to him.

So she does what she does best: explode. Then continue to explode. As much at him as at her own naiveté. How could she fall for a Greek? She should've studied the culture. She should've had him checked out. But his charm was magnetic. His accent elegantly sexy. His social skills, polished. She swears if he were here, she would take him. She knows she could. She would karate-punch him silly until he agreed to...what? Be devoted only to her? Reserve his passion only for her. God! It all sounds so schmaltzy. So unhip. So un-evolved. So unrealistic.

Her chest, her very soul, burns from the mistake of her love. She needs to run with this heat, out of his villa, to beat at the cool sea. Needs to swim until she feels nothing but salty fluid scraping her skin. Needs to counteract the sting inflicted on her very soul. Needs to breathe hard—a lover's rhythm...needs to let the sea—and its tough love—have her...all the way to Italy if necessary...the sea is a safe lover...a lover that is her equal...a lover that...

"Stop it!" screams her inner voice, "Don't let yourself slip into the vastness. Shut your eyes and keep them shut. Don't look at the blue. It will capture you. Stay strong. Stay angry. Stay strong. Stay angr..."

Wham! Sheryl is nearly jolted out of her own body…by him…the bastard himself…Kostas, the cheater. His very name makes her gag. He's found her. Who else would resort to knock-out violence? His jealous, possessive spirit hunts her, hits her, wants to choke her…but the ocean is *her* turf. Here she has cunning. Can feign injury…calculate…steady…

Now!…Go!…Squirm out…twist around…counterattack…aim for the black-out meridian…avenge your honor…make him hurt like you hurt and…charge him…and…hit…hit…and…hit…hit.

Sheryl surfaces onto the turbulent ocean to glimpse the object of her rage floating inert on the choppy sea. The erratic current is carrying him away from her. His head is down. All she can see are his snow-white trunks. Assuming he's playing possum with intent to assault, she draws a breath and drops underwater to scout him. Combat him.

Instead she is shocked from her fury when she sees a limp, defeated form begin to sink, leaving a delicate bubble trail in its wake. From its *blonde* head.

3

Sheryl and blue-Sheryl

Jesus, what is this...Holy Christ! Kostas is not blond! She has...she is... killing this...other...guy. His white trunks are a beacon visible in the blue backdrop a scant four feet below. She is sending some innocent man to the bottom—by mistake.

Instinctively she plunges after him. Below into the noiseless, welcoming void. So much less awkward than above in the wind chop. It's pure harmony down here. Now seven feet down, angling beneath the limp man, Sheryl nestles a shoulder against his midsection and pushes upwards, bending her legs only at the knees and kick-thrusting—on that edge of exertion where near violence meets grace. Oddly, this moment is the most lucid she's experienced in the two hours since the phone call.

She intuits this refulgent moment as a celestial cue, ceases her resistance, and lapses into a *blue-Sheryl* experience. A state she's had no choice but to name. Because it's extraordinary. And frightening. Her and not her, both at once. She's named it "blue-Sheryl" because the blue of sky and water fully infuses her with its quintessence.

The hue below the surface is beyond astonishing. Intense sunlight refracts through the prismatic water and plays off the unseen bottom. This submerged arena is so all-embracing, there is no separation between her and the light that suspends her.

No thoughts to think. Her rhythmic kicking and the exquisite rush of sunlit blue are the entire universe. All going on around her. And inside her. So intimate with them that she disappears from her own mind and enters—becomes really—something much more vast. Much more alive. Yet much more haunting.

Since that first time in her Indigo-Lake adolescence, she's longed to know if this experience lasts longer than a normal human breath would have allowed her to stay underwater. She's been afraid to confide in anyone lest they think she is crazy. So she has had no way to find out. Or to know anything about the origin of this eternal moment of blue-Sheryl, this out-of-time moment that holds her again as she penetrates the surface, rejoining—for better or worse—the rarified air of a Grecian-island morning.

4

Kostas and Stefanos

Kostas, now hidden away in the cargo bay of a covered produce truck, is trying everything he knows to calm himself. He holds his breath. He deep-breathes. But he can't stop his stomach from churning with the angst that he has poisoned his bond with Sheryl. His one shred of hope is knowing she is stuck at his villa. He fools himself into thinking he can charm away her rage when he returns.

He tolerates these disruptive forays into Athens only because they are lucrative. A necessity of perpetuating his extravagant lifestyle. Today, as usual, he's hand delivering a cache of smallish precious artifacts for his partner to liquidate. In turn, he'll bring home a brief case bulging with cash. *But we could have done this next week. Why does he summon me when Sheryl is out on Solagros? It's almost as if he knows.*

Kostas would much rather be relaxing on his patio out on Solagros—with Sheryl. Then the temptation to indulge his sexual appetite would not have arisen. Up to now, he's been comfortable with his pattern. He sees, he meets, he conquers. He then tires, brushing them away without concern for any wreckage he might leave in his wake—until Sheryl.

The past twelve years have been a steady diet of willing women and fast cash interspersed with lengthy, pleasurable stays at his hideaway. And the deliveries of course. To Brindisi, Rhodes, or Crete. A second chance to embrace the seafaring life he had fancied so much as a teenager.

In his day, Kostas' father was a master smuggler and would surely be proud of his son. Especially of his capture of Sheryl. Kostas is pleased that in every way he's gone beyond his father, who lost his stomach for smuggling, having turned to fishing before his terrible demise.

Kostas, curled and hidden inside a crate, grimaces more at the thought of the coming meeting than at the danger of his "prison" overturning. He imagines the impact might bring some sort of relief.

Finally the truck comes to a permanent stop and Kostas feels the familiar sensation that he's being hand-trucked into the receiving bay of their headquarters.

Stefanos takes every precaution never to be seen with Kostas. His distrust in people permeates the entire operation. Kostas always thought this strange since Stefanos controls the disbursement of all profits. Kostas originally thought that this edgy atmosphere surrounding his partner was the result of some savvy business strategy. Instead he has come to realize that constant worry—paranoia plain and simple—is simply the man's underlying nature.

Thus, he's always felt secretly superior to Stefanos because, even in crime, he's managed to remain a trusting person. If the truth be told, he trusts everyone, even himself—except that thick-skinned part which cunningly cheats on women. Up to now, he's never had to absorb any torment from that quarter.

The operation—a trinket export business and wholesale produce front—is housed in one of those blocky-looking, stucco office buildings that sprung up after the war. Its only redeeming quality is the fact that it looks from its hillside out across a tree-studded valley to the Parthenon on the distant Acropolis. It had been a kind of tourist trap hotel at one point—in fact at exactly the point Stefanos' father had cheated Kostas' father out of it in a high-stakes poker game. Little Kostas had witnessed the game. And it haunts him still.

Stefanos had grown up five years ahead of Kostas in different districts of the city. He'd inherited the business after his father drowned when he fell from his yacht in a storm off the south shore of Crete. Or so the official story goes. Kostas suspects there's a different version.

"Morning Stefanos", offers Kostas, squeezing out of the crate and brushing off some leafy produce remnants.

Stefanos can only utter a grunt. He practically pushes Kostas into his office and kicks the door closed behind him.

"Sit down Kostas." Kostas winces at the menacing tone in Stefanos' voice, then turns it into sigh. "Tomorrow's transport has been delayed in Tangier. No details came with the communique. I don't like it." He looks at Kostas half expecting him to proffer some calming line of reasoning. At least it seems that way to Kostas.

"I know there are codes. Was there any explanation hinted at?"

"Of course not. We don't have codes for explanations." Stefanos isn't getting to the point. Kostas knows there is a point. There is always a point.

"Did they say when it is coming?" asks Kostas.

"How much do you know about your girlfriend?" Stefanos' gaze pierces right through Kostas' forehead.

"What do you mean..." Kostas starts to boil over then quickly checks himself..."by how much?"

"You must know she works at the U.S. Embassy. What's she doing there? Have you tried to catch her in any contradictions? Are you sure she's not an agent?"

Kostas holds back a laugh. For all his machismo, he can always find humor under strained conditions. He is now going to defend the lover at whom he'd screamed venomous epithets a scant hour before. He becomes so amused by this he is smiling. Intuitively, he knows this is the best way to defuse Stefanos' crap.

"Tell me what's funny!" snarls Stefanos.

"Of course she's a spy. Spying is the nature of the female, is it not?" Kostas is going off now. "She busted me this morning. She knows everything!"

"What! This must be handled immediately." He reaches for the phone.

Kostas knows he has him now.

"She called at the exact moment Landi and I were at climax. Sheryl could feel it so strongly in her own groin, she…I mean, how could I lie to such a woman?"

"You mean you told her the truth? Right then?"

Kostas nods.

"That's cruel! That's so perfectly cruel." Stefanos snickers, letting his guard down a bit.

The moment hangs for a tense second or two until Kostas mimics Stefanos still holding the phone. Kostas tries not to, then cracks a huge grin.

This boyish act disarms Stefanos sending him into howls of laughter. "I've been pushing you for weeks to show her who's boss. Now you told her she's just a plaything! You are my man—my man on the phone," says Stefanos, holding an imaginary receiver to his ear.

His renewed laughter becomes a grotesque celebration of his perceived mentoring triumph.

Witnessing the abrupt change in his partner, Kostas cannot refrain from reacting to the comedy of the situation. He laughs with such gusto he too loses his breath in his release of angst. He laughs all the more recklessly because he has successfully blocked Stefanos' psychic attack—at Stefanos' expense—not with an overt lie, but with a truth so regretful that his callused laughter is the only impediment that keeps him from slipping into the restroom and inflicting instant, deliberate pain on his own head and face.

5

Pull and Kick

Sheryl and her limp cargo pop into the air where a stiffening wind is pushing up the swell. Blue-Sheryl instantly gives way to a calm yet affected Sheryl.

I've got to get this poor guy to a beach in order to resuscitate him. Between breaths she pleads. *God. I'm so sorry…Are you dead?…Don't die on me…You weren't under that long…I know you kept your mouth shut after I hit you.*

Sheryl detects a heart beat against the underside of her forearm.

Somewhat comforted, she evaluates their situation. *Damn you wind.* She hisses out loud. *So you want to push us against the cliff. Let me get the angle right. Slip past the point. Should just take us another minute.*

They clear the point by a long half-yard. Now she knows the wind will be an ally and push her and her cargo into the soft sand of Kostas' private beach cove, forty yards away.

Sheryl doesn't doubt she'll get him there. She just wants to arrive in time to save him. *Thirty yards and closing. Pull and kick. Pull and kick. Twenty yards. So much of life is repetition. Repetition in between short, intense events. Pull and kick. Meet a Greek. Have an affair. Pull and kick. Have a blow up. Pull and kick. Yell and scream. Pull and kick. Kill the wrong person. Pull and kick. Bring him back to life. Ten yards. Pull and kick. Pull and kick.*

As the wind pushes them onto Kostas' beach, Sheryl is beaming at her ability to make life amusing in the midst of possible peril. She drags Andre out of the shore break and begins to go through the resuscitation procedure.

You've only been out a total of no more than five minutes. "Here goes, mister." She begins mouth-to-mouth only to discover he is already breathing. And he has the warmth associated with life.

Perhaps you just passed out. From my blows? From panic? Sheryl blocks herself from continuing to reason it out. She smiles, recalling the image of practicing revival skills from her lifeguard training. But this is not someone from her high-school. How odd to put her mouth on a total stranger, yet one with whom she is rather intimate, in a life-and-death kind of way.

A sudden indignation floods into Sheryl. *Why isn't this fellow coming to? That's what's supposed to happen. Better call for help.* She concedes. But halfway to the villa, glancing back, she sees him jerk to a sitting position. She sprints back, lands gently and crouches in front of him.

"Hi," she offers, "I'm Sheryl and I'll be your executioner today."

"Hi…uh…my…my… what? Am I dead? Wait. There's this girl out there and she was drowning and…"

"That would be me."

"But then she?…you…hit me?…and we both…are we dead?"

"No but we might have been. That wind swell is wicked. Anyway, I got us over here. After I knocked you out and dredged you up and…"

"Where is here?" Andre glances about erratically. "I don't recognize this beach."

"This is Kostas Terzi's place. My classic lov…uh, ex-lover. It's around the corner from Kapetan Yanni's. Swim out fifty yards and you'll see his beach. You must be staying there."

"Yes…Wait a minute. You *did* hit me. What was that about?"

"I lost it. I thought you were Kostas choking me. I was so pissed at him. Typical story. I just found out this morning he was cheating on me. I guess I took leave of my senses. I was trying to swim him out of my life. I lost it. I was on my way out to sea when we collided. I thought you were him

16

and I smashed your head and…look, I'm really sorry. Are you okay? I was on my way to call rescue. I can…"

"No. No…I'm okay. Just a serious headache. Good thing I wasn't your actual boyfriend."

Sheryl stifles a laugh, unable to find a clean response to his amusing remark.

"There are some pain killers in the house. And a warm shower. You're a little blue."

Andre is in no position to argue. He stands up and almost faints, feeling the full impact of the trauma. Sheryl catches him and they hobble to the villa like two drunks on their way back home from an all night binge.

6

Regret

Thud…Thud…Thud. Kostas' head impacts a whitewashed, block wall in the alley behind a market where he was dropped.

Although Kostas doesn't have the language—or the tools—to know himself, he is grieving. The more he hits his head, the more he gets a repeating flash that Landi, the woman he'd had last night, means little more than a boyish outlet. Yet he is driven to have her, this tough girl, ready to oblige with sexual favors—without the attachments and maintenance schedule of sophisticated Sheryl.

Not that Landi isn't alluring. A half-Greek, half Puerto-Rican raised in Spanish Harlem, she looks like a cross between a biker queen and a Siren. *God she's just so sensual looking.* She is the kind of high-octane woman a man like him is supposed to go for.

As he is smashing his head, it occurs to Kostas that as much as Landi is built for pleasure, Sheryl has the odor of class. And status. With her he could pull himself out of the dangerous web Stefanos has woven around him. He could bail to America, play the charming Greek husband. Have a couple kids. Maybe even work for her father in the government. A translator perhaps? A well-connected ambassador would be able to pull some strings, especially for a new son-in-law.

Do I love her? Does it matter whether or not I do? Kostas alternately laughs and beats his head harder every time the concept of love comes up in his mind.

"Love is dangerous. Play is where it's at," he hears Stefanos instruct.

"*Act* like you love them, even when you don't," his father said once. "It's far easier than honesty."

"I love you Sheryl," he'd told her many times in and out of bed. *Did I mean that? What did I mean by that? Am I imagining I have an obligation to say it? If I say it enough will I start to believe it? Is that the goal? Don't I really love her after all?*

Kostas ends up with a very sore cranium knowing two things. One, he really is driving himself crazy. Two, he has to get to Sheryl and do something, anything, to get her back, and he has to do it immediately.

7

The Villa

A showered, robed Andre treads into the great room of the villa. The pain killers have kicked in, posing an interesting counterpoint to his grogginess. Then there is this intriguing woman and her intensity. Like an island that needs to be combed for valuables after a natural disaster.

"Are you sure we haven't died, and this isn't heaven?" he says.

"Actually, it's hell. The Devil's house. Especially if Kostas were to come back. He's the jealous type. Once he wanted to fight some poor guy in a cafe who struck up an innocent conversation with me. Not that he'd have any reason to want to…." She drops it to avoid any awkwardness.

Andre wishes he could pick up the thread and respond. He can already feel the nausea welling up at the thought. And behind the nausea lurks a minefield of dread. He senses it but cannot begin to go there. This process takes place in an instant. The net effect is automatic. He acts like he doesn't even hear her comment. He instinctively lurches for the nearest chair.

"Are you hungry? If you haven't had breakfast perhaps something light? Juice?"

"Sure. Maybe some orange juice…and a banana," says Andre eyeing a clump of them in a bowl on the table. "Hope Kostas won't mind," says Andre risking a smile.

"He'll never know," says Sheryl setting a tall glass down in front of Andre.

Andre drinks half of it in two long gulps, which triggers his hunger. He reaches for a banana. Sheryl who has been monitoring Andre for signs of lingering trauma, smiles at this normal behavior.

Andre the architect methodically scans the great room and actually grows astonished at the craftsmanship. At the quality of the sculptures and paintings. At the finesse of the spatial design.

"What's this guy's story? What's he do to afford a place like this? These roof trusses are really intricate. And these floor tiles, I've never seen them anywhere else in Greece. And this wall finish."

"Exporting. Some type of exporting is all I can get out of him. He never wanted to bring business into our relationship."

"I believe that. Hey Sheryl, check this out." His eye finally settles on a serpentine-colored, half-life-size statue of a mermaid lounging on an elliptical disc. But his lips continue to ring, well after the enchantment of her name has graced them.

"Are you an art dealer or something?"

"Not really. I'm more of an 'or something.' Actually, an architect who's addicted to the marriage of art and form. My firm specializes in clients who wish to display antiquities in their homes. Sometimes we'll design an entire home as a mini-museum. Sometimes the antiquities are even designed into the structural elements of the building...This mermaid is fascinating. I've seen the style before in a gallery...no, an actual museum. I don't remember where."

"I'm sold. I hereby *encourage* you to check it out. It's the one thing Kostas always told me to leave alone. Said it was super fragile." There is that grin again. Sheryl is pleased to be amusing herself this much. Pleased at this awkwardly-timed humor.

When Andre looks at the statue, his trained eye goes to the pedestal on which it is mounted. To him the mounting of a piece of art is often as noteworthy as the piece itself. In this case, the artist had chosen an ellipse to gracefully accent the shape of the mermaid, going so far—Andre thinks—as to hypnotically counterbalance her organic, curvy sensuality with a pure geometrical shape.

"I wish I could have designed such a perfect mount for this treasure," confesses Andre with near blatant jealousy.

The piece quite naturally occupies an un-prominent corner, yet contrasts elegantly with the white marble floor. Though at first glance appearing flawlessly accomplished, as Andre is drawn closer, he notices a crescent-shaped void along the base on the back side, no more than one-quarter inch at the widest point. When his hand instinctively goes to it, Andre feels a draft of cool air issuing from the slit.

'What's with this?"

"With what?" Sheryl blurts out, overexcited at being a party to violating Kostas' taboo on the statue.

"This statue's not on the floor, it's covering a hole *in* the floor. And look at this.

It's actually floating a fraction above the floor!"

Instinctively, they both start pushing and pulling on the sculpture, wiggling it until Andre infers that the whole assembly is on rollers and pivots about one end.

"Push here!" Applying force in the correct direction, they rotate the statue, revealing an oval-shaped hole in the floor. Sturdy metal ladder rungs are fastened to one end of the oval's concrete walls. They squint but can't make out the bottom of the dark space below.

"Flashlight!…Sorry I seem to be reverting to this guy that runs around at construction sites barking orders." Andre is at once light-headed and excited. He lies on the floor next to the statue collecting himself until Sheryl retrieves a flashlight from her travel bag. She climbs first down the ladder onto another floor twelve feet below.

The exertion of moving the statue and the rush of excitement from finding this unexpected hatchway combine to push the still disoriented Andre past his limit. Halfway down, he momentarily blacks out. Luckily, Sheryl is facing the ladder guiding him down. She perceives him slip and on impulse gets a shoulder under his butt preventing a serious fall.

"Andre! Andre!" she yells. The intensity of her voice blasting through the silence jars him back to full consciousness. Though her heart is pounding, Sheryl helps him deftly down to a soft landing.

"Guess you're gonna have to keep rescuing me today. Sorry I'm not...."

"Hey, it's my fault you're groggy. We've got to take it slow from now on." Sheryl says. She almost blushes as she catches the word "we" hanging in the air. *What the hell's with that? Are we involved in some sort of teenage parlor game here?*

Andre struggles to regain his focus. He spots a lighted rocker switch and pushes it. The chamber becomes a lit tunnel, somewhat crudely hewn from the rock.

Without speaking, they shuffle through and down a ramped, windowless hall which descends in the general direction of the sea. At some distance, they enter a stark, well-lit chamber equipped with a lone desk and two brand new computers. Some other sophisticated-looking electronics gear is mounted to the wall near them.

Andre kneels and rifles through the drawers, finding nothing of note. Then, instinctively, he looks under all of the equipment housings and discovers a small black book filled with dates, account numbers and amounts.

Sheryl spots some current tide charts on the wall. High tide at 8:03 PM on Tuesday, the 22nd is circled. *Tomorrow night. How convenient. The bastard has planned my departure on the Santorini ferry tomorrow afternoon. Two o'clock. Around some use of this cave. He'd be here now with me but for the "emergency" he needed to attend to. The other-woman emergency. Bitch!*

Andre and Sheryl discover that the chamber ends at a stairway which descends into an unaltered room somehow connected to the ocean. It's too natural to be a man-made tunnel. Along one wall hang scuba tanks, wet suits, flippers and some kind of space-age watertight container. Like something she's seen used on deep-diving expeditions.

They detect reflected daylight in the water thirty or so yards away. The water surges and subsides, probably mimicking the waves as they slap the cliff. The same cliff they'd just avoided being smashed against only an hour before.

Andre surmises that the chamber they are in was once an ancient sea cave that has been overhauled. And that connector ramp to the villa. Andre figures that 200-plus yards excavation alone had to cost at least a quarter-million dollars.

"Your ex-boyfriend is a professional eccentric, I'd say." He breaks the silence which had begun to feel uncomfortable. "Wonder where that cable goes?"

"I'll let you know in a couple minutes," she smiles and disappears into the water toward the sunlight, then circles back and pops up again. "You feeling alright?"

"I'm okay now. As long as I don't exert myself, I'll be useful. Besides, this is more fun than I've had on this entire vacation," says Andre, realizing the joke is more true than not.

Sheryl smiles back and disappears again. Andre traces the other cable end back to a switch on the wall. He deduces that it controls some heavy load, such as a beacon or a winch perhaps. He waits a long minute for Sheryl to reach the open sea. Then he flicks the switch three times.

Just prior to Andre's action, Sheryl surfaces for air. As she dives back toward the underwater cave mouth, she lurches at Andre's signal—multiple light beams so powerful she becomes disoriented by the dancing blue rectangle they leave behind her reflex-slamming lids. She suspects that a person without light-filtering goggles would literally be blinded by this intensity, especially at night.

What can all this possibly mean? Even an independently wealthy Greek could not chalk this kind of installation up to some nocturnal marine fetish. He's bragged about everything else in his villa. Why hide something this unique?

Sheryl turns her back to the lights in case Andre tries to flash them again and invents a stroke to get her body inside the cave, where she can feel safe to keep her eyes open. She fights an surging explosive sensation in the back of her throat.

The robed Andre, waiting on the steps in waist-deep water for her approach, is relieved to glimpse the turquoise fabric of her suit streaking toward him. Because the jarring light beams caused an autonomic exhale, Sheryl has miscalculated her air and is way beyond running out. She hits the surface and grabs for Andre's midsection.

"I'm okay! I'm okay! We've...got...to get...out...."

"Easy, easy." But he doesn't feel easy. It is almost their first encounter all over again, except in reverse. He gently boosts her up to the edge.

Andre can't help noticing that there is not one ounce of excess on this woman's body. *She must spend hours a day training. She is well-tanned, bronze even. Yet her skin is amazingly rich and smooth.*

This contact is starting to feel familiar, even intimate, but with a heavy dose of dismay. He knows himself well enough to admit he is becoming addicted to being in Sheryl's presence. But, true to all his earlier similar encounters, Andre absolutely will not act on it. Cannot act on it. He can't stomach anything that smacks of a contrivance. He cannot know that deeper still lurks the specter of "violation." But intimacy with this demon remains below his conscious mind. Thus the ability to act in synch with his desire is a chasm within him that he cannot cross.

He'd once gone to a shrink at the urging of his best friend, Ray. Ray was concerned about Andre's lack of forward motion around women and shaped his brotherly advice accordingly.

"Man, you'd have so many more chances if you'd just push it a little. Say something suggestive. Something racy. Something flattering. Women like that kind of aggressiveness, and if they don't respond, you've not lost anything. Today's woman wants a real man. A *sensitive* cowboy, if you will, but a cowboy first and foremost."

Then Andre would protest, "But I'd lose track of who I am. If I compliment them, they'll think it's because I want to sleep with them."

"Well, don't you?" Ray would grin. "You're in shape. Well employed. Wouldn't break a camera. Get some cajones. What kind of American male are you anyway?"

If for no other reason than to hire a referee, Andre went to the shrink. The way Andre tells it, "The shrink was good. Too good. He brought out my unprocessed lust, my repressed sexuality, and the deprivation that started when I was weaned too early. He said we needed about a year to work through each of those, and another year to process the as-yet-undiscovered core issue of which the others were just symptoms. I ran screaming straight off his leather couch to the self-help section at the book store and have never looked back."

If Ray were here he'd collar him and ask if he's now supposed to tell the panting Sheryl that her face is resplendent flushed against her sun-tinted auburn hair. Tell her that her near-death experience unleashes her primal desirability. That the way she grabbed for him reminds him of mating rituals of apes he's witnessed at the San Diego Zoo.

No way. He will use the formula he's developed in the darkroom of his own soul. The one that gets him his clients. The one that tells him when and where to go on vacation. The one that's helped him conquer his fear of death: "Watch the signs which occur around you for validation that you're on course, and let your actions arise spontaneously. Don't force anything—especially your will—on anyone, and embrace the miracle of each moment of life as if you were to die and be frozen in that instant."

Of course Andre is the first to admit this is on a good day. A bad day still involves the gut-wrenching lament of not having stuck his neck out. Not having created the luxury of a healthy relationship with a woman.

The trick—he has come to know—is to control one's movie to the point where these ideals become automatic. Andre knows enough to know he is not there, but at times he's observed these traits active in a few others. He knows this is possible and will stop at nothing to achieve it continuously. As he's begun to live this course of action, old friends like Ray think him hopelessly warped and shy away. Andre shrugs it off as the price of his evolution.

Andre holds the distressed Sheryl until her breathing normalizes, savoring every second.

"Wow, that was a close call. Another second and I'd have opened my mouth and swallowed all the water in this cave."

"What happened out there?" says Andre, releasing her cleanly.

"I got stunned by the flashes from the lights and…"

"Oh God, I'm sorry. I never thought they'd have that much…That wasn't too bright of me." Andre says innocently. His words hang in the air for a long instant.

They simultaneously get the unintended pun and cannot disallow themselves the release that accompanies unconsciously-induced, out-of-the-blue laughter.

8

Athens Airport

The Athens airport is one of those crossroads of humanity that more rightfully belongs in another dimension. Due to its placement at the eastern edge of Europe, on the horizon of Asia Minor, and immediately to the north of Africa, the traveler is treated to an ever-stirring cultural human stew. Hindus with rice-anointed foreheads; chain-smoking Israeli teens in American t-shirts on leave from their mandatory stint in the military; Tunisian businessmen nursing their ouzo-induced hangovers; pairs of Britons on holiday with their twelve bags of luggage; weathered men in turbans sitting motionless; Greek security trying to keep an imaginary lid on the psychic intercourse.

It is the last place Kostas wants to be. Especially flying standby to Santorini at the apex of high season. A couple more good deliveries and they'll have their own plane and bypass this tourist-driven bottleneck.

He hopes but doubts that Sheryl will cool down on her own time, in her own way. He considers calling but knows her well enough to concede that his only chance is in person.

Of course she will still be there. Where would she go? Kostas laughs out loud at his wishful reasoning, startling the Muslim family in line next to him. He suspects the truth is that she'll move heaven and earth to get off that rock. He also knows that most days the rock is practically a prison. Almost no private boats stop there.

Today is Monday. The public ferries arrive only on Tuesdays and Fridays. No, she will not be at the villa. I hope she doesn't trash the place. No matter, I know everyone. A distressed American woman will be easy to track.

Kostas rehearses, then revises, then re-rehearses his flawed excuses until his brain feels like mashed string beans. *Sheryl can you forgive me? It's you I really want...Wait...No...It's you I love more than anything...I'm flawed...*

No…It won't happen again…It was a moment of weakness. He thinks *I'm sorry* but can't bring himself to utter it—even in practice. He looks for a wall to head butt. With none in sight, he paces.

Kostas secures one of the last seats on the hour-long flight, just before it departs. The time is 2:45 in the afternoon. With his love blinders on, he has no reason to notice a plainly-clothed, red-headed female halfway across the terminal turned slightly away from him, talking into a cell phone. He has no way of knowing Landi is watching his every move.

9

Intelligence

They put the villa back in order and erase all traces of their search for clues to the purpose of the underground chamber. In the process, Andre has let his mind explore the few facts he knows. He puts them in the form of a question to Sheryl.

"I wonder if the Kapetan is a party to keeping Kostas' secret. He is the next-door neighbor. And he repeatedly warns his guests to stay away from the cliff. Coincidence?"

She stops gathering and throwing her stuff into a travel bag and perches herself on the edge of a chair straining to resurrect everything Kostas has ever mentioned about Kapetan Yanni. Which isn't much, she concludes.

"Kostas seldom speaks of him, and when he does, it is not with affection."

"What do you mean?"

"The way he talks, they had some sort of falling out...Wait! Not between them, but between the Kapetan and Kostas' father. Or some other older man. Something about a shipwreck, I think. Maybe it was a drowning... It was a while ago. That he mentioned it, I mean. I wanted to go over there for dinner one night and he wouldn't. I remember he seemed a little uneasy...God, we've got to get out of here. I can feel him racing toward me. He hasn't called back because he knows his only chance is to try and charm me in person."

Andre suppresses a twinge of jealousy. Then, true to his self-help training, he concentrates on experiencing it fully. Suppression of such emotions leads to their retention—or so all the books proclaim. But deep down, Andre suspects he's fooling himself. As quickly as he starts the exercise, he abandons it. He's jealous and there's no getting rid of it. *You really are a phony. And you're probably involved in all sorts of cover-ups and denials.*

"Do you think you'll take him back?"

"Never. And after that little book you found under his computer, I'm afraid of what he might do to me if he gets any idea I've been in that chamber. Do you realize what kind of danger I...we...are in? He's probably some sort of smuggler. Maybe arms. Or drugs. And he covers it up with this place, this opulent lifestyle. Any legitimate export operation would deal with two maybe three banks. There were fifteen banks on that list."

"Is that why you had me write them all down? What are you going to do with the list?

"Have them checked out."

"Can you afford that?"

"I work at the American embassy in Athens. In security...I'm just a glorified clerk but trying to work my way up—to intelligence. This could be my ticket."

Sheryl grimaces at how opportunistic that must sound. *After all, Andre is just a naive tourist. A nice...no, a very nice naive tourist. Does he think I'm callous? And vengeful? So ready to turn in my freshly estranged lover.* She is surprised she cares about what he thinks. Just as quickly she stops her internal chatter. *This is not worth exploring right now. Kostas' whereabouts are my immediate concern.*

Andre too cannot keep from sizing up their situation. *Four solid months of Sheryl would be a major intoxicant. To have it turned abruptly off would not be healthy for anyone in this guy's path. From all she's said, Kostas is not a cold-turkey kind of guy. But he sure appears to be a guy with some major funding behind him.*

"Kostas is either a big time criminal or an extremely rich eccentric. We've got to get you off this rock and out of his bull's eye," he announces.

10

Santorini Eyes

Kostas stares out his window. *His* window because he's paid the man sitting next to him to trade places. He always gets answers looking out of an airplane window.

To his dread, Kostas can no longer deny that his heart is racing. In fact has been racing since leaving Stefanos. He's been caustically berating himself for screwing it up with Sheryl. In his world, you cheat, you use, you hide the truth to secure what you desire. This dependence upon another—for anything—is pure poison. A virus that makes his demons ill—these parts of him whose ruthless demeanor pushes him. And right now, each part of him wishes all the others would die.

Kostas is still staring into the sea when the crescent-shaped island of Santorini comes into view. Santorini is the kind of place that takes one's breath away. Even Kostas' breath with its litany of distress signals.

There are thirty-two calderas in the world. The earth manufactures them by collapsing volcanoes in on themselves leaving extremely deep craters filled with water. Like Crater Lake. Lake Tahoe. Taupo. Molokini. Perhaps the most dramatic is Santorini, that crescent-shaped remnant of a round volcanic island which collapsed into the sea in 2500 BC sending a tidal wave so epic it erased the entire Minoan civilization in seconds as it washed over Crete.

The colors of the Santorini caldera can haunt a man to his soul, whether from gazing into it through a diving mask or being awed by its grandeur from the air. For a moment Kostas forgets his mission as he stares into the cobalt of the abyss. In contrast to the lighter surrounding blue, and the dark eyebrow of the landform, the center becomes a giant eye that peers into space. This eerie beauty brings him right back to Sheryl. She is its human equivalent. Her sapphire-like eyes are equally as devastating.

They land at 3:55 PM. Kostas runs for a taxi to take him through Thira and down the switchback road to his launch in the harbor. At 4:35, he and two crewmen immediately cast off for Solagros.

11

Kapetan Yanni

Sheryl and Andre agree to jog over the hill to Kapetan Yanni's. After twenty yards, Andre makes it known he needs to walk. Ten eternal minutes later they steal up to the Kapetan as he half dozes upright in a chair near his small olive grove.

Sheryl is surprised that the Kapetan does not appear ogre-like. Instead she finds a kindly-looking gentleman in a white dress shirt, khaki shorts and one of those black-billed, white hats that cruise ship officers wear. He senses movement and opens an eye. He recognizes Andre as one of his guests but puzzles over Sheryl.

The Kapetan stands and bows in the formal manner of Greek hospitality.

"You American? " he asks Sheryl before she or Andre can speak.

"Yes American. Was staying with Kostas. Need to go to Santorini now. Will pay you to take me."

"Us," blurts Andre, looking straight at Sheryl. "Now. We have very serious need."

Kapetan Yanni, in his eighteen years of catering to tourists at the resort, has seen it all. Has heard all the crazy requests, overheard all the lover's quarrels. But he realizes this is different. Different because he knows this to be Kostas' girl, his American prize. The whole island knows it. He'd not met Sheryl, but he's heard the descriptions. Brunette mermaid who's surely lost her tailfin. Muscular with a velvet smile. "Daphne has returned and graces Solagros," the teenage girls say.

The Kapetan scratches the side of his head. *Without warning she comes here to me. Something big is going on.*

"For you, $400 American. Fifteen minutes at the cove."

Andre checks his watch. It reads 4:05.

Sheryl is relieved that Andre is coming along. She considers a mild protest but realizes he can corroborate her story. She is careful to tell herself that she isn't just being calculating. She is scared and appreciates his concern, his steady presence. Until they discovered the cave, she figured she could take care of herself in this separation from Kostas. But she's come to doubt if that's true.

What if the Kapetan delivers her (them!) to Kostas? Why is Kapetan Yanni so willing? The money? She senses it's something else. Her heart thumps as she helps pack Andre's stuff. It thumps all the more as they rush to the cove. They arrive out of breath, stride to the end of the dock, scramble aboard the *Oracle II*, and cast off.

No matter how riled a person gets on land, the sea has a way of softening one's sharp corners. Even a fast boat has a comforting rhythm. The sun will soon set bringing a greater sense of security. They huddle behind the windshield, to avoid the wind which can bring a slight chill on the open sea, even in August.

Sheryl calms enough to see the futility in trying to size up Kapetan Yanni. She wants to ask Andre, *How'd you know to look under the computer?* but is seduced by the delicious salt mist spraying her face and arms. The sensation decides for her that now is not the right time.

12

Aboard Oracle II

Sheryl feels downright sexual. The act of being transported in a launch on a bright afternoon on the Aegean Sea in August is simply sexual. Mythologically sexual. As if she were engaged in outmaneuvering some horny god or rival goddess. And aboard the namesake of the *Oracle* no less.

Jesus Sheryl, you're really starting to lose it. You're done with this jerk. You're safe. You're on a private yacht with a hired crew and a personal bodyguard. What about this bodyguard? Kostas would want to break him in half. Hah! That might not be so easy. He's nothing but wire. Nothing like a normal cubicle jockey who sits around drawing blueprints—or whatever architects do.

Sheryl privately studies Andre like a stranded climber might study a route down a cliff. She notes the golden body hair. The boyish grin. The well-formed calves. *The last thing I want to do is...*

"In the head. NOW!" shouts Kapetan Yanni, pointing at Sheryl. "You... Mr. Andre stay here! Put on vest. Sit in chair. Hold breath long time. Look like sick seagull!"

There's a certain awareness on the sea that all seasoned captains possess. Kapetan Yanni knows shortly after Kostas' launch clears the horizon that the boats are destined to pass. He's learned to read boats like a taster reads wine. Color, body type, displacement. He knows that stopping for a lengthy chat is not an option. On Solagros, he and Kostas keep their distance. But out here, altering course to avoid contact will arouse suspicion.

The Kapetan chuckles to himself. *Looks like I'm taking sides.*

He knows more about Kostas than he wants to admit—even to himself. He knows that money—big money—is involved. He'd seen and heard the construction noise when the villa was being built. Seen it from the ocean while passing by on his launch. Heard the imported workers in the restaurants at night, bombed on ouzo, cursing the rock.

Yanni eyes his pistol and knife and smiles wryly. *I always knew this day would come. My chance to change the score. Must not let the man with the faster boat and tougher crew suspect that their unfaithful treasure is stowed on board. Or some very old, very ugly wounds may be forced open. With violent consequences.*

In the ship's head, Sheryl's internal battle rages on. It is, she curses, as a result of her proximity to Kostas. She remembers that first night they'd been out in the festive Plaka at an outdoor dinner with some of her friends from work. He'd put his hand on her thigh and with the warmth of the night, in the aura of the Acropolis, she melted. She felt like Daphne all the way back to his flat. Her chest, vibrating, her nipples, erect. Unbeknownst to her, she had become blest with the ancient ache of the Grecian Feminine, and with the poise of an erotic goddess, knew it was her destiny for the throbbing to be appeased.

Now weary from resisting the thoughts, much as one surrenders to a flood, Sheryl not only allows them, but also lets them envelop and deliver her for the first time ever into an unfamiliar, previously un-experienced blue-Sheryl event: blue-Sheryl-out-of-water.

13

Virtual Collision

To prepare himself for the encounter with Kostas, Kapetan Yanni muses about how absurdly entangled certain human's lives can become and chuckles himself into a jovial mood. Shortly after 5PM, at the point where the boats were closest, Kostas gets the distinct impression of Sheryl's naked, fit body, sauntering around his villa. Both captains cut their speed to a crawl as they pass one another, Yanni to show some civil form of camaraderie for a neighbor here on the open sea, Kostas in response to Yanni in case he was being hailed for a communication. "Got a sick one here," a grinning Yanni calls out in Greek. "How're the swells ahead?"

Andre, at this point, is panicking. He doesn't have to fake having the shakes but is prepared to put up a fight if need be. *An old man, a fit woman, and a strong but untrained, unarmed man against three tough, probably armed, male criminals.* He steals a glance at Kostas and sees the silhouette of a desperate man against the lowering sun. Andre is nearly catapulted out of the boat as Kapetan Yanni hits the throttle at Kostas' thumbs up.

Perhaps it is the fact that the *Oracle II*, though adequate for Kapetan Yanni's purposes, is a small enough craft that all decks are open and can easily be viewed from a passing vessel. Thus all Kostas sees is a pitiful tourist wearing a life vest. Perhaps Kostas is so focused on bee-lining for Solagros that he neglects to act on his inner impression and connect the dots that would put Sheryl—now fifty yards away and lengthening—back into his grip.

Instead he vacuously returns Kapetan Yanni's wave, fixing a gloating grin over the wimpy figure crouching in the smaller vessel. Kostas' oversize ego won't allow that Sheryl would run from him on that puny boat, let alone be able to flee his island at all. If he were able to think clearly about ways for her to escape, he'd surely come about, cut off the *Oracle II,* and board and search her.

To have such a thought would require that he possess a scrap of humility. Or possess at least a scrap of ability to question his perception. No such scraps are to be found on the shelves in Kostas' internal, under-stocked cupboard.

Then too, there is the matter of Kostas' father and the Kapetan, which has always kept—and continues to keep—a wedge between them. A wedge they willfully maintain. A wedge with a life of its own, improbably helping to guarantee Sheryl's escape.

For a time, Kostas' thoughts meander around this unease with Kapetan Yanni. One of his earliest memories is the summer the Kapetan piloted a launch for his father and Stefanos' father. On days while the men conducted business ashore and the boat was docked, Kapetan Yanni taught Kostas the fundamentals of backgammon, poker, and fishing.

Stephenos had strained his back in a freak soccer accident and was laid up. Otherwise the boys would have met and perhaps bonded, though Stefanos was five years older. In truth, Kostas' father did not wish for the boys to meet. Even then he sensed that Stefanos would be bad news, even within a caustic yet prideful enterprise run by thieves.

One early September morning, Kostas' father announced that Kapetan Yanni had been fired for stealing from them. Out of loyalty, Kostas stopped relating to the Kapetan. In retrospect, he's curious at why he'd never pressed his father for details about Kapetan Yanni's abrupt departure. His gut told him the stealing was untrue. He has always linked that event with his sleeping problem, though he doesn't know why.

He lets out a laugh at the irony that he and the Kapetan ended up as neighbors on the same obscure rock, chalking it up to life in a small country. How could he know that his partner Stefanos' shrewd handiwork lurks at the core of this coincidence?

14

Shred of Memory

"Sheryl, you okay? Sheryl!" Andre knocks then pounds on the head's door.

Sheryl, who first merged with the small chamber, then with the hum of the engines, then the presence of the whole vessel and finally the entire Mediterranean basin, exits blue-Sheryl reluctantly. As always, a significant shred of memory from blue-Sheryl remains.

She opens the door still enthralled by the sweet lingering music of sexual ecstasy and stares Andre down from blonde head to long feet and back up to those much-more-kind-than-hers-sapphire eyes, realizing to her shock it is he—not Kostas—with whom she has just fantasized sharing her body and immense soul in her private ocean of blue-Sheryl.

15

Interiors

Five minutes after the *Oracle II* docks at Monolithos Beach on the east shore of Santorini, Sheryl and Andre are in a taxi bound for the small airport about eight kilometers distant. Just as they near the last turnoff, simultaneously they turn to each other almost shouting, "Wait!"

The gravity of their situation hits them like they've each swallowed a live grenade. By now, Kostas has searched his villa plus all of tiny Solagros and has found no trace of Sheryl. They imagine that if he, in fact, has some type of network, he may already know they've been whisked away by Kapetan Yanni. Worse, he may have contacts here—and the small, confined Santorini airport would be an obvious point of intercept.

The driver pulls off, inwardly chuckling at the crazy Americans. They methodically engage him in a discussion of other ways to quickly leave the island. Using broken Greek and by pointing to the driver's map, within two minutes they hatch a new plan. In response, the taxi speeds across the fattest part of the crescent-shaped island bound for the deep-water port of Athinios.

Inside the car, rock slides are occurring in the psyches of the passengers.

Andre is fully aware he is sitting next to a rare find. *She's so much more magnetic than anyone else I've ever met. I feel merged with her. Even though our time together has progressed like a quirky set of crash landings, we've reached an unspoken level of intimacy.*

Doesn't this count? Aren't I creating this—even if it's imperfect? This is so different from Galen. I went so slow with her—we both wanted to go slow—so tediously slow, that we gradually drove ourselves off different cliffs...without even noticing until long after we hit the rocks at the bottom.

Grimacing at his distrust of this exquisite moment, he knows that he's gotten too far into his hyperactive mind for his own good. Whenever he becomes aware enough to notice his mind trying to dominate, his self-help training urges him into the immediacy of his surroundings. He scoffs at people who need a live teacher. He'll read their books, thank you. *No, he can do this solo. Anyway, aren't spiritual teachers just shrinks in white robes?* There goes his mind again.

Andre leans back, closes his eyes and concentrates on being with his breathing. All the books talk about breathing. This most basic of human activities, when focused on, almost always brings him into a calm place. So simple. In...Out. Fullness...Emptiness. Everything...Nothing.

His process evolves naturally into a vital inhaling of Sheryl's essence. Not just Sheryl the Aquamarine Angel but Sheryl the Athlete. Sheryl of Melodious Laughter. Sheryl the Cunning. Sheryl of a Million Dazzling Facets.

He lets her fullness into him, lets her presence merge with the sound of air rushing by the open window. Lets the Greek summer heat inhabit him. He breathes through moment after moment of this interior festivity so completely, at first he doesn't notice that it's Sheryl's hand caressing his forehead. It could be Aphrodite's—or his own—for all he knows.

On her side of the taxi, Sheryl is swimming into uncharted waters. This day started so serenely. A glorious sunrise. A few stretches, some fruit, then the pang. She went dizzy, not out-of-body, but rather, a tumbling into herself. And way inside the tumbling, a clear picture of Kostas in bed with a hot, dark-haired, browned-skinned beauty. More than a picture. A three-dimensional scene that made her nauseous. She couldn't block it out. So she called his satellite phone. The idiot actually picked up, still panting from his sexual exertion. They yelled and screamed at each other and she ran into the sea and smashed into Andre.

This brings her to now, when she has become very tuned into this appealing man. Very aware of his nearness. His smell. His lanky frame. *Ha. He's the only man I've been this close to in years who's taller than me.*

42

Their taxi is a compact, small enough to cause them to sit quite closely. Sheryl realizes, to her surprise, her complete ease around this man. *He's so familiar it's strange.* Perhaps it's his average American looks that both excite and calm her all at once. She can literally feel his gently beautiful spirit shining through. And this completes the attraction. He seems agenda-less, at least regarding any intention of putting a move on her.

Though she can't put a reason to her response, she instinctively rolls onto her right side, snuggles against him and begins stroking his forehead ever so lightly with the fingers of her left hand. This goes on for a few eternal minutes until Andre rolls his head over, opens his eyes and they interlock with hers.

16

Bad Blood

Kostas returns to his villa and darts through all the rooms, checking even the closets and, aside from a little sand on the floor, finds no trace of Sheryl. He searches the cave and is ambivalently relieved to find it untouched. His crew, who've been dispatched to scour the small island, phone in to report that at about four in the afternoon, Sheryl had been sighted leaving with Kapetan Yanni and one of his American guests—a man.

Kostas is livid. The picture of that brief encounter with Kapetan Yannis' launch now imbeds itself in his mind like a hornet sting. Less than three short hours ago, he'd been within a few meters of her. Despite his prowess at deception, she's managed to blunt his instincts to the point where he lulled himself into underestimating her resourcefulness. What is worse, in very short order, this enchantress has managed to mangle his pride, shrink his machismo, and take his focus off his enterprise.

Grabbing his satellite phone, Kostas begins screaming instructions to associates in Santorini and Athens to watch the airports and ferry terminals, including the vast harbor at Piraeus. He knows this is futile, but he has to try. Why exactly he can't say. If he catches her, what will he do? Interrogate her? Make her love him—somehow? Force himself upon her? No, that is pointless. But perhaps facing her is not. What of this American dog she's traveling with? Perhaps Kapetan Yanni is simply ferrying him back after his stay. Maybe he has food poisoning. If he's with her, he'll rip him apart.

The evening is a weight on Kostas. He paces, he plots, he daydreams. Every now and then he beats his head into a wall. Hard at first only once, then more and more gently until it becomes a symbolic act. *This morning I really hurt my head doing the same thing for much the same reason. I must get under control. My head simply can't take any more abuse.*

The chime of the phone interrupts his love-hate communion with the wall. His heart leaps for an instant until he hears Stefanos begin grunting over the surface line with orders for him to receive the shipment at 8 AM the day after tomorrow.

"Yes Stefanos, I'll be sure everything is set. Yes Stefanos, I'll crate it up and haul it off to Simi by the following morning. Yes, the *Star of Datcha*. Yes, I've met the kapetan before. Mehmet. Yes, pure Turkish, but trustworthy. Yes I have the payment for them. Okay. I'll call you when I'm enroute. I need rest. Goodbye Stefanos."

Kostas softly hangs up the phone then punches the wall with his fist until his knuckles bleed.

17

Overnight Ferry

Sheryl and Andre's taxi descends the dramatic switchbacks into the port of Athinios. They pay the driver to purchase their tickets on the soon-departing overnight ferry to Skyros. From there Sheryl knows a local ferry they can catch to an obscure port an hour's bus ride southwest into Athens.

The gates open and the stew of sunburned vagabonds rush the large vessel. Sheryl and Andre, who've been slumped in the cab, exit separately and blend in. To hide their hair color, Sheryl wears a headscarf and Andre a cap the driver sold him.

Greek ferries in the high season are floating slumber parties by night and pre-parties for island night life by day. There is no known limit to the number of passengers the ferry companies will allow. Greece throws a party for the rest of Europe every summer, and the islands are center stage. The big boats faithfully serve those who choose to hop between revelries—and of course those who must leave the scene altogether. Cell phone signals are weak or spotty. It's often difficult for friends on the same ship to find each other and beyond impossible for anyone to find anyone else in the islands at large unless it has been thoughtfully arranged.

Once aboard, Sheryl and Andre find a semi-private corner on the floor in one of the recreation rooms and settle in. Exhausted, they become over-whelmed by the gnawing feeling of leaving the islands for the reality of Athens. The gnawing always waits to start until one boards the ferry, then it grows with each successive kilometer sailed in the direction of Athens. For Sheryl and Andre, it has everything to do with the end of their brief liaison.

"So far this has all been about me," Sheryl said. "Tell me about yourself. How did you find Solagros? It's way off the beaten track."

"Right now, I'm just here. Feels like I've always been here. On my way to Skyros, with the honorary yet tragic Queen of the Aegean. Please don't take this the wrong way, but...I guess—no, I know—this is...this is our time together." His foot was in his mouth now and he'd better just keep chewing.

"Most likely I'll return to my obligations, my clients and friends in San Francisco. Right now though, I'm just here camping on a Grecian ferry with a mysterious beauty, avoiding a phantom menace, on our way to an island I've never heard of. For all I know, it doesn't exist. But we exist, of that I'm sure. It's all quite exciting."

"Exciting?..." That he calls her a beauty is like a lotion fondly absorbed into her chest. "Just exciting?" is all she can muster, wrapping her arms around his torso.

"Okay," says Andre, overriding the alarms going off in his throat and allowing himself to enjoy her advance, "how about thrilling bordering on miraculously ecstatic? Aren't you thrilled? I mean, this set of circumstances has never happened before in all of existence. And tomorrow is wide open. Anything can happen. But it's no different from any other day."

"Why not?" Sheryl feels a dispirited twinge.

"Well, every day you wake up, you don't really know what's going to happen. You have ideas but they're not necessarily the truth—usually not the truth. I mean, after tomorrow, we may never see each other again—or we might. I find that deeply exciting—again, because we're here now and that makes the moment sacred."

Sheryl melts a bit more into Andre, stares into the darkness out a large round window, and really feels into what he's saying. *There are the stars doing their thing. And here we lie among the mass of humanity shoveled onto this ship. And here is the ship pitching and rolling in the swells on its way north. Here is this sea beneath us, drenched in mythology. This sea that Cleopatra had known. That Jesus' feet had probably touched.*

She sighs, trying to let the day go so she can be right here with Andre. *Everything he says is true and the point of view is so simple, yet so compelling. Seems like a familiar song playing. But the lyrics have more meaning now.* She draws him closer to her desiring to absorb his essence.

47

Last night she'd gone to bed alone in love with a hot Greek eccentric who's probably a cold-blooded criminal. Twenty hours later, her alternate self is dreaming up exquisite fantasies with a man she nearly drowned. To the unbiased observer, she knows her behavior would be considered well outside the norm.

So who if anyone is normal anyway? Certainly not me. I have blue-Sheryl to thank for that. Who is this blue-Sheryl character that's claiming more and more of my time? Toying with me. Like it's got an agenda all its own. And I'm just the servant. The impression strikes her that slipping into blue-Sheryl at some inopportune moment could result in her harm, even her death. Her back muscles shudder as if to protest such a fate.

"You okay?" Andre is jolted from the ecstasy of her closeness by her involuntary movement.

"Yeah—and no. It's not just that this has been one of the weirder days of my life. It's more that I'm having a hard time just staying inside my skin."

You mean like nerves—or something deeper?'

"Deep. I think."

"How so?"

"Let's just say that who I am moment-to-moment is questionable."

"Me too."

"I don't mean it in the way you do. With me there's this…this other thing… not really a thing, more of a reality shift into some other realm…I've never tried to articulate this before, not even to myself."

"I'm with you so far. You're doing great." Andre covers his intoxication with her nearness with his encouragement, perfectly. *Stop being such a phony and just listen. This sounds like soul talk.*

Sheryl, ear against his chest, hears his heart, squeezes him and knows she must get this out.

48

"Sometimes…when I'm in water…or around water—like on the boat today—I go into this place…where the 'I' I know myself to be is just not there and it's all very vast and very enticing…like I have no control, don't even want control. When I come back I remember much of being there. And the impressions—the visuals—remain."

"Wow. That's incredible! I've read about that. It's the state where master yogi's dwell."

"They can probably control it. I can't. It's beginning to freak me out. Today, just since I met you, I shifted into it—twice."

"Really. When?"

"Once as I was I rescuing you. And then again in the head as the launches crossed paths."

"I don't understand. How could you rescue me and be in that state at the same time?"

"That's right! I did do that. I remember I didn't want to panic so I let myself relax into it as we were rising to the surface. Then I did come out of it as I took that first delicious breath."

"So you see, you were able to use it to actually keep you—and me—safe. That's a powerful and beautiful ally. Probably helped you use your air efficiently."

Sheryl realizes he is right. *Even in the head on Kapetan Yanni's launch, going into blue-Sheryl had calmed me in one sense. Calmed me and pleasured me as well. It truly is an ally. At least it was then.*

"It came again when I was hiding in the head," she confesses. "That's the first time it ever happened out of the water. I was the whole Mediterranean and I was completely turned on sexually."

Andre remembers pounding on the door a while. "Wow! Sorry I interrupted you. Timing has never been my forte."

49

Sheryl lifts her lips to Andre's ear and purrs, "It's ironic that you brought me out of it because you were the sweet centerpiece of my desire."

18

Secrets

It's said that keeping a secret in Greece is like trying to take one's eyes off the Mediterranean. Thus, word of Kostas' dragnet for Sheryl has gotten quickly back to Stefanos. He's heard enough of the story to know that Sheryl had been left alone in the villa—the vital hub of their operation. To Stefanos, this is the equivalent of sleeping with the enemy, then letting her snoop around at will behind your lines.

It is Stefanos' turn to pace. Unlike Kostas, he is paranoid but has become adept at covering it up with an edgy mixture of coolness and heartlessness. He can't possibly possess the awareness that his ugly demeanor stems from the affairs surrounding his father's death—and his calculated response to it.

He also would never be able to unearth the source of his pre-occupation with Sheryl-as-enemy. Stefanos, the classic loner, has adopted a rigid stance with women. Like most adolescents, he'd had some hormonally-based puppy loves but at age fourteen, when his father was killed, a cloud of fierce bitterness had sucked him in. In the years following, no girl or woman cared enough to get near his vile exterior, let alone navigate his rage. Still, he noticed women but had resigned himself to paying for his sexual release because, he consoled himself, that a woman's getting too close could bring down his enterprise. And his enterprise is his essence. Without it, his world would cease to exist. And he would be swept into non-existence as well.

He had often tried to export this philosophy to Kostas, always encouraging him to move from conquest to conquest before any of them could get wind of what they were up to. The strategy was working—until Sheryl appeared on the scene. Stefanos only knew Kostas' previous conquests by name—never by sight. He was comfortable, even eager, for them to share their exploits, always with the unspoken agreement that the whole deal was transitory. Nothing should last more than a week or two. This thing with Sheryl is going on four months and Stefanos' paranoia is hitting the red line.

But something deeper is operative. Something Stefanos can never confess to Kostas. In one of those rare, fateful congruities, Stefanos happened to catch sight of Kostas and Sheryl walking together through the Sunday flea market around Monastiraki Square. Stefanos religiously avoided this locale, as, in happier times, his parents often loved to bargain there with him in tow.

But this particular Sunday, he'd impulsively decided to rendezvous with his hooker from the previous night, at one of the outdoor restaurants. She'd managed to seriously unlock his passion and, against his better judgment, he thought he'd repay her with some lunch. He didn't have any idea why he was doing this. Yet it seemed significant.

Stefanos managed to avoid Kostas and the woman on his arm. To say she registered her presence is to blankly mumble that Greeks love life. In a short skirt, bare midriff and tropical halter top, Sheryl turned the heads of men and women, Greek or tourist. Stefanos' head was no exception.

There were other women about with comparable looks but Sheryl possesses that rare quality that springs from beyond the physical. That quality which registers even in a person whose wounds blur his vision of the world. All Stefanos saw in that instant of vulnerability was a real-time image of a world he would never enter. A glimpse of a delight he knew he would never have.

Before the suddenly repulsive hooker could find him, he fled to the emptiness of his flat, pulled the curtains, and furiously set about pleasuring himself—failing pitiably.

19

The Pull of the World

Andre and Sheryl enjoy a frustratingly sweet night of French kissing, exploratory caressing, and heavy breathing. Andre is grateful that out-and-out sex is not an option. After all, they are within inches of other passengers attempting to sleep. And he has an uneasy feeling about going that far too fast. Even this level of intimacy would, under any other circumstance, make him anxious. But with Sheryl it feels as right and natural as enjoying a new, unforgettable song.

To both of them, each and every moment is delicious just as it is. The constraint posed by the other passengers simply adds a hushed tension to their passion. They don't choose to confuse these moments with dialogue. In fact, the only choices they need to make become when to stop a long, hard embrace in favor of an extended kiss. When to engage in mutual flesh exploration or alternate with the other as explorer and exploree. Sheryl really enjoys being explored or doing the exploring—not so much both at once, although alternating all three modes proves rapturous.

Even though she's on a ship on the sea, even though because it happened on the Oracle II and Sheryl is half expecting it, blue-Sheryl does not come. *I wonder if so much human ecstasy crowds out the more cosmic variety.*

"I want to be right here with you right now in all of my humanness," she whispers to Andre.

The ferry docks and jolts, exchanges its human cargo, and casts off again for its next port, repeating the process through the night. The two lovers fall into this rhythm, savoring the stretches between ports for allowing the passion to build, only to let it subside upon docking. For them, it becomes the in-breath and out-breath of love itself.

Studying him at close range in the early morning light, Sheryl looks past Andre's pleasant face and slim, yet toned body to a depth of soul that is illuminated with rare and genuine exuberance. Yet tempered with humility. And not the acquired or skin-deep variety. *He appears to vibrate to me. I want to touch the source of this, so to vibrate in unison. Okay Sheryl, if once again you're throwing caution to the wind, why should you care? Besides, the calculating part of you has it all reasoned out. You've only invested all of twenty-three hours so far.*

Andre for his part can scarcely believe his good fortune. *I've stumbled upon a most exceptional woman. Besides the rugged, subtle physical beauty, there is this other-worldliness to Sheryl. Something akin to a Greek goddess with one foot on earth and one on Olympus. Like she knows intimately the pleasures of both worlds. Along with her base honesty and playful spirit, I just melt in her presence. That she would give me so much more than the time of day, brings me to an altered state—one where I feel alternately uneasy and at ease. Something about the rhythm of that dynamic makes my whole being feel like it's levitating. Or being levitated.* If Sheryl knew this detail of Andre's inner experience, she would proclaim him a candidate for "blue-Andre".

"I feel so good with you," Andre hears her say as they unhurriedly untangle from their all-night embrace, discreetly slipping into their jeans under a blanket Andre had finagled the night before.

"And I with you, although *good* just isn't enough. I think they've yet to invent the appropriate adjective."

"I want us to invent that adjective then," says Sheryl. They are standing now, actually wobbling under the pitch of the ship and holding each other up. "But first we've got a huge decision to make."

"Breakfast to go on the deck or in style in the dining room?" Andre quips.

"So 'in the moment' aren't we my sweet? I mean when we dock at Skyros, do we follow our hearts and bodies, find the nearest bungalow, and make love for five days straight? Or do we act like grown ups?"

"You mean bee line to the Embassy and tell somebody about the cave?"

"Unfortunately I do," says Sheryl, stifling the ache exploding slowly through her.

Andre falls silent. *God knows I want nothing more than to spend a week discovering the many wonders of Sheryl, showering her with every ounce of my attention. I want to share our essences, and deepen into—ugh, you are so corny—unbridled, yet sacred, love.*

But try as he will to hold that picture, he has this nagging feeling about Kostas. After all, this is his turf and he has to be looking for them. If ignored, he sees this wild card escalating into something which may ultimately destroy them—or at least alter the trajectory of their togetherness. Now at only twenty-four hours with Sheryl, he will camp out in Antarctica to be with her.

Out of the bright sky, a bolt of clarity zaps Andre with the insight that he is projecting into any number of alternative futures, all of which are pure conjecture having nothing to do with present reality. Gently, he pulls himself back to her azure eyes and they become his entire world.

Without speaking, they stroll hand in hand out to the nearest open deck, merge with the unbroken blue sea spread before them like a huge orchid petal, and embrace like their time together will never end.

20

Counterforce

Stefanos pours over maps of the greater Athens region and laments his conclusion that Sheryl is too smart to enter the city via the airports or main harbor at Piraeus.

Someone like her with local knowledge can arrive by at least twenty different ferry & bus scenarios. And she can—and probably will—elect to disembark from a bus somewhere. Then she could hire any of hundreds of taxis to bring her to the Embassy. If she gets there, I am probably cooked. Has she discovered the cave? Has she already called it in? The fact that she vanished into thin air on Santorini tells me she suspects something. She surely knows what she's doing.

Of the two main companies, Stefanos has high contacts only in the one called Taxi Athena. Deciding that fifty-fifty is decent odds, he calls its owner, Mikos, offering the equivalent of four thousand American dollars should one of his people be able to deliver Sheryl and her male escort to a van parked a block away from the American Embassy. *After all, how many women of her description will be bee-lining there from the outskirts.*

If Stefanos is to capture Sheryl and Andre, he's already decided to leave Kostas out of the loop and simply disappear them. *Curses! This means purging Kostas' villa due to the inevitable investigation of two missing Americans, at least one of whom worked for the government. On the other hand, if Sheryl and friend know nothing of the contraband, is their disappearance worth the dismantling of my operation? My "baby" that has taken so many years to construct. Perhaps I am over-reacting.*

Just as he's deciding to ascertain where her flat is and watch it—figuring that if she knows nothing about the operation she'll return there first— a call comes through that a woman matching Sheryl's description, and that of her male American companion, are approaching the city from the northeast, enroute to their Embassy in a cab provided by Taxi Athena. Even as they speak, the driver is dialoging with the dispatcher about the exact location of the intercept van.

21

Reentry

As the Acropolis looms into view in the distance, perhaps as a result of clinging to sweet, blue-jeaned Andre, perhaps from the colorful fish decals on the cab's blue dash, or from the dolphin medallion swinging and dangling from the rear-view mirror, Sheryl finds herself willingly slipping into blue-Sheryl right there in the taxi.

She finds herself in a Grecian moment where the magic of ancient Athens reverberates through her. Not harshly. But rhythmically. Unveilingly. As if the aggregate of lives once lived here were weighing in. Bringing clarity. Insight. Awareness. Merging with the world within the vehicle. Now expanding into the street engulfing the facades of the buildings, intuiting the mood, yes the very collective soul of the passersby, the shopkeepers, the fellow occupants of this school of multicolored mechanical fish wending along the boulevard under an anemic cobalt sky.

All the while the driver has been talking back at a voice in his radio and Sheryl has engulfed that as well. First the inflections, then the meaning begin to come through. All as natural as swimming, even though Sheryl's Greek is basic at best.

So as Taxi Athena #588 slows for a light at a crowded intersection, with a fully in-tune movement, blue-Sheryl leans harder into Andre, all to more easily lift a concealed foot against the door latch pulling it down, kicking open the door and pulling Andre out of the still-braking car with her—into and across the street in the opposite direction to which they were traveling. Leaving blue-Sheryl to fend for itself in the ethers above the pavement. Landing fully back into her athletic body.

"Sheryl! What is going…"

"Trust me! Run! In there!" Sheryl whisper-yells. "The cab was a trap!"

Day packs in hand, they sprint. Into a deli and out the back door. Down an alley, into a laundry, back onto and across the same boulevard. Through a maze of narrow back streets evading taxis, avoiding police, dodging dark-colored cars. Buying a head scarf and shawl for her, a peasant hat for him. Onto the lower level of a double-deck, sight-seeing bus bound for the Parthenon via the Plaka District—the "Old City." Not speaking—just moving like a pair of carp along the bottom of a very large tank.

Slipping off the bus just inside the entrance to the Plaka, they duck into one of its plentiful, two-star pensions with cheap rooms, a lot of local color, and a telephone in the claustrophobic lobby. Within twenty minutes, they are bound for the Embassy in a secure van with smoked windows and an armed escort.

22

Hollow Homecoming

The lurch of his plane impacting the runway at San Francisco International is a fitting punctuation mark on the end of the most bizarre chapter in Andre's life. His purported debriefing at the embassy in Athens had morphed quickly into a hostile interrogation.

Half a world away, he's still unable to get Special Agent Frank Mankowski's fire-red hair and irritating tenor voice out of his head. "How did you know to operate the entry mechanism to the underground chamber? Do you really think we're stupid enough to buy that this improbable meeting with Sheryl wasn't staged? How did you just happen to find the bank list under the computer?"

Mankowski simply knew he, Andre, must have some covert agenda and grilled him for several hours. "You just happened to be swimming half a mile offshore in dangerous currents? Right. What under-the-radar cartel do you work for? None? Right. If Kostas is a criminal, why would you want to be the chosen one to ruin his operation? Is there something in this for you? Who is paying you?"

Through it all he managed to stay calm, letting the accusations break over him like small waves. Except when Mankowski got right in his face firing questions about he and Sheryl.

"Whose decision was it to flee the island? Mutual. I see. Exactly how did you and Ms. Jensen get tickets for the ferry? A taxi driver. I see. At what point did things get cozy between the two of you? None of my business? Don't push me. You're one smart answer from being detained indefinitely. Now, what were the sleeping arrangements? I'm asking the questions. It matters because I say it matters. What do you mean I sound envious. What kind of bullshit is that? Okay Bud. You're on the next plane out of here."

Andre had laughed at the one-dimensional stupidity of federal agents on TV dramas, but to see it unleashed up close and real was deeply unsettling. But not as unsettling as the funeral-like limo ride to the airport and personal escort onto a direct flight stateside.

Andre wants to turn right around and grab the next flight back to Athens and Sheryl. Wants to scoop her up and run off to a love bungalow on some pristine beach. Wants to be there when she is commended for bringing down Kostas' operation. Wants to show Special Agent Frank Mankowski what a moronic set of assumptions he's made. Wants mostly to wake up in Sheryl's arms. Drink her smile. Inhale her freshness. Become whole again. Like that morning on the ferry.

Instead he's 9000 miles away with a cage around him—a passport no longer valid for entry into Europe—or anywhere offshore. Courtesy of Uncle Sam. "For your own protection," he was told. He's spent the past eighteen hours swallowing this pill. His conclusion: *This is what is. You'll just have to deal with it—Bud.*

Aside from the fact that his entire being feels rent in two, Andre almost believes—then rejects the belief—that his self-help platitudes will get him though this all-too-real nightmare.

23

Warnings

Stefanos' paranoia is hitting the red line. Because of the manner in which Sheryl slipped through his grasp, he knows in his gut that the artifacts shipment is in certain jeopardy.

In a perfect world, he would call the transfer off. But he knows that is not an option. His contact was most definite. "This is your last shipment. We are delaying it exactly 24 hours. The sub is already parked offshore and its communications are blacked out. There will be no changes. Should something go wrong, we hold you and your partner responsible."

Stefanos' blood runs suddenly cold. *These people have never issued such a threat. What if they have a mechanical failure? What if there's a storm? High waves?* He paces. He plots. He packs. *Just in case grab the cash, emergency rations, crucial records. Leave no trail. If they find me, the dogs will kill me.*

Then he stops himself. He even allows a brief smirk. *Maybe I'm overreacting. Maybe I'll wait until Kostas checks in…Maybe everything will go smoothly and this is all in my mind.*

Then the panic comes back with renewed force. *If there is a glitch, Kostas is surely dead. He deserves it for his stupidity. If they find me, I'm dead.* As Stefanos stuffs the last of his clothes into his bag and is about to sneak out of his own building, his phone rings.

"Meli Productos—Stefanos."

The party on the other end speaks five words and hangs up: "Your cave is raided—now."

Without any forethought, Stefanos' dials Kostas' emergency phone. The second it rings, he considers hanging up, thereby throwing Kostas under the bus for sure. *The bastard should rot in jail.* But the chance to be superior and scold him overrules all other factors. Before he can reconsider, Kostas answers.

24

Anger Management

Sheryl wants to kill. Is so livid with her embassy superiors for dumping Andre on a plane she wants them skewered. Why wasn't she allowed to see him? Console him. Make plans. She's alone in the basement gym screaming on the weight-resistance machines. Pounding, high-leg-kicking, Karate-chopping the seats. Wishing they were Frank and Ben Andrews, the Deputy Ambassador.

"Ignorant, arrogant pricks! I'll rip your throats out! I'll feed your dicks to the seagulls! I'll have your testicles on a stick!"

Sheryl stomps on a padded mat and attacks another hanging from a wall. With a patented Kung-Fu move she tears its "skin" like it is thin paper. "I'll shred your faces! I'll squeeze the gunk out of your brains! Bastards! I'll kill, I'll make you...wish...you'd...never..." She drops to her knees, slams the pads with clenched fists. She's a discordant symphony. Half guttural groans, half screams. Finally spent, she collapses onto her side... "I'll... take you apart...I'll"... She curls up on the mat. Fists still clenched...rasps of air raking her throat...gradually aware of a touch... a soothing touch, hand on her shoulder...no strength to resist...now both hands gently...and a voice—*so smooth...a sister's voice...so kindly so wise....*

"It's okay sweetness...Jus' let it out, it's all gotta come out...tranquillo..."

Like a birthing whale, Sheryl moans, now sobs, now utters from her innermost private place..."Men are so stupid...so hopeless and stupid," after which Sheryl lets out a wail that would have sent Zeus running for an exit. Eventually the wail returns to moans, the moans back to sobs, the sobs to tender heaves. Then a calmness. A private peace almost startling in the depth of its emptiness. In due course, Sheryl rolls over and begins to willingly drown into the serene eyes of a vaguely familiar, ebony-haired jaguar of a woman.

"H'lo Sheryl, I'm Landi Riquelme."

25

The Shipment

Wednesday night at precisely 8:45, Kostas activates the under water lights to assist the sub crewmen in dispatching their cargo through the tunnel into the cavern. These transfers never take more than 30 minutes. This evening however, the cargo is especially large and heavy—a prize statue of a Roman Charioteer unearthed in a Tunisian cemetery. Perhaps Kostas is too preoccupied with Sheryl's whereabouts and emotional state to have taken his normal precautions.

He hasn't left the villa to observe if any suspicious visitors were afoot in the village. Hasn't casually strolled the market and outdoor restaurants. Hasn't posted extra men to watch the beach, nor the docks. Instead he is possessed with the absence of Sheryl. The loss of her affection. The magic light she brings into a room. He's rung her phone until the ringing feels like a virus in his brain.

Above all Kostas hasn't bothered to thoroughly scrutinize the disabled trawler being repaired a ways off Kapetan Yanni's dock. A team of two men weld a patch on the hull. Their blue flashes in the amber dusk lend legitimacy to the ruse: the trawler is a command post for a large intercept team.

At this moment, Kostas is entirely unsuspecting of the armed divers being disgorged from hatches below the trawler's waterline to disable the sub and block any attempted escape of its crew. Simultaneously, he's ignored a group of plain-clothed Greek undercover police posing as tourists on Solagros for a holiday. They sing a bawdy ballad and feign a drunken stroll near the villa to block any would-be escapees.

The squeeze nears its zenith as the statue is being beached inside the cave. At the same time, Kostas retreats to a wall-mounted phone, halfway back to the beginning of the ramp to the villa, to field a call that could only be Stefanos, selfishly interrupting the pace of the operation.

"Hallo. Stefanos! You know better than to call when the sub is…"

"Careless bastard dog!" Stefanos spits the words. "You and your damned high-class bitch have cost us our fortunes. Grab what you can and get out now. I'll try to meet you at the rendezvous place twenty evenings from now."

Even before Kostas can get the phone out of his hand, through the distance, he makes out harsh commands issuing from a cluster of black-clad figures surrounding the cask. And just as abruptly he hears a startling commotion in the tunnel emanating from the direction of the villa as well.

26

Comparing Notes

"You mean you were in deep undercover trying to bust this guy for smuggling while I was…Didn't you…Don't you…I mean next you're gonna tell me Andre is working for you!" Sheryl is incredulous.

"I just heard about Andre," says Landi with disarming integrity. "Seems like an innocent bystander to me…We really don't care that much about Kostas either. We are trying to nail the people supplying him with artifacts. We suspect they're Islamic terrorists, using the money Kostas and his partner pays them to buy equipment and explosives for suicide bombers."

"Wow! But what's Mankowski's game? He grills Andre for hours, then shoves him back to the states without letting him see me. If he thinks Andre is innocent…I mean, the man isn't consistent."

"I came to the 'innocent-bystander' conclusion on my own. Mankowski is under strict orders from the State Department to leave me alone. We don't speak. I think he's just flexing his wounded-pride muscle. He has a suspicion he's a little man in a little puddle and it eats away at him. He hates me b'cuz he thinks I'm trespassing on his fiefdom—miniature though it may be. But his pride is swollen now. Muy macho. He gets to orchestrate the raid on the cave."

"Why?"

"B'cuz you uncovered the whole damn operation an' you're one of his troops. Don't be surprised if you're promoted."

Sheryl starts to relax now, seeing Landi as an ally. Besides, Landi is so alluring that Sheryl at once impulsively trusts her and wants to be liked by her. In fact Sheryl can't take her eyes off her.

"How well did you know Kostas?" Sheryl asks.

"Very intimately I'm afraid. Lo siento mucho."

"You mean…were you with him last Monday?"

"Ya, I mean sexually intimately. And ya, Monday morning."

"Oh. I had you pictured. But I had no idea the image would not do you justice," says Sheryl trying to be generous. "Ha." Sheryl stifles a laugh.

"What's funny?" Landi wants to know.

"It occurs to me, I could be hostile—but I'm spent. I could withdraw—but I'd eventually explode. I could be philosophical—and puke. Or I could simply accept the obvious."

"Really? What's obvious?" says Landi, confused.

"I guess this makes us relatives. Sister-in-lusts."

In an altered state to begin with, Sheryl can't help herself and giggles. Then the sudden release urges her to wax into full sorority-girl laughter. Landi catches it too and they both convulse together for a precious half-minute, leaving the fallout from their awkward encounter on pause on a padded mat at 8:30 PM Wednesday night on the Embassy gymnasium floor.

27

The Call

Andre loves a fast walk from his urban wilderness home up the Mt. Tamalpais trail. Usually a mile, sometimes two, occasionally more. Wherever he stops, he does conscious breathing exercises he found in some obscure article he happened upon called "Breathe Your Way Into Bliss." *Inhale with the whole body…Inhale the entire universe…Now release…Exhale until totally empty…no air, no ego. Repeat until nothing of you but breath exists.*

Then… just simple, sweet nothing.

Ten minutes of this deep attunement, then run hard down the mountain. Run and only touch the ground to lift off again. Stay airborne. Stay light.

Andre alternates between taking in the sacred panorama of forest life and looking down at his muscular, pumping leg muscles. *What a great gift to have strength and mobility. I'm so thankful.*

He's been home almost three days and this is the first time he feels unburdened enough to bound down the mountain. Maybe it's just the air working its magic. But to Andre it feels more like a cork has popped. Something is changing in him. He literally leaps off the trail up onto his deck.

He doesn't even mind the ring of the phone. *Probably a client who also just got home from work, wondering why his permit's not ready.*

"Hello, Andre Bell speaking."

"Hi Baby."

"Hi who?…Sheryl!…Sweetheart…Are you alright?…I…"

"I'm better now that I beat the crap out of everything in the Embassy gym. It's 5AM and I'm still totally wired. And I'm furious that they yanked you out of here. I told them so. Told my father too."

"Your father?"

"Yea. He's kind of a big mucky-muck. Long story. Hey, they busted Kostas…I mean his smuggling ring. Rare artifacts. Anyway, Kostas and a silent partner escaped. Vanished. Not easy in Greece. They must've been ready. Could be hiding anywhere in the world."

"They don't think I…"

"Listen, I really miss you—miss *us*…"

"Sheryl, I want to see you more than I want to take my next breath."

"Then let's meet somewhere—anywhere. Paris, Africa, the Caribbean."

"You don't know? The bastards have quarantined me here. Says so on my passport. 'Cannot leave continental U.S. by order of Dept. of State.'"

"Wonder why I wasn't told? Let me work on fixing that."

"Aren't you concerned about your safety? I mean…these guys are still on the loose and they know you were the key to busting them."

"So sweet of you to worry! Very unlike Mr. Accepting-of-Everything." She laughs and Andre swears the fading sun just got warmer. "It's totally under control. They assigned a bodyguard to me full time—actually she volunteered…We hang together when I'm not at work. It's a good thing I'm not a man. She's drop-dead exotic. And tough as nails. There's no way I'd ever leave the two of you alone."

28

Confession

"Bless me Father for I have sinned, I cannot remember my last confession...I haven't been to church for over five years. I've been sexual with more women than I can count. I've had more than one woman at a time. I am not married. I am not an honest man. I am a sinner. I am sorry. Please help me."

Kostas is shaking in front of the shocked priest. He can not look him in the eye. Nor can he go into his dishonest business dealings. He doesn't want to have to explain it. The priest might even alert the police. Confession in the Greek Orthodox Church is face to face. No curtain. No dark stall. No hiding.

For his part, the priest's countenance has broken out in a four-alarm blush. His parish consists of twenty-two remote islands where the biggest sin going is petty theft or coveting the neighbor's olive crop. No one talks about sexual exploits except the occasional, misguided adolescent. The priest doesn't know this new arrival to his congregation. But his litany of sins suggests he came from one of the larger cities or party islands.

In the Orthodox Church, the priest typically questions the penitent. The nuances of his sinning must be known intimately because, as the theory goes, only then can effective, spirit-directed guidance be given. But in this case, Kostas blurts out his sins before the overmatched priest can use the leverage of interrogation.

"My advice to you is to spend the next twenty-four hours on your knees asking God's forgiveness. I will grant you absolution from your sins. But you must return weekly for more counsel. Until then, I will pray that the angel of clarity bestows grace upon both of us. For your penance, say..."

Kostas barely listens as the rote prayers are prescribed. He was hoping for a sense of comfort—some drip of wisdom. Hoping for anything except the humiliation of mimicking a snail's posture. Instead he gets promised an angel will straighten his life out. And this blessed event will take place next week? Kostas needs something now.

He mumbles his penance and leaves the little church still feeling sick at heart. Betrayed again. Not the outcome he needs. He thought God would help him. He must be losing it. God didn't help his father. Why should he start believing now?

Kostas doesn't know it but he needs mothering for comfort—and fathering for clarity. But he never had true mothering. And he despises his father's memory which has failure etched all over it.

Through his own doing, he's lost the love of his life. His livelihood is in shambles because of her. His partner in crime is so angry with him, he fears for his life. He's sleeping with one eye open. The law is after him. He's feeling like Achilles. His tragic flaw is his obsession with one woman. He was surely born with this fate. He doesn't know how this obsession will kill him, but he's sure it will.

29

Andre's High

At least once in every life, a day dawns with a realization that despite your up-bringing, despite your foibles, you stumble onto the nature of the heavenly realm. You know it from the little things. Your morning orange juice bursts with the intensity of the tropical grove from which it sprang. The sun slanting through the lingering mist surely leapt off Seurat's brush only moments ago. And who is this god looking back at you from the mirror?

Andre is on fire, but not with the ruthless blaze that dwarfs the light hidden within the soul, ultimately to consume it along with any shred of guarded self worth. "This is the real deal, the real Andre," he says out loud, emerging from the tunnel and getting that first breathtaking glimpse of the towers of the Golden Gate. He draws a long breath. The superstructure of the bridge, the cars in front, the tree-studded far shore—all of this earthly embellishment moves into and through him. Like divine wind.

The phone call from Sheryl was not the product of his imagination. It really happened. Okay. It's not happening right now, so...so what! "Give it up you tight-ass!" He actually yells at himself! Wow! In that instant, Andre has to admit that he is tired of his own rhetoric. *Why not just simply be— and stop this incessant analysis. Last time you looked, you were an architect, not a shrink, for Chrissakes.*

They were on the phone for over an hour, making plans, rejecting them. Neither of them cared. They are in love and in touch. The loose ends of Kostas and company seem insignificant. They considered everything. Sheryl quitting the Embassy and jetting to him—tomorrow. Andre sneaking off to the Bahamas in a private boat for a beach-time reunion. Or both of them, waiting out the capture and confessions of the Greek fugitives—finally clearing Andre of the ridiculous suspicions Frank continues to entertain— and a reunion in Santorini.

They decided to give it three weeks and then take action. They talked honestly about the pitfalls of long-distance relationships. They vowed this one would be short and that they would check in every other day. It sounded perfect. Solid. Each even spoke about their bond as if it had its own life. As if it had never not been.

But Sheryl, given her track record of failed liaisons should know that love is unpredictable. And Andre, given his experience with abrupt changes of the climate in his clients' minds, should know that nothing in this world is solid even if it actually appears to be happening.

And right now pulling into the parking garage below his office, all Andre sees is he and Sheryl swimming side by side in the stunning sea off Santorini—or Eleuthra—not the man in the dark sedan who's pulled in behind him, parking a few spaces away.

30

Nightmare

Stefanos jolts awake at 4AM from a nightmare. Even in his wakefulness, he still sees Demitrios' hated face, first hanging dead from his mast, then morphing into a pained Demitrios reaching in vain for Nikos, Stefanos' own father—*not* pushing him overboard.

With a chill, he realizes this is not the first time he's had this dream. He tries to block it out, becomes enraged, curses his weakness at having invited Demitrios' son Kostas into his world. In the next moment, he's admitting that their partnership was the perfect course of action. A cunning move at the time. Now he pictures bludgeoning him. His mother's voice scolds him. He hates her memory. He's drained from all this thinking. And he can't stop.

Ten months after his father's death, his mother overdosed on barbiturates, having lost the will to live without her husband to attend to her. Stefanos still feels guilty that he was unable to fill the void left by the father's untimely demise. Now Sheryl floods into his brain. He has an erection. He fights a dry heave. He knows that to harbor any hope of regaining sleep is pointless.

So, to calm himself, he reverts to analyzing the assets. For the third time today. Up until now they were fat. So as not to attract attention, Stefanos diversified their funds into bite-size amounts. He could access any of the funds. Kostas could do so only if Stefanos cosigned. Or upon presentation of his death certificate.

Hah! I knew how to handle lots of money. Twenty-two bank accounts, over half of them Swiss or Cayman, hence untouchable by the law. But most likely no longer accessible from anywhere in the world lest alarms be set off. If I show up at one of these places in person I won't make it out the door. The other half, eight hundred fifty thousand dollars in U.S. currency, sits in plain sight. Traceable. Completely frozen.

The only good news is that, in his paranoia, he kept a large amount of cash in a walk-in vault below the office, in a duffel bag which he grabbed on the way out. If he's careful, he can stretch it seven, maybe ten years. By then he may be able to somehow tap one of the accounts. The challenge, he counsels himself, is to stay hidden that long.

Remaining in Greece in the long term is out of the question. No one will think to look in an out-of-the way Turkish village on the southern coast. Lots of foreigners there.

He can stomach the Muslim calls to prayer. The food is much the same. He'll study English or Dutch, get rid of his accent, pass himself off. The whole thing stinks. He's not happy about it. But then, if he were honest with himself—which he's not—he'd realize he's not been happy for as long as he can remember.

His only real decision is whether or not to make the prearranged meet with Kostas, or continue his wide arc toward Turkey. *Any meeting is risky. Best to stay away. Keep using minor bus lines. Sleep in cheap pensions. Better to sever all ties. Move on. Let Kostas, the naïve lady's man, keep anything above 50-50.*

Still, in the relative safety of a northern, rustic bed and breakfast, Stefanos can't help but feed his overwhelming urge to beat the crap out of Kostas—no, to beat him savagely. He tries to imagine it, tries to picture Kostas' smashed-in face. Instead he can only see the unacceptable: Kostas' father Demitrios' despairing look as Nikos, his own desperately-loved father, slips overboard into oblivion.

31

Facing Stillness

"Damn it!" Kostas kicks his covers off and lies wide awake for most of the night. "I don't deserve this!"

He can't stop looking at a picture of his mother, who died due to complications during the birth of her second child, when Kostas was five. The baby suffocated in utero before the father could get her to the hospital. Kostas was raised by his mother's sister until he was old enough to live with his father at age twelve. His memories of mother had mostly faded by the age of fourteen, when his father's suicide occurred.

His father's death was a huge blow. He was never comfortable with the circumstances surrounding it. Demitrios had abandoned the criminal mode of making a living, and, after helping Nikos' widow and son Stefanos, he had just enough capital to turn the ship into a fishing vessel. He was content to live out his days on the sea, training his son Kostas to become his partner and take over when he was ready to retire.

The two became close during the four years leading up to his death. Kostas would accompany him on weekends and during school vacations to the best spots where they would work the catch. It was a healthy, natural life, giving the boy a grounding in seamanship enjoyed by none of his peers in the throes of urban Athens.

Demitrios was found hanging from his mast on a Wednesday in late April, in open water off Lesbos with a suicide note stating to his family that he was sorry. It didn't apologize for anything specific—just that he was sorry. Kostas knew that this was not the behavior of the man whose values he had come to know so intimately. Values he has long since abandoned because they had gotten his father nowhere.

From that day forward, he has followed a new creed.

I've been a god-damned orphan for sixteen years. And I hate the hand life has dealt me. But I am Greek, I am young, I am strong, I will make my life rich. I will choose how I will do this. I will use any means, and I will make my own good fortune.

To live his creed, a conflict has come to define Kostas. Of necessity he has had to become two different people in one body: affectionate sensual charmer and cutthroat criminal. When the two don't mesh, he inflicts physical pain on himself. He does not want to know why. It would never occur to him to ask.

Once again, on this night, he cannot stop his private highlight reel. The normal highlights—first dance, first love, first drunk—have been displaced by the untimely loss of his parents. Added to that is the loss of the love of his life.

Kostas' unrelenting highlight reel includes seeing three dead persons: his mother at age five—which he can recall vaguely as if she were asleep, and his father at age fourteen—which to this day brings up only rage. Along with the insomnia which is its bedfellow.

Perhaps more impactful was Nikos, his father's partner at age ten. He didn't want to look at the body. When they told him to be a brave boy, took his hand, and said, "Come in and say a prayer for him," he thought he was going to faint. Then, when he got fairly close to the casket, he did faint, because it brought back the last time he saw Nikos alive—at the card game. The sight of those large, lifeless hands clamping the beads of a rosary was just macabre. Just a week earlier he'd seen them move deftly, shuffling and dealing cards. Now they were permanently still.

These reels of his mother, father Nikos, and Demitrios flash alternately in Kostas' mind throughout the wee hours of night. Dawns, including this one, at least provide a reason to rise. Sheryl's face floods into him like the new day's light, crowding out the dead. Then just as quickly he replays the angry phone call and she fades. So he stumbles out of his lean-to, dives off a rock, and considers swallowing sea water until he too is still.

After almost opening his mouth underwater, he breaks for the surface. "I am the worst dog of a coward," he confesses to the seagulls who scatter off the rocks of his hideout toward the crowning sun out on the eastern horizon.

32

Intelligence

"I can't imagine it, let alone believe it!" barks Sheryl when Frank tells her he has intelligence that identifies Andre Bell as a small-time fence dealing in stolen artifacts.

"He staged that whole meeting with you. Think about it. He went right to the cave entrance. Knew to look under the computer for the bank lists..."

"Suppose—but I don't for a minute believe it—suppose you're right. What did he gain by coming half way around the world? Where's his payoff? It only cost him money. There were no funds to be had. Not even any artifacts!"

"Even a couple of rare, fist-sized artifacts to the right buyer could bring tens of thousands. We think his plan was to stake out the villa from Captain Yanni's place, then swim over and rob whatever he could get his hands on, when he was sure Kostas was gone. He didn't plan on running into you. He was winging it after that. He probably figured he'd at least get some revenge by stealing Kostas' girl. You two did get close, didn't you?"

Sheryl grows downright pissed. "Look, the guy's a working architect in San Francisco! He doesn't need to resort to criminality to pull a paycheck. I spent some concentrated time with him. I know this man is genuine. He...could not lie!"

Frank stifles a smirk. "Look Sheryl, I want to be sensitive about this, I do. But you were with Kostas three, maybe four months, and never detected his other life."

"But that was..."

"And I hope you've not forgotten the reason you're in Greece. The reason your Dad and I arranged this job for you?"

"That's not fair, Frank! That was practically in another life. My head's been on straight for way over a year now. Kostas is a well-camouflaged schizoid. And I did pick up on it. I just took a little time, but I got there."

Sheryl turns curtly and barely avoids stumbling out into the hall. *Is my reality shattering again? Did I misjudge Andre? I need my friend. My sounding board. My listening post. The only one who can be objective about Frank. And smart about Andre. I need my Landi!*

But Landi is indisposed—fencing with her own demons—until quitting time.

Shaken and shaking, Sheryl manages to drag herself up on the roof, and proceeds to bawl like she's just been told she is infertile, she is never destined to have a true friend, and there is absolutely no man on Planet Earth worthy of loving her.

33

Landi's Perfect Demon

"So what are you telling me? That I'm having a slight relapse. Just because I have the thought I want to binge?" Landi yells, wanting to rip her therapist's head off but knows she can't over the phone.

"That's not what I said."

"Well then would you mind translating what you said into street talk? Habla direcha, por favor."

"I'll try. It's going on a year since you've binged and purged, and…"

"Tell me something I don't know," says Landi scowling into the mouthpiece.

"The fact that it's been in your recent thoughts to overeat means you're dealing with the same trigger that caused your condition. That's not a relapse. That's an honest reaction."

"I'm not any more stressed now than I have been."

"Maybe not. But perhaps you're down on yourself because you think you're not responding to your latest stressors—perfectly."

"Okay. I got one big stressor. I'm babysitting a new girlfriend who's so damn fine I'm threatened. I mean she's not what you'd call gorgeous, but she's fine in a fun-loving, deeply healthy way. Like the way that I'm not. Besides that, I love her to pieces. Probably take a bullet for her…No, I *would* take a bullet."

"What comes up when you first see her?"

"First awe, I guess. Then jealousy creeps up its—my—ugly little head."

"And how would perfection respond?"

Landi digs down deep into her private-most place. "I'd tell her, 'Girlfriend if you get any more perfect, I'll have to lock you up where the real good men—los hombres perfectos—won't find you.' Ha!" Landi laughs out loud at her "perfect" joke.

"Great! So…are you two competing for the same guy?"

"Not exactly. We *were* but she didn't know it. The competition wasn't real to begin with. And now it's over. We actually think it's funny." Landi gives an honest chuckle.

"So you have similar tastes in men?"

"It wasn't like that. My interest in the guy was strictly professional. Anyway, what's this got to do with my bestial desire to gorge myself?"

The therapist sighs. "I was trolling for active stressors. Most career women your age start wanting a husband and kids."

"That might be me in a year or two. But right now, it ain't poppin' my cork… Look, ever since I blasted out of Harlem, I've been looking back over my shoulder to make sure I haven't slipped into reverse—in the direction of that trap."

"Elaborate on *trap*."

"You know as well as me, if you go too far toward your past you might get captured by it. I've decided to make it my life's mission never to return there. I'll visit, but there's no way I'm returning."

"I see. What happened there that gives you this sense of needing to move in the other direction?"

"Because everybody there—parents included—told me I'd never get out. Every step I take away from there is another way of proving them—and their negative bullshit—wrong."

"So is it fair to say that when shit happens now, you must respond perfectly or you run the risk of backsliding?"

"I suppose. I remember studying for tests at Howard thinking, 'Girl, you gotta get one hundred percent of these answers right, cause if you do, they got no grounds to hold your ass back.' So I usually got them all right."

"Is this strategy still working? What I mean is this: When will you know that you've come sufficiently far that there is no danger of falling back?"

"I know this much. That'll be the day I say sayonara, au revoir, and adios to your ass. And believe me, that day can't rear its sweet cabesa fast enough."

"I'd say you're pretty close."

"That's good to know. Now I gotta drag my overly perfect butt outta here. Looks like I missed my last period. I need to figure out if it means Harlem is calling. That kind of shit happens there. If they are really and truly calling, I need to concoct some perfectly sane way of blowing up the damn phone."

34

No Answer

Andre rings Sheryl's flat for the fifth time this evening. No answer. So he keeps replaying their last conversation.

"I may not be in for a few days," she'd said.

"Where you off to? Hope it's not the islands. I'll be jealous."

"There's a pressing matter I have to deal with."

"A work thing?"

"Not exactly. I'm not at liberty to say."

"Alright my sweet Aegean Queen. I'll stop prying. Just promise me you'll keep yourself safe. Only sixteen more days until our twenty-one day waiting period is over. I'm so ready to hold you, it's all I can do to stay in my skin. Any refined ideas about where we can meet? We should be thinking about booking flights and all that."

"Nothing concrete yet. There are plenty of options. I haven't called my folks... My father is a factor in any travel I do. Another long story I can't go into now."

"You really are a bundle of stories—and secrets."

"Aren't we all pretty much that?" she'd said almost accusingly. "Listen, it's nearly one in the morning here. I'll talk to you in a few days. You be well. Goodnight Andre."

"Bye Sheryl. Love you."

Sheryl hung up the phone without her typical "Love you baby!" She knew—no she hoped—Andre would be confused. In a strange, somewhat teenage way, she wanted to inflict some cruelty. "I wanted him to know that something was very wrong. Wanted to ask him if he was really a disgruntled associate of Kostas. Wanted to stab him if he was," she later confessed to Landi. "But I couldn't bring myself to ask. So it came out tempered and covert and callous—and borderline hateful. God, I'm a friggin' adolescent mess!"

Andre for his part is hurt. He feels the not-so-subtle cruelty like a kick in the groin. *This is my worst nightmare. I open up and finally feel easy with a woman, only to find that my long-sought island in the rough seas of relationship is sinking as rapidly as it has arisen.*

Andre can only assume he's been using a faulty compass. He'd read that when one is truly open with another, you are God's eyes looking at Godself expressed in the other. They had this. They'd been there. In the unity. Now, without warning, the diamond-like atmosphere they were in has cracked. Has begun to crumble. Is turning to coal. The metamorphosis feels tangible. Terrible.

"What happened? What did I do wrong?" cries Andre to the walls of his house.

Running on the trail is no help. The surge of endorphins only serve to make his ever-present image of Sheryl more sharpened and pervasive. He's never gone out of his way to listen to country music, but now he's craving the lost-love exploits of Hank Williams. "Cold, Cold Heart" plays constantly in his head.

He's like a lovesick teen. All over the map—and he doesn't care. When he knows Sheryl is at work, he calls the Embassy switchboard, is politely shoved onto her voice mail, and stammers through some of Shelley's third movement of "Ode to the West Wind."

The next day he leaves only four lines from Shelley's friend Keats:

> *A thing of beauty is a joy forever:*
> *its loveliness increases;*
> *it will never pass into*
> *nothingness.*

35

Salim's Jihad

Salim Hafiz sits in his private office in a wing of his suburban Atlanta mansion. Software designer's home office. Cosmetically-perfect family compound. One-acre paradise-become-prison.

He stares at a near-perfect oil reproduction of Rousseau's masterpiece *The Sleeping Gypsy* by a Moroccan artist. He's perspiring even though the air-conditioning is on.

"Allah. Allah. What do I do? What do I do?" Salim whispers over and over. A knock jars him from his reverie.

"Master? Would this be a good time to talk?" says Naib, the head "caretaker" who works in the on-premises, clean-room lab Salim has installed for his business software research.

"Yes, of course. Come in."

Naib chooses his words carefully.

"We have determined that the last shipment has put us over the top, as they would say here. Once it is processed and integrated, we will have the desired capability. We only need your blessing to proceed. Are you ready to give it?"

"Nearly," Salim lies. "I must council one last time with Sarfaraz."

"I thought that had already taken place." Naib's usual stoicism is betrayed by a momentary frown, like a shadow crossing his face. This warning sign does not go unnoticed by Salim—especially in his hair-trigger emotional state.

Salim sizes up his faux employee. Naib is another driven genius like himself, he concedes, but that is where the similarity ends. In contrast to his own robustness and genial manner, Naib is so emaciated he could pass for a Halloween skeleton. *I can't tell which came first, his social ineptitude or his frightening looks. Careful Salim. Feel superior to this wretched man at your peril. Naib is revered within the organization. You know too well, to cross him would be certain suicide.* Salim suppresses a shudder and relies on his lightning-quick mind to cover his momentary lapse into dread.

"Are you absolutely certain we now have all the critical material we need to produce the result? I don't want to be embarrassed later and have to tell Sarfaraz that we miscalculated. Then we would have to wait for another shipment of the artifacts. This would set us back considerably as that channel is now blocked. I would ask you to recheck your methods and calculations once more. And bring the results to me."

"I did not know the channel is blocked. I will do as you wish," Naib replies, all trace of darkness on his countenance gone. He begins to bow, then stops himself. "And if we are correct, when do you plan to confer with Sarfaraz?"

"As soon as I can arrange the link. It's a bit tedious to get a secure feed in and out of Pakistan right now. It can take up to a week."

"That puts our go date at least fifteen days away!" laments Naib, the shadow returning, this time lingering.

"We must proceed in an orderly manner," retorts Salim, ever the boss. "If we fail, Allah will not be pleased."

At that statement of finality, Naib bows, mumbles an "Allah be praised!" and treads respectfully out of the house and back to the underground lab.

36

Promotion

Sheryl tosses through another night. Mostly awake. Replaying events. As if her soul is swimming through an ocean thick with drama. She feels herself pulling away from Andre. *There are simply too many coincidences for his side of the story to be true. But didn't she rescue him? He would have drowned. Maybe he was faking it. He did regain consciousness at the perfect time. And he did find the passageway—almost like he knew it should be there. But didn't Landi say he was an innocent bystander? Landi has the superior intel.*

Nauseous and out of synch with her own gut, she plays his last message again. Just one haunting sentence: "All is well for the Blue Jack of Diamonds." *What the hell does that mean?* "He's losing it," she says out loud.

Sheryl is grateful to have Landi to lug her raw carcass into the office. Day twenty-one of her and Andre's decision time table is on the horizon. She's dreading the call. They've not spoken. She's remained strangely withdrawn. Despite his poetic messages. Despite his apparent genuine wounded heart. Despite her ache to feel that spirit-level love they'd had on the ferry. *What if he's the real deal? And what if, like all the others, he's not?*

She's taken to reading Greek myths in an attempt to gain some insight as to what esoteric law might be governing this mess. She hopes she'll fit the pattern of Psyche who was elevated by the gods to be the wife of soulful Eros. But with a string of loser men in her wake, she fears she's more like Eurydice, fated to be the bride of Pluto, ruler of the underworld.

"Hey Sheryl, 'Uncle Frank' wants to see you in his office." It is Mike, one of the new college interns.

"Thanks Mike. And he's not my uncle!" It comes out with misdirected hostility. She almost doesn't care.

"Sorry. He just said, 'Go tell Sheryl Uncle Frank needs to see her.'"

She sprints up the two flights of stairs hoping the rush of oxygen will erase some of the emotional fatigue she knows is evident on her face. While Frank's secretary goes through the stuffy Miss-Jansen-is here to see-you-sir protocol, her anxiety starts to approach the red line.

Upon entering, Sheryl remembers why. On her last visit to the chief's office she became acutely uneasy. Though Frank's office overlooks the Embassy's pleasant courtyard through floor-to-ceiling windows, Sheryl felt like she needed to get out. And here it is again. In this moment.

"Morning Sir. You wanted to see me?" Then, spotting a new, well-stocked, rather large home aquarium tank along a side wall, she exclaims, "Wow. When did that arrive?" She practically runs over to the tank though it is only four steps away.

"Yesterday." Frank is beaming. "You like it? I just thought, I live so close to this watery paradise, and I'm usually stuck in this room and can't get out there, so why not bring some of it in here?"

"Good call. And it's beautiful. Really livens up the room," says Sheryl noting her own sincerity. Noting how good easing her self pity feels. "Wow look at the yellow-and-black-stripe citizen! And that indigo-orange character. So gorgeous."

The longer Sheryl looks, the more detail she notices. The shells, the shimmering fish, the subtle green shades of the plants, the shafts of light penetrating through. She is drifting into blue-Sheryl and there is nothing she can do about it—nothing she wants to do about it. Her life has become stale. Blue-Sheryl is exponentially fresh. And it has been so long.

At first Frank appreciates her interest. After all, he's grown tired of his frugal self-image, deciding to start making some noticeable changes in his work environment, his diet, his interactions. He can envision the day when this will even extend to his wardrobe. So Sheryl's interest is more than a small validation.

Though he is friends with her father, Sam Jansen is always two cuts above and three steps ahead. *Such an elegant man. Smart as they come. Like father, like daughter. And she appreciates my décor! Sweet Jesus! I am getting somewhere!*

But this pause is bordering on awkward. It appears to Frank as if Sheryl's transfixion is open-ended. He apologetically breaks the silence.

"Sheryl...Let me show you something," he says, reaching for a paper on his desk.

Sheryl, lost in the tank, feels as though a harpoon has crashed through the glass sides. "Let me show you something...Let me show you something." It keeps echoing through her. Eerily. So eerily.

Frank offers her the paper and, out of reflex, she takes it, staring through it.

"This is the latest intelligence report on your boy, Andre Bell." Frank recites from memory:

"'Subject observed entering Arabian Antiquities specializing in middle-eastern artifacts, mostly sculptures. Subject observed in animated conversation with owner. Exited premises after 33 minutes.'

"And let me show you something else."

Now Sheryl is recoiling internally, as if her soul is locked in a cacophony of pulsations from which a buried memory begins to emerge. She is four. In her playroom. After dark. A much younger Frank is there too. He's given her a very beautiful, brightly-painted wooden bird which he's brought from South America. 'Let me show you something else,' he says. He unzips his pants and pulls a long object out. "It's pretty, don't you think?"

Current Frank, thinking Sheryl is too overwhelmed by the intelligence to speak, decides to continue his train of thought.

"Partly because of your leading us to Mr. Bell, as of last Friday, you've been promoted to a Step 10. I think you'll enjoy the extra three hundred per month." He hands her the paperwork. "And you're now officially in Intelligence. You'll report directly to me. I'll fill you in on the..." Ring,

ring, ring. Frank's phone cuts in. "Must be important to interrupt me. We'll talk later."

Just as Frank reaches for the phone, he waves Sheryl off, mouthing, "Later…" —without volume.

"Later," says Sheryl weakly shuffling out, now returned from the realm of blue-Sheryl, with full knowledge that her boss, this family friend, this avuncular figure who's been in and out of her life from early childhood, exposed himself to her, or perhaps worse, at a tender age.

On the stairs, she pulls out her cell phone, then puts it back in her pocket and returns to her desk. A slow rage begins to rise within her. Her face feels like a burning tire. She's afraid her heart is pounding so loudly her officemates might notice. *Dammit! Why can't I just call Andre? He's my man. And I need him right now. What's keeping me?*

"*You do not trust man,*" says a voice.

Sheryl looks around. No one looks up. She concludes no one heard the voice. She laughs to herself, thinking it's her mind playing tricks on her. She doodles for a few minutes before deciding she needs to go to the restroom and splash some water on her face.

Sheryl looks hard at herself in the mirror and picks on all her flaws. *Yes darling, you possess a kind of desolate beauty but you carry a lot of visible problems. You're too tall. You've never stopped being gangly. Your hair isn't hair. It's a snarled struggle. And then there's the scar. Like a friggin' facial snake tattoo. Ha! Andre named it "The Mark of the Warrior." Told me it had no doubt bled over from another lifetime where I was a sword-wielding Amazon in some exotic cult. I can't tell him it is from a battle in a cult in this life. I told him about blue-Sheryl. That's enough craziness for a first date.*

It's still early but nearly 10 PM on the West Coast. She plods back to her desk and stares at a calendar. *What day were we supposed to decide when to meet? And where? Who was to call whom?* It's impossible for her to focus because she gets the feeling this whole disturbing business with Andre and Frank is one of those one-way conversations God is trying to have with her. *Who—or what—else could it be?*

But Sheryl is in too much turmoil to listen to God or anyone else. So she climbs up to the roof and finally dials Andre, hoping to the worse half of herself that he doesn't answer either.

To her relief she gets his answering machine and hangs up.

37

Ray's Challenge

"Well then, when are you going to ask a *real* woman out?" says Ray. "I hope you're not waiting until you think you're ready. That day may never come."

"I told you. I have a girlfriend in Greece…"

"…who's stopped calling. Wake up and smell the dead roses. She's not real anymore. Most likely it's over."

"Maybe. Or maybe she's not calling for a good reason." Andre has no idea what that reason might be, but it gives him some fragment to cling to.

"Look pal, I know I haven't had the market cornered on successful relationships. But at the risk of blowing what's left of our friendship, it feels like you have some built-in stumbling block. Something that keeps you from being free, being normal, with the opposite sex."

"What do you mean by free and normal? Putting moves on them so I'll be able to screw them? No thanks."

"Okay. I did try to push you into that. And I'm sorry. That's been my identity. I thought every man should have it. I got busted on it big time. I'm trying to change."

Ray seems oddly genuine for once. This catches Andre off guard.

"When did this happen? And who busted you? I mean, who did you let get close enough to allow that?" Andre cannot mask his shock. *Ray just doesn't talk like this.*

"Whoa. These are all good questions. Okay, I was dating this girl. Started out normal. We had a bunch of fun times. And then she springs him on me."

"Him? Her big brother?"

"No. Her teacher," says Ray, his face reddening.

"Teacher? Is she in high school?" Andre hopes his thirty-four-year-old friend isn't chasing some underage beauty.

"No!"

"Okay then, what kind of teacher?"

"All right. If you must know…a spiritual teacher."

Andre falls silent and takes a long pull on his Australian stout. He looks calmly around the restaurant, becoming aware of the combined mumble of the other patrons.

"For God's sake, what's this world coming to? My friend Ray is letting his guard down enough to take advice from a spiritual teacher? This bodes well for our species."

"Okay. I know I've been down on this sort of thing. Especially after that egomaniac with the shaved head. But this guy is different. He's regular. Except that he seems to have a wisdom and a way that blows your mind. Literally."

"What's that supposed to mean?" Andre notices that he's on the edge of anger. It's not like him and yet he can't deny the feeling.

"Look, I know I've leaned on you to try every fad that's come down the pike. And this thing with pushing you toward women, that's just my twisted way of trying to be your friend. It hurts me to see you suffer. I really should own that. It's my thing. Wow! I'm realizing this for the first time. From where I sit now, I can honestly say I have no investment in whether or not you check out Vincent."

"So that's his name? Vincent?"

"Yeah. He comes to the Corte Madera Best Western every Thursday evening. Seven PM sharp. Rents one of the conference rooms and does his thing."

"So are you going this Thursday?"

"No."

"Why not? Sounds like he's your man."

"He gave me some homework."

"So."

"I haven't completed it."

"So what?

"He told me not to come back until I did."

"Okay. That does it. If this guy can jerk Ray Manners around—make him behave like a schoolboy—then this guy I've got to meet."

38

The Slip

Disturbed to the core from her encounter with Frank barely an hour before, Sheryl easily eludes her stand-in body guard by sending her for coffee. She then hurries outside and hails a taxi for Piraeus Harbor. She instructs the driver to drop her at the ferry to the nearby Saronic Islands— to the southwest of Athens. Within fifteen minutes she is on a half-hour hydrofoil to Aegina.

The port there is much too busy for her liking so on a whim she disembarks and quickly boards another ferry for the more obscure island of Angistri. Sheryl is driven to find some clean, deep, quiet water. *You're probably crazy but you've got to get some answers. You need to get them from your own source. In your own way. You need to get them from blue-Sheryl.*

Angistri is so small, over half of it can be viewed on the ferry approach from the northwest. And Sheryl loves what she sees. Rock cliffs interspersed with sandy beaches ringed with greenery. Small, partly vegetated mountains rising to the center of the island. Dots of gardens, splashes of olive groves, clusters of modest, weather-defying homes. *If I wanted to, I could fool myself that I'm approaching Solagros after a rain.*

Disembarking, she runs for one of two taxis in sight and asks to be taken to the best beach next to a cliff on the island.

"Aponissos is where we go," says the middle-aged driver with a sparkle in his eye and music in his voice.

The beach is nestled in a small, secluded bay 15 kilometers distant on the southern side of the island. It is ringed with pine trees and lush, flowering bushes. So much so it's almost tropical. The exotic, blue-green water of Aponissos is a well-kept secret. With one look at Sheryl, the driver knew she was destined to meet the place.

Sheryl offers to pay him three additional Euros to stay but he refuses the money.

"This is my pay," he says, exiting his cab and waving his arm at the bay. "You walk. You swim. I wait." He removes his cap and bows to her like a youngster in a skit. "Now I sleep," he announces, slips back into his cab, slouches into the seat, and pulls his cap over his eyes.

Sheryl is coming to see the Mediterranean as a vast lake with an endless mélange of under-water rooms. And under water has been her physical and emotional sanctuary. Her therapist. And, she's starting to think, her soul mate.

Having already slipped her suit under her working clothes on the last ferry, she peels off her yellow cami and navy cargo pants, piles them over her purse, and dives off a six-foot cliff into the lapis-and-emerald bay.

Blue-Sheryl meets her instantly.

39

Card Game

It's 1979. Ten-year-old Kostas is sipping orange soda. He's hanging around his dad and two other men playing cards. He loves the sound of the chips clicking against each other as they're tossed into the pile in the center of the table. Loves the look of the face cards. Especially the King of Spades and Queen of Hearts. Loves the sounds of betting and checking. The men squinting at their cards. The winner raking in his chips.

He is far from grown, so from his vantage, he easily sees goings-on under the table. Even in his ten-year-old gut, Kostas has a nagging queasiness that something is not right.

The men's friendly game has abruptly become like a vase that just shattered against a wall. They are yelling about who gets to own the hotel. Demetrios, Kostas' father, is betting his half of the hotel that he has the better hand. His partner and rival, Nikos, is just as certain he holds the winner. Zafiris, the third player and first mate, who has folded, is dealing. All the men have downed several shots of ouzo—a complex hard liquor made from grapes, herbs, and berries that, to the uninitiated, tastes like a blend of cheap gin, white vinegar, and turpentine. The smell of it permeates the room.

Little Kostas half notices Zafiris—with a cupped palm—deftly lift a card from his thigh, place it on the top of the deck, and deal it to Nikos to replace his discard. He then deals one card to Demetrios. Nikos wins the hand with three aces beating Demetrios' two queens and two eights.

What little Kostas could not fully bring to consciousness was his observation of the cheating. He saw it but he couldn't see it, since it didn't fit his ten-year-old innocence. He drains his soda and keeps quiet—obedient to some instilled notion that life is held together by the cement of fairness.

40

Underwater Cinema

Sheryl has never expected anything of blue-Sheryl before this plunge into the pure water off Aponissos Beach. But this time she welcomes—no is owed—answers to Andre's behavior, answers to Frank's obsession with Andre, and some resolution as to the wisdom of confronting Frank about whether or not he exposed himself to her when she was very young.

"You are one star in a dazzling galaxy."

Not responding to—but internally recording—the voice, Sheryl gets a replay of the images of events that led her to Greece. Her body swims, yet it's as if her soul is watching a movie of itself four years ago.

There are images of Gabriel, an ex-lover. Images of him lecturing at one of his seminars that he is above earthly pleasures. Images of her mesmerized. Images of him nevertheless regularly indulging in tantric sex with the female followers. A psychic portrait of his self-deluded ego thinking this is some form of humble gift.

Sheryl's tan, lithe body swims mechanically through images of her becoming hooked into Gabriel's cult. Through an image of his charisma convincing her that he has the red phone to God. Now she enters the image of Gabriel wanting her exclusively and him pledging—at her insistence—that he is willing to forego the pleasures of the other women in exchange for her.

Now come images of sex with him, with close-ups of his astonished face recognizing her as a being so uniquely pure, that he knows she is the natural embodiment of the love about which he preaches: the love that emanates from within. Images of his fractured ego in the equivalent of seismic shock, knowing but unwilling to admit that she is as direct a channel to Source as he's seen. A purer channel than himself. Which is a small self. A second-rate Grand Manipulator.

Friendly, but troubled eyes watch from the bluff seeing only a submerged swimmer in a turquoise bikini and not Gabriel's crushed ego whose only move is to capture and exploit her, so to siphon this energy into himself. The eyes cannot see the images of the contrived love in the seminar room being so viscous in the air, one can literally drink it in by simply breathing deeply. They cannot see the carefully rehearsed exercises, the meticulously honed—but fake—in-service personalities so ingrained that the followers cannot distinguish them from their more authentic selves.

The manipulation now illustrated to Sheryl is so effective, the leader and core followers continually drop what they call "the love bomb" so that newcomers—especially the ones from broken, troubled, or emotionally sterile homes—find it irresistible.

And then, out of the underwater silence a kindly, centered voice speaks to Sheryl.

"Gabriel's dilemma is that he did have some form of an awakening. But even when he thought he was acting purely, he was in a deluded state. Because the lurking ego is the one thinking. the one commenting on its own supposed purity. He could not know what elements of his message were true insight, but told himself he could sort them out through his own inner guidance. Much of his message did not spring from the eternal, that is to say, the message was unbalanced. He soon came to treat his every thought as true insight. He became what is known as a rogue teacher. As it has been said, 'One must learn from one who knows.'"

If Sheryl were herself she would check into a mental institution for hearing voices. But in the transparent, harmonious state that is blue-Sheryl, the words travel through her much the same as the images. Much the same as the magical shafts of light splaying into the richly-colored sea, courtesy of the afternoon sun.

41

Seeking a Teacher

Here sits train-wreck Andre on a Thursday evening, all because his friend Ray has somehow become mildly self aware by being in the presence of this man without a last name.

Andre's mind comes full of pre-judgments. *Strange place for a spiritual teacher to hold forth. A sterile conference room in a Best Western next to a six-lane freeway is more suited to a tax-seminar leader.*

A salty-looking sound man sits in the corner piloting a small mixing board, looking fully attentive yet oddly blissful. *These people already come off psychotic. Ha!* Andre has to laugh at his harsh musings.

Four rows of fifteen chairs each are arranged in a flat arc about the teacher. An attractive, cheerful assistant completes her welcoming and announcements, then introduces Vincent.

The room becomes instantly and completely still as Vincent strolls to the front. He sits on a high stool next to a table holding a beautiful array of cut flowers, a lighted candle and a tumbler of cold water.

"If there are any new people here tonight please raise your hand so I can try to sense why in Hades you would venture out through this insipid blanket of fog ," intones a genial, forty-something man dressed down in a Hawaiian shirt with traces of an aristocratic demeanor. Andre was expecting a feral, tie-dyed, Renaissance man. Now he doesn't know what to think about this light-hearted, slightly graying—and, as it turns out—Italian transplant. The guy comes off as normal as espresso.

Andre, and a wildly-dressed, thirty-something woman raise their hands.

"Welcome and Francois has an offering for each of you," says Vincent. "This may well be the only no-strings-attached gift you'll ever get from me, so I suggest you savor it." This elicits a healthy burst of laughter. Andre laughs along, more in relief of his own pent-up anxiety.

Francois, a bright-eyed, curly brunette, hands over an introductory CD as Vincent launches into a treatise on the sacredness of the present moment. How our personality and previous wounding continually conspires to hijack the moment by trapping us in the imprinted past or projected future. Trapping us in our theories, points of view and beliefs—including belief in God.

"I'll give anybody a thousand dollars cash—right now—if they can demonstrate that there is genuine life outside this particular moment. Any takers?"

No one even shifts in their chair. Andre considers how he would structure a challenge. Something tells him he'll never succeed. Mainly because, while staring at Vincent, an immense wave of timelessness breaks over him, washing any semblance of logic out of his being, leaving him feeling at once vast—and empty.

"Being right here, right now, is to experience the fullness of life. It's the only way we can know God directly. And what is God? I submit to you that everything in this moment is God revealing Godself. These flowers, the sounds of the freeway, the light fixtures. Tune deeply into this truth and you can save yourselves years of spiritual practice—which only serves the hope that you'll reap some earned reward at a point in the far-distant future. The future does not exist. There is only now."

Andre's inner vastness takes a momentary quantum leap—until Sheryl parachutes into his mind—whereupon he contracts almost violently, feeling his head itch, and his legs stiffen. He tries to regain the feeling but only grows more uncomfortable. He manages to hide his discomfort by sheer will. He feels like an over-inflated balloon breaking out in a rash.

"Who'd like to share?" says Vincent, entreating the ardent seekers in the packed room. "Remember, we're not interested in your history. Just what's genuinely up for you right now."

Several hands shoot up. "Pass the mic to Mara." Mara launches into a monolog that, at Vincent's urging, quickly evolves into a torrent of tears and moans. She ends up laughing. The regulars sit there in varying degrees of stillness and focus. A few strays blow their noses. Andre notes the abundance of tissue boxes strategically placed around the room.

The personal attention rolls on, through Stefan and Alicia and Dan. Vincent encourages each one to express their feelings through what seems like totally unique channels. Andre senses the energy in the room is very still, yet alive. He wonders if he's part of a mass hypnotism. His neophyte counterpart, the wild, thirty-something raises her hand. The cordless mic is passed over to her.

"My name is Barbara."

"Hi Barbara!" echoes the room.

"I'm addicted to men," she says.

"How are you addicted?" asks Vincent.

"I can't stand them, yet I'm miserable if I'm not involved in a relationship with one of them."

"Quite a dilemma, it would seem," says Vincent. "Perhaps you should have a cage built in your room then lure some unsuspecting male in there. Would that satisfy you?"

Barbara appears to actually consider the idea. The room erupts in laughter.

"Wait a minute. That's your advice? A cage?" yells Barbara, fully realizing what that would entail.

"Why not? It would seem from your remarks that men belong in one. Why not do it? Start with one, then lure in more. Punish the bastards. You can have it both ways! When you want to relate, they're fully available. When you want to hate…fully available! Hate, relate. What's wrong with that?"

"Sounds sick."

"Exactly my point. You need to take responsibility for your sickness. Ultimately, it's a statement about you. When you've invited them into your space, then can't stand them—as you've stated—you're basically saying, 'I reject my creation'. I submit to you that this is not healthy.

"Look out in the audience at all the men. Each one is a potential lover. Make eye contact with one at a time. Say to someone, 'I reject you.' And truly feel that as you say it. And men, stay fully awake! " As far as Andre could discern, this meant sit still, let your mind empty, and simply allow any onslaught directed at you to be received with the deepest neutrality, if not compassion.

At first, Barbara is unable to comply, appearing to be deeply embarrassed. But with Vincent's guidance, she soon spits out several venomous "I reject you's"—until she breaks down crying. Vincent intervenes again, gently asking her what her true feelings are for the men.

"I really do love them. But I carry so much hatred."

"Did your father reject you when you were a little girl?" whispers Vincent gently.

Barbara nods. Vincent goes on to soothe her with perfectly-worded reassurances that ultimately lead her to the realization that she is not crazy, not unloved, and not alone in her humanness. She ends up beaming. The audience gives her a resounding round of applause.

But for hyper-sensitive Andre, this only further triggers his feelings of rejection by Sheryl, linking his unworthiness to his own father's seeming disinterest in him. And there is no way he's raising his hand.

Vincent finishes off the evening's festivities by inviting everyone to turn their attention to the vase of flowers on the table next to him for a long minute and be with their uniqueness and beauty. Andre tries to focus on the exquisite colors and shapes, but the torch that he carries for Sheryl only flares ever more hotly in his brain.

Anything stunning reminds him of his Queen of the Aegean, whereupon he drowns in the memory. And according to Vincent, memory is the mind dragging the awakened you into the past where awakening cannot exist. Andre drives home feeling very lonely and very screwed.

42

The Tracker

Sheryl continues to swim through an undersea slideshow off the picturesque rocky coast of Angistri. Upwards of a hundred insight-heavy tableaus—and counting. But Sheryl is not counting because in blue-Sheryl the paradigm cannot encompass anything that is not of oneness. Thus even the many seeming pictures are one great picture of a soul's flow. All occurring within one breath. The timelessness of this dimension defies every convention of normal reality. In her experience, she's witnessing years of psychic records occurring in a cosmic instant which, to an observer on the shore would amount to a handful of earth seconds.

She literally sees pain—the pain of her father sensing his sweet daughter fall into a trap. Observes the love and resolve it took for him to rise up and use his influence to have the group infiltrated. Watches Gabriel's denial as he's busted for tax evasion, enslavement, and embezzlement. Swims through her six months of deprogramming at an exclusive facility on a barrier island off South Carolina. Stares blankly at her therapist who becomes Sheryl's personal lifeline, easing her back into a world where people, especially good-looking men, could be "scanned" thence trusted— or not—if the scan was applied effectively.

Again her father appears in the form of unconditional love, pulling strings and arranging her position at the US Embassy in Athens where his protégé, Frank Mankowski, Chief of Intelligence, can keep tabs on her. The sight of Frank's image jars her out of blue-Sheryl.

On cue she surfaces, drawing in a long glorious breath. Then a tremor wrenches the serenity from her as she spots Landi sitting next to her clothes intently watching her from the small cliff.

"Dammit girl! You scare the crap outta me." Landi yells, making certain Sheryl knows she is quite pissed. "And I thought you were gonna swim forever in that figure eight pattern. Que pasa with that? And maybe you snuck a breath—but I don't think so. You were under at least five minutes that I saw. Nobody can do that. Who the hell are you?"

"I came out here to be alone," Sheryl almost screams. "What are you—a stalker? Only a psychic could find me this fast? How is that possible?" says Sheryl, scaling the six-foot rock face like it isn't there.

"I will tell you that when I know I can trust your ass. *Don't even think about telling her you put that micro-size tracking device on her purse.* Now listen girl. You wrecked the lives of these Greek bad boys. They have got to be ballistic. They have allies in dark places. Prob'ly have a friggin' contract out on your hide."

"A what? You mean…"

"Yeah I mean. And I suspect Al Qaeda is after them too. Cluster of fanatic killing machines…Allah my ass. I ain't religious but even I know any Allah worth his weight doesn't sanction murder. Bunch of glorified goons. Relentless assholes. Sticklers for erasing loose ends. You stumble into a crossfire, it'll mess up more than your suntan. This isn't some TV show. It's your life."

"But…then you're not…just…watching out for me? Oh, I get it. You're using me for bait! I thought…damn it, damn it, damn it!"

"Whoa there, girl. What's with the bad wishes? Surely you knew this wasn't all just simple sisterhood."

"I knew there was some danger. But I thought I was owed protection. And I thought we had something. A real friendship. Never has happened to me."

"Friendship goes both ways. Real friends don't just up and run off without checking in. And what d'you mean, never. Everybody has friends."

"*Everybody* doesn't include me. Never has." Says Sheryl, eyes starting to water.

"C'mon. High school. College. No way you didn't have girl friends." Landi looks hard at Sheryl, trying to picture her going years without something so basic.

Sheryl sighs. "In school, I was the guy magnet. Ruined so many couples 'cause the male always seemed to want to conquer me. Conquer the Amazon. Subdue the She-Dragon. So I let them try. Felt good. Powerful. But so wrong. Same story in college. Girls, women, they all hated me. Can't blame them. Can't for the life of me figure it out. I'm just not that hot. It's a curse. I finally just gave up on the female. Until you showed up. And now..."

"Whoa all over again. Turn off the pity machine. First off, you're not just hot. You're a living breathing blast furnace. Hotter than hot."

Sheryl laughs.

"What? What's funny?"

"I had a sort of man-friend once. Was just flashing on him in the water. He used to say that," Sheryl says.

"See. I know whereof I speak."

"Ha! He thought he did too. He was a self-styled guru. Charismatic asshole. Guess you could call him a cult leader. Made me the queen of the coven. Got me hooked real good. Like being drugged."

"Sounds like a heavy chapter." Landi says, playing it like she doesn't know.

"Definitely. I'm still in recovery from that one."

"What hooked you? His voice, eyes, body? His message? What?"

"Great question. A lot of things. His name itself cast a spell. Gabriel. He claimed to be the physical incarnation of the archangel. Can't believe I fell for that B.S. But he made it seem as normal as toast."

"Sounds nutty as hell. Did he have some irresistible set of virtues? Did he like… promise you wings and halos—with some cosmic sex thrown in."

"His message was not even that complicated," says Sheryl blowing past the suggestion. "The simplicity of it was the hook. He drilled the notion into us that God's benign love resides at the core of everything. The body, the dirt, the stars, our thoughts. Even if we are momentarily caught up in judgment or depression, these are just masks. Peel them away and direct contact with the love is assured."

"Damn! I ain't all that pious and shit…but that shit sounds pretty good."

"Exactly. But boiled down, it's simply another New-Age, sweep-the-shadow-side-under-the-rug philosophy. The minute anyone expressed a real concern—say an illness, a parent flipping out, a doubt if the lifestyle was right—you were brought before the group and publicly flogged."

"You mean beaten?"

"No, humiliated. Felt like a psychic crucifixion. So eventually no one spoke up. We all just collectively stuffed our dark sides. It took a few months— and some serious martial arts training—for me to accept that being able to dance with one's shadow is a major key to true liberation. Balance is where it's at. I thought I was there—until Kostas came along."

"That part doesn't compute," Landi says, unable to resist talking about Kostas. "Given your history, how is it you trusted this shadowy Casanova?"

"Looking at it in the rear view mirror, I was ripe. I don't have to tell you, he could ooze sincerity and lace it with charm. The looks distracted me. The accent excited me. And he was able to so wall off his dark side, my scan apparatus never was able to detect it. If you hadn't read his file, would you have caught that?"

Landi shrugs. And wonders. And admits, *the guy was a great lover. But his mistake was that his dark side should have scanned beyond my body.* "I guess not," she finally answers.

"I think not either. He has that boyish innocence going. But when the man is sincere, he is sincere. In such moments, I can only deduce that he even fools himself. There's no defense against that."

43

Chatter

Andre eases his silver Porsche into a space near one of the upscale waterfront shops on the main drag in Sausalito. Upon exiting his car, he makes momentary eye contact with one of those glowing northern California women who seemingly cause heaven to reveal itself on earth. *What if she says "Hello"? Would I be able to reciprocate the interest—a little? Do I even want to? Why shouldn't I? Why can't I say hello and initiate a conversation? Other guys can. Am I missing some critical gene? And how would Sheryl react if she were watching?*

Despite Andre's decent education and successful career, on the woman front, he knows now, more than ever, that he's the strikeout king. His father was a womanizer, having left his mother flat when she was pregnant after promising to marry her if she'd have their child. The man just couldn't get over that hurdle of giving up his freedom to settle down with only one woman. Andre knows intellectually it's a bridge every man confronts and usually crosses gracefully. *Cross the marriage bridge? Ha. I don't have any idea what galaxy that's in.*

But both Andre and his father have failed to cross over—for opposing reasons.

Daily he carries the baggage left by Gordon, his father, last heard from living in a ramshackle, expat community on the Costa Rican west coast. *How perfect for him. An abundance of transient women. Warm ocean. No real law. The ultimate in non-commitment. On the cheap.*

On his side, Andre is so blocked by the fear of duplicating his father's miserable track record, he's been essentially frozen from any unburdened pursuit of the opposite sex. That is, until the unusual circumstances surrounding his encounter with Sheryl dramatically thawed him. *What shift in the solar wind caused Sheryl to land in my life?*

Andre now moves through time and space believing that their meeting was not only mere destiny, but also that once-in-a-lifetime chance for the brass ring. *I lose her, I lose my soul.*

What he doesn't know is that to lose her will result in a long, painful recovery from the blow to his ego—which he, like most, has mistaken for his very soul.

He's relieved that the glowing woman doesn't give him a second glance.

In reality she's attracted by his athletic image and does gaze back, but he's too involved with his tedious self-analysis to notice.

44

Tell Me

"Hi Daddy!"

"Sheryl! How are you sweetheart?"

"I'm okay. Listen, Daddy, I really need a break. I'd like to come home for a couple weeks.

"What happened?" says Sam Jansen, going immediately glum.

"Nothing major," Sheryl offers, knowing her father knows it's a lie.

"Have you talked to Frank about taking time off?"

"It's none of Frank's business." Sheryl is doing some violent doodling to stay calm. "Is it a crime to take a time-out and come home?"

"Frank tells me you've become an important part of his organization."

"You've talked to Frank?" Sheryl presses so hard on her pad, the pen snaps in half. "I don't want my every move analyzed by the two of you."

"Sweetheart, he's practically a family member. We're just looking out for you. Hey, I hear you got a promotion! I'm really proud of you."

"Thanks Daddy. But I'm not sure why I got promoted. It doesn't add up."

"Tell me." This is Sam Jansen's blood-hound-mode expression. He rose up through the ranks of the Foreign Service by his tenacity at digging into the incongruous muck people leave behind when they're not operating with integrity. He simply assumes that there is a pervasive atmosphere of compromised ethics afoot—especially in the corporate-government complex.

With the skill set of a detective, he's been able to spot this phenomenon and exploit it to his gain—and that of his country.

"I'm not sure where to start without going into a drawn-out story." Sheryl knows she has to be concise or her father will tune out. For all of his vaunted people-skill prowess, she is amazed at why he simply can't hear that she needs to come home without having to plead a damn court case? She makes a fist and takes a punch in God's direction.

"Give it your best shot sweetheart."

Sheryl sighs, knowing before she dialed that it would come to this surrender.

"I'll try. It's complicated. I've been involved with a Greek entrepreneur named Kostas. The same morning I found out he was cheating on me, I collided in the water with an architect from San Francisco named Andre. I had to rescue him. Dragged him to Kostas' villa where I was staying. Kostas was unexpectedly called to Athens on business. Andre and I discovered a secret chamber under the villa that connected to a cave that connected to the Mediterranean. Turns out Kostas is involved in laundering artifacts, using the chamber as a collection point. Anyway, Andre and I decided to…"

"Whoa!" cries Sam. "I'm diagramming this out, and can barely keep up. What's all this got to do with your promotion?"

"You tell me. But let me finish first. At this point, Andre and I sensed we were in danger and paid a private boat captain to get us off the island. Kostas and his partner had a dragnet out for us, which we managed to elude and get to the Embassy where I thought we'd be safe. Next thing I know, Frank personally interrogates Andre, then ships him back to the States without letting me see him. It's not even his department that's carrying the thrust of the case."

"Tell me."

"Well, there's this agent named Landi from Counter Terrorism, CIA. Frank had explicit orders to not interfere in what she was doing. They've been onto Kostas for a while. They think his artifact supplier is a money conduit to Al Qaeda."

"So why did Frank get involved?"

"I don't know. Maybe he wants to make a name for himself. And he's still involved. He's having Andre tailed. He says Andre is part of the network. Daddy, I've come to know Andre. He would never be mixed up in this kind of thing. At least, I don't think so.

"Tell me…About the promotion."

"One morning Frank calls me into his office. Says because of my work in fingering Andre, he's pushing me up to a Step 10. Daddy, you know I wanted this. I love intelligence. I've wanted to be more than a clerk. Funny thing is, I'm still a glorified clerk. I'm just making more money. I still don't get to sit in on briefings. Maybe that's coming."

"This man Andre. How well do you really know him?"

"I'll be totally straight with you. I spent all of twenty-eight hours with him. I can't say we are lovers, but I can say we deeply care for each other. At least it felt that way when we were together. It was soulful."

"It's hard to argue with that feeling if it's genuine." Sam has his doubts, but his devotion to his daughter has always won out and it's winning again now.

"I know this must sound crazy. And I know my track record with men isn't stellar. But this guy isn't some wild, charismatic alpha-male. He's very ordinary actually. Kind of a worker bee. Great sense of humor. A truly gentle man. On the other hand, Frank keeps hammering this intelligence at me that implicates him. I'm pretty confused. That's why I want to come home."

"Tell you what. Your mother's in Miami babysitting her Save-the-Key project for a couple days. When she gets back, we'll talk. Meanwhile, let me look into this from my end. Can you call me Tuesday the 3rd about this time?"

116

"Sure Daddy. Sorry I'm so much trouble. Thanks for hearing me out. I didn't realize how much I needed that."

"Okay sweetheart. So glad you called. You're doing a good job in life."

"Thanks. Oh! One more thing. I've been having a recurrent memory of Frank doing something icky when I was little."

Sam starts to say "Tell me!" but just can't begin to pile that on top of what he's already heard. And Sheryl is in no mood to elaborate.

"Let's address that when you come home. Goodbye for now sweetheart. We'll talk Tuesday." Sam Jansen hangs up the phone and buries his now aching head in his hands. But only for a moment.

45

Demetrios' Demise

Under a crescent moon, Kostas is rowing, steadily, rhythmically. He has killed the engine on the zodiac a mile and a quarter off Solagros. *Are you crazy? Risking imprisonment to get answers. What if there are no answers? Stefanos would tongue-lash you for this stupid display of emotion...Screw him!*

Alone on the hushed, star-lit sea, his thoughts turn naturally to his father, Demetrios, who, in this moment, he misses terribly. He imagines the seamen's last moments. Climbing up the mast with a tie-down rope. Fixing it to a cleat high up on the mast. Rigging the noose. Cinching it around his neck. Jumping out into space. Slamming back against the mast, Neck snapped. Eyes unable to shut. Gone.

Kostas stops rowing. His own breathing is stifled. He has the dry heaves. He's back in the next room listening from behind the door to the police inspector going over the results of the investigation.

"What do you mean you couldn't find anything substantial?" says Makis, Kostas' uncle.

"There's a couple small things that don't add up. Very minor. Nothing we could justify as the basis for opening a murder case," replies Inspector Vitros.

"What small things? Nothing is too small! I know my brother! He was at peace in his life. His only goal was to build a fishing business to turn over to his son, Kostas. Somebody did this to him!"

"I'm sorry for your loss. There's absolutely no motive we could uncover."

"Then you're not looking hard enough. He must have had some enemies from past business dealings. There's some man he called the Kapetan. My brother gave him a lot of money as I remember. Maybe it was blackmail."

"We checked that out. The Kapetan is clean. Runs a little resort out on Solagros…He did give us some interesting background on your brother's ex-partner, though. Name of Nikos. Was washed overboard in a storm off Simi. Has a son named Stefanos. Seems your brother felt so badly, he set up the widow and the son—plus the Kapetan, a family man who was left stranded with no income. He kept much less than half the assets from the sale of their hotel for himself.

Kostas remembers Makis grunting at this news. And when Makis leans hard on the Inspector for the "couple of small things that don't add up," all the official would offer is "no *obvious* trauma to any part of the body but the neck," and "the suicide note was written on paper not found anywhere else on the boat—or on none they could find here in the house." This makes Kostas more crazy right now than it has in years.

He opens a beer and rinses his mouth with one great swig, pitching the rest in the sea. He renews his obsession of rowing the bulky zodiac toward a small light perhaps a mile distant. Expertly, he's timed it so the tide is with him. *I must find out why my father helped out the Kapetan. Why would he tell us he fired the man for stealing from him, then help him with a lot of money. And I must know the details of Sheryl's departure from Solagros. Who is this American?*

46

Kostas and the Kapetan

Shortly before midnight, moving in synch with the stealth of a slight current, Kostas ties his zodiac to the dock at Kapetan Yanni's. His hands are blistering and his adrenaline is up.

He's been surviving alone on a small, scrubby island the size of a half a soccer field about three hours away. It has a big enough niche in the rock to hide the zodiac from the air. As an emergency plan, he had previously cached outboard fuel, water, and enough food staples to last a couple of months. He's been sleeping under the stars and spear fishing for exercise and fresh food. Very occasional nighttime runs to Oia on Santorini to use the public phone are risky but possible.

The rugged life's been good for building Kostas' toughness, but emotionally hellish because he's addicted to social interaction to an extreme. Women normally fill that void for him. Even though he's dreading confronting the Kapetan, he's unconsciously elated at the impending human contact.

"Kapetan. Kapetan!" Kostas exhales in a loud whisper. "Kapetan!"

Without switching on the light so as not to disturb his guests, Yanni comes to his side of the residence door. "Who is it making this noise?"

"It's Kostas. I am sorry for waking you. We must talk. Will you oblige me?"

"Kostas! One moment. I will come." Kapetan Yanni calms his wife, throws on his white shirt and shorts, and starts to conceal his ever-present knife. He hesitates then reverses course, thinking it better to remain unarmed. Didn't he just hear Kostas actually use the word *sorry*?

Yanni slips out the door & motions Kostas toward the dock where the gentle lapping of the waves will muffle their conversation. They sit dangling their legs over the dark water.

"I need to know why my father helped you so much after Nikos died."

Kostas is more surprised by his own question than is the Kapetan. They both thought he would be driven to find out about Sheryl's departure.

"Your father was a very kind man."

"Too kind for his own good. But something does not add up. Wasn't there a card game where Stefanos' father Nikos won the hotel from him? I was there. I remember something funny about the game. Why did he give the hotel over to Stefanos and his mother when it wasn't his to give if he'd lost it?"

Yanni lets out a long breath. "Even though I was steering the ship at the time, this game has haunted me every day since."

"Why would it do this?"

"Demetri, your father, confided to me he figured out the card game was rigged. His plan was to confront Nikos. No papers had actually been filed on the hotel. They had yet to speak about it. He was waiting for the right moment and was willing to give his friend an out by saying that he knew the whole thing was a practical joke."

"This is the behavior of a loser!"

The Kapetan is a simple man, and with that territory, comes patience, and at his seventy-plus years, a measure of wisdom. He keeps calm.

"He couldn't really lose either way. If Nikos took the honorable way out, they were still 50-50 partners in a risky but lucrative enterprise. If Nikos persisted, then Demetri would know it was best to exit the relationship, as greed had trumped friendship. He still had enough nest egg to start some thing else—and more legitimate. Strangely, this is what happened."

"It cost him his life—and could have ruined mine!" Kostas wants to cry but goes to anger instead to mask it.

121

"Perhaps. Or perhaps God has a larger plan."

"Don't give me that God crap. It only works for the blind and deaf."

"And your way is working?" Yanni knows this is a risk. He also knows Kostas needs more from him than he's gotten.

"Not right now. But at least I'm here talking to you and not rotting in jail."

"And I salute your courage to look for answers. I have yet to tell you why the card game haunts me. Do you want to know or would you rather move on to the girl?" Yanni bets some more imaginary chips and smiles inwardly.

"You haven't changed from my early years when you taught me poker. Still know when to hold a knife to a person to make him listen."

Yanni senses an opening. An opening in a man he assumed would be overrun with anger and thus unable to approach.

"Everything changed when Nikos drowned. I was in the wheelhouse trying to keep the ship from capsizing. Demetri and Nikos were struggling to lash down their cargo. Some Turkish hashish we picked up off Simi. I thought at first Demetri pushed him. Pushed him because of the card game.

I thought this for a long while. I was hard on him. Through it all he swore the ship lurching in a wave knocked him into Nikos. It was getting dark. I was steering the ship. I only caught a glimpse. I could have seen him trying to reach out and grab his friend. Sometimes the mind makes us see things according to what we already think."

"Where was Stefanos when this was happening? Did he see it?"

"Stefanos was fifteen. Too young to be above deck. He was riding out the storm in the lower cabin, staring through a porthole. He told me he was watching the two men struggle with the lashings. Demitri's back was to him and all he saw was his father going over the side with the other man lunging at him. He too saw it as a murder. I doubt if to this day he's ever changed his mind."

"Even after my father was so generous to him and his mother?"

"After the drowning, as you may remember, Demitri unceasingly expressed his grief at not having saved Nikos. For whatever reason, Stefanos had already become so hardened, he could consider no alternative possibility but murder. Even when Demitri gave much of his share from the business to him and the widow, Stefanos' rage was not to be quelled."

"What changed your mind? You saw my father as a killer also."

"I studied Demitri for months after. He never acted like a guilt-ridden man. He never changed his story. And he never stopped grieving for Nikos. Only a caring soul could do these things.

"I still don't understand why he would put someone else's family ahead of his own." Kostas wants to beat his head into a wall at his father's altruism. Yet a fledgling pride is emerging that he's never before allowed.

"I suppose Demitri figured, in the larger movings of the planets, it would bring him relief to be free of the whole affair. His good heart thought the generosity would provide a graceful exit. Sadly all the good gestures had no effect. A couple months after the funeral, as I was moving Demitri's papers from the old hotel, Stefanos charged in, throwing things and screaming into my face, "There has been no justice for my father."

"Why didn't you tell this to the police?" Kostas stifles a yell.

Yanni shushes him. "Because I wanted to steer away from retaliation. Even when I last saw Stefanos in the flesh at fifteen, I feared him. I have a family. And I must tell you, I did not want the police snooping around to discover the smuggling that lay below the cover of the trinkets they were exporting. When I realized what they were doing, it was too late. I was already involved. And it has not stopped to this day. I have been forced to do favors for Stefanos. "

"What favors?"

"These shipments you get, I tell Stefanos when they are coming."

"How is this possible?" Kostas feels as if the dock where he sits is coming unmoored from its pilings and is drifting away.

"Either a letter would come, or a courier, depending on how soon the shipment was to arrive. I then would leave a coded produce order on Meli Productos' answering machine," sighs Yanni, knowing he has now crossed beyond his own long-secret border.

"I had no idea of this," says Kostas dumbfounded.

"It is unfortunate. And now, I wonder when one of these couriers will come for me with a knife. Or a silencer. If Demitri were alive, he would be able to make all of this go away. Just like he did the last time. He made it all go away," says Yanni with watery eyes.

"So this is why my father concocted that story about why he fired you. So you wouldn't turn on him and go to the police. He must have paid you off. He bought you this property. Didn't he?"

"It wasn't like that. Demetri and I had already been close friends for many years. He lured me in but always felt badly because he could see I was most uncomfortable. I have terrible ulcers to show for that time. Probably my debt for not just walking away."

"Debt to whom? Not the God thing again!"

"Call it what you will. Everything we do has consequences—good or bad."

"Sounds like bullshit. I believe we make our own luck."

"My son, this is exactly what I am saying. You too have made your own luck."

Kostas is stunned. *__Now your soul knows this utterance is the reason you have risked arrest to see the Kapetan.__* Kostas ignores what he deems to be a loud thought. He focuses intently on his father Demetrios, and pictures him in complete synch with his life at the helm of his fishing boat.

He grows extremely quiet as the events of the last months and years replay themselves on the screen of his mind. *Could my father have displayed great insight? A savvy I cannot see. A brand of wisdom I shun. Or was he weak and guilt-ridden? Wisdom or fear, was this worth paying with his life?*

In a profound way, the conversation—like all catalysts—is rendered irrelevant. Only the innocent sound of the lapping waves remains as the two men sit motionless on a dock in the Grecian midsummer night.

47

Nazzy & Salim

"Of course I'm a bit confused lately," admits Salim as he sips his mid-morning tea in the nook off the kitchen. "Not much is working for me professionally right now. Do you think I'm a has-been?"

Nazneem—Nazzy as he affectionately calls her—covers her shock at his question. "Of course not. I see you like the jackal. Surveying the landscape. Waiting for the perfect time and location to strike—with another of your brilliant triumphs."

Salim fights a shiver. His wife's metaphor is more real than she could ever think possible. "Oh Nazzy! You have such faith in me. I don't deserve you!"

"It is I who don't deserve you. You are the sun that sustains my brightness."

Salim tears up. Not because she is correct. Because he has fallen from such grace. And because she is so innocent.

"Do you ever long for Pakistan? For our ancestral mountain home? For the ways of the place."

It's Nazzy's turn to shudder. "We've been gone so long. Every time I call, the family tells another story of how bad it is there. The Taliban always watch them. The daily pressure chews on them like a pack of hyenas."

"The Taliban leave you alone within your compound. They still respect family sovereignty," counters Salim.

"Ha! Have you been smoking opium for breakfast?" Nazzy retorts. "Freedom has become an emptier word than even a year ago. And the year before that. And the year before that. We've not been back for over ten years. It gets worse by the day. Why would I wish to trade what we have here for oppression? For danger?"

"But our daughter will never know her…"

"Our daughter is an American citizen. She feels a belonging here. An acceptance. Even in Atlanta, heart of the American South. Do you think she would enjoy going about in a bourka?" Nazzy is nine-tenths of the way to livid. "Why are you saying these things?"

"I do not know." But Salim does know. He is floating a trial balloon and it just popped. In his face.

"And tell me again why we left Palo Alto? If you tell me it's because you wanted to move in the direction of Mecca, we're going to counseling!"

"I can't explain it right now—but I promise I will soon," is all poor, cornered Salim can muster.

The dazed man dashes out, lying that he has an appointment downtown which he's just remembered, leaving Nazzy in tears.

48

Mermaids in a Cove

"I feel like a mermaid who's been out of the water too long and gotten banished to land," sighs Sheryl.

"Damn girl, I just rescued your behind four piddly days ago! Remember? When you up an' ran off in the middle of your work day? You some kind of mermaid or what?"

Instead of bantering back Sheryl surprises herself and takes hold of Landi's hand pulling her hard toward the water. *Okay just shut your trap, reach out, and see what happens. Even if she's using you to lure in the bad asses, she's the closest thing to a friend you've known. Remember when you felt like you could access the love at the center of all things? When you were exploding with that grace? Maybe this time that gift will become real in a the form of a genuine friend…*

Like a pair of school girls, they run to the sunlit sea, jump in off a small cliff still holding hands, and revel in the diamond liquid. The rock and plant formations below the water are exquisite. Though it's fairly near the ferry lanes, but on the far Peloponnesus side from them, the water is miraculously clear. A cacophony of animated sea creatures greets them: spotted weevers, blue manna crabs, silvery bream, and—looking like miniature moving murals—a school of painted combers. To simply view them puts the swimmers in an altered state.

It turns out Landi is no slouch in the water. At first she and Sheryl go into near hysterics, then ease into a state of sensual delight. Soon they are diving deeper and deeper, getting more ballet-like with each descent. They help each other with cartwheels and lifts. It is as if blue-Sheryl has been waiting down there to reunite with its vehicle, the entity known as Sheryl Jansen.

On their sixth or seventh dive, Sheryl's blue-self becomes as big as the Mediterranean. The transition is seamless. She merges with the aquatic life, the light shafts beaming in, the undersea plants waving, even Landi hovering then twirling beside her. Now she becomes the container the sea sits in. And expands out into the container of that container.

Off in the distance a figure—white trunks, blonde hair—searches for her. Even though she could not and can not begin to define the term, this elevated dimension of her knows it's a soul—Andre's soul.

When Sheryl naturally expands to encompass him, the joyousness of the inclusion causes her immense being to undulate. Like a ripple through a galaxy.

A brief eternity later, Sheryl becomes aware of Landi moving away, toward the soul of an olive-skinned, dark-haired being she knows to belong to Kostas. This awareness coaxes her out of blue-Sheryl, whereupon she meanders to the surface for a long drink of treasured air.

Landi immediately slips under Sheryl's back and assumes the lifeguard's standard rescue position.

"Hey, Landi, I'm okay! Really, I'm fine. See?" Sheryl wiggles free and swims a quick circle and a half around her shocked counterpart.

"My God, woman! When you pulled that out on Angistri I thought I coulda' been seein' things. But not this time. How'd you learn to hold your breath that long?"

"Long is right. It's a long story. One that's not in my dossier...Hey, I'm famished and that restaurant out on the point is one of the best-kept secrets in Greece. And we mermaids have some scaly things to dissect."

49

Kostas Calling

On the sunset walk to the point, the ringtone on Landi's cell phone breaks the mermaid spell.

"Landi speaking."

"How are you, my sweet delight? It's Kostas!"

"Wild thang! Como le va? Where have you been? I thought you dropped off the planet." She tugs at Sheryl and silently mouths 'Kostas!'"

"I've been to Rhodos on business. It took longer than I thought. Where are you now?"

Landi has dropped onto the sand, opened her purse and is frantically writing a note to a confused Sheryl which reads, "Use you for bait?"

On impulse, Sheryl nods.

"…Hello…Funny connection. And funny you should ask. I'm about to dine out on the Peloponnesus with a new friend. Met her at the Plaka. Says she knows you. Her name is Sheryl Jansen."

"You know Sheryl? And she's there? Right now?" *I can't believe this good fortune. Word of the bust must never have reached into her world.* "I'll say hello for a moment. Then we must talk." He handles this news so smoothly he almost believes his own lie.

Sheryl takes the phone while Landi frantically scribbles instructions. "Hello Kostas. This is Sheryl."

"I can't tell you how much I've longed just to hear your voice. I am so sorry for putting you through hell and I will do anything to make it up to you."

"Yes, it's been a while. So what are *you* up to?" Sheryl is intuitively aware she needs to play it as if she were hiding their relationship from Landi. It would be funny were they not talking to one of the most wanted men in Europe.

"Listen. I must see you. Is that even possible?"

"I would enjoy that sometime. Perhaps we could make it a threesome." Sheryl winks and Landi nearly loses all semblance of composure."

The innuendo goes right past Kostas.

"Thank you for keeping this from Landi. She is so spicy-sweet and I do not wish to hurt her. There's an out-of-the-way café at the base of the long stairs at Oia. Right on the water. In English, *The Fish Lady Grill*. How about in 3 days? Monday night around 10 PM?"

"We'd love to meet you in Santorini. Call Landi sometime next week and we'll have a plan. Does that work for you?"

"If you'll be there just say *yes*…once. Then put Landi back on."

"Yes. You too. Here's Landi."

"Yo boyfriend! We gotta spend some one-on-one downtime. Real soon. I ain't waitin' for Santorini. When you comin' back to town?"

"I can't get free for a few days. I need you badly. You know you are my tiger woman…"

"All parts of me are missin' you. Call me when you get it figured out. We got some sweet catchin' up to do!" Landi teases.

"I will call soon. I promise. We'll spend a whole day in bed at my flat."

"Umm. Sweet. But this time we do everything I want. Kiss, kiss baby." Landi hangs up quickly before she snorts violent laughter into the phone. Then, along with Sheryl. she unloads it to the point of gasping for air.

Calculating all the while. *Okay girl. You gotta get a sting op in place. And who is this chick?*

She looks Sheryl up and down as if truly seeing her potential for the first time, then fixes her gaze square into Sheryl's eyes.

"Honey, I'm already comin' to love you like my own sister but I'd be damn jealous if I weren't Special Ops and trying to trap this creep. You are crazy, classy, and best-actress material to boot. This beach outing has turned into a workout—and a workday. I'm famished. And I'm buying—but only if you're gonna tell me how you stayed under so long."

50

Andre's Process

Andre sits in Vincent's Thursday session not understanding why he's even there—except for the fact that he has nowhere else to turn. He's lost in his thoughts during the opening remarks and finally tunes in. He doesn't even notice his friend Ray slip into a seat in the second-last row.

Vincent strolls in with the ease of a seasoned surfer on a chest-high wave.

"We humans are taking ourselves down a dangerous path. The ego is far too dominant in our lives and we have no sense of the implications of that. We're all living in our own separate worlds and the further we go into those worlds the more destructive we are. To ourselves, our fellow humans, and our planet."

"Our only hope is to awaken out of the separation and realize the Oneness that is at the very heart of everything. It is like awakening out of a dream. There are many spiritual teachers now emerging with this message. But who will hear, who will respond?"

Along with several others, Andre tentatively raises his hand. Rather, his hand seems to have raised itself. Vincent is always happy to involve new people, and calls on him. Feeling exposed, Andre immediately goes into a state of regret, but it's too late. Besides, he has a genuine question that predates all of his current craziness.

"Are you implying a person can't wake himself up by himself? He has to have a teacher? Isn't it possible to do it by oneself?"

"Ultimately you are correct. You are responsible for your own awakening. But there are so many forces of resistance that without the clearest possible guidance, awakening for most people is unattainable."

"I thought I was making progress. But right now nothing seems to be working," Andre confesses.

"What's not working?"

"All I can think about is the girl I lost when I had to leave Greece abruptly."

"You Marin people and your relationship dramas…All right then," sighs Vincent. "Why did you leave abruptly? Were you such a bad guy they kicked you out? What did you do, run naked through the Parthenon? Actually, they might approve of that!"

"I wish it were that simple," sighs Andre after the laughter subsides.

"Would you be willing to come up front and sit here in the hot seat right next to me?" coaxes Vincent. "Nothing's so complicated we can't get to the bottom of it in a minute or two."

Andre hesitates and finally complies, feeling even more exposed.

"So, what sordid behavior got you kicked out of paradise?"

"It wasn't like that. There was this smuggler and the girl was mixed up with him without knowing he was a criminal. I collided with her in the water and after she rescued me, we stumbled onto this secret cave the smuggler uses. I helped her escape. And we were almost kidnapped but made it to the American Embassy where she works. This jerk interrogated me, accused me of collusion…and put me on a plane…and I wasn't able to say goodbye and…"

Virtually everyone in the room breaks into fits of laughter as Vincent cocks his head back and rolls his eyes. Andre is shocked at their heartlessness. Vincent senses Andre's dismay.

"Don't you see it's just your story. It's a good one—but just a story nonetheless. Stories only serve to keep us trapped in the mind. Tell me, what's the feeling associated with the story?"

134

"Helpless. Like a victim," replies Andre glumly.

"There's no joy in victimhood. You need to become empowered. I can lead you through a process, or I can simply open you into the power that's already there. Which do you choose?" says Vincent.

There is a generosity in Vincent's voice which enables Andre to calm himself and reflect a moment. "All I know is, I feel helpless to do anything about the situation. I think I need something immediate."

Vincent stares directly into Andre's eyes. To Andre, it feels as though his whole being is being penetrated—yet he does not feel threatened.

"You have much rage repressed within you. You will never be at peace until that rage is brought to consciousness. Bring it forth responsibly and you will come into true power."

Vincent's suggestion causes a flood gate in Andre to open. Simultaneously, he locks eyes with a man in a dark polo shirt in the back row. The man stays with him for several long, interconnected moments then morphs into Frank, his interrogator, but in some primitive setting.

Andre's eyes close automatically. Tightly. In his inner vision, without his wanting or willing it, Frank remains there. Andre's fists clench. "I want to tear you apart! I will tear you apart!" He gets out the words so gutturally that no one comprehends. Instantly, he pulls a stick from the fire at his feet and considers plunging it through Frank's heart.

"You goddam moron! If you don't let me see Sheryl right now, I'll put a hot stake through your heart. I'll sever your testicles. I'll hand you your head on a stick. You're not a man. You're a disgusting bag of rancid flesh."

Now Andre makes his hands into claws, lets out a prolonged, ruthless yell, and stands ready for mortal combat.

In that moment, if Frank were to walk through the door, Andre would tear the larynx out of his neck. Everyone in the room knows it.

135

Instead, something strange happens. It's as if Andre's body itself is made of powerful armor. "Frank! Frank! Frank!" He calls out repeatedly to his adversary, confronting him at every level, exposing him for the worm he surely is. Frank shrinks before Andre's gaze into some amorphous, cowering entity. Andre's sense of power and competence is exhilarating. He watches the whole room drift freely and beautifully through time and space. Andre feels like a god.

"What was that?" exclaims Andre, his awareness unexpectedly plummeting back to the room.

"That was you fully awake and invincible. And you got there by accessing your humanness—through your anger," replies Vincent. "Let's all join with Andre and celebrate this moment with our collective Presence."

The ensuing deeply-shared silence is so enchantingly delicate, the slightest unconscious noise or movement could wreck it.

Everyone senses this and the room remains absolutely still for perhaps three minutes, though the experience seems like a miniature slice of timeless infinity.

Andre can only look at Vincent and wonder who in the world he is and how the hell he and this wild man just had the synchronous collision they had.

51

Coming Clean

"My God dude, you made more movement in an evening than I've made in two months," complains Ray Manners, Andre's somewhat estranged friend. "I could be jealous but I can't help but be excited for you. Looks like you got a major slice of your inner pie tonight."

"Hey, thanks man. I still don't know what happened in here. But it felt right. Like some ground-zero course correction."

Ray squeezes him gently on the shoulder and fades off into the fog-induced chill.

Several other people come up to him, either expressing their thanks for his inspiration to them or offering their encouragement for him to stay involved in the work. He presumes *the work* means following Vincent's teachings. This gives him a not unwelcome chill.

Andre floats out of the Best Western fully impacted. *Unbelievable. It's one thing to intellectualize about living in the moment and quite another to actually be there. One thing to read about the awakened state in books and quite another to have the direct experience.*

His buoyancy prevents Andre from becoming deservedly embarrassed about his catalog of past pseudo spiritual practices. And the reams of nauseating rhetoric. All because he's still swimming in the essence of the real deal. *Is this actually happening to me? Is my soul's journey altered—forever? Is this thing called Presence now truly anchored down in the depths of me?*

Vincent himself had spoken to him briefly, and even now, ten minutes later, he can't reproduce any of the substance of his comments. Though he certainly carries the sustenance they have generated. He wishes Sheryl could've been in the room to bask in the drifting, the Oneness, the...

"Andre!" A voice calls from the interior of a dark Buick sedan parked next to his Porsche.

"Yes…who is it?"

"It's Darryl. We had some eye contact before you went into your process. Let me get out so we can talk," says Darryl already nearly up and out and facing Andre. Even though Darryl has an imposing stature—aided by a black leather jacket—Andre notes that the guy's voice has a very slight tremor. He also notes the hypersensitivity from his process remains active in him.

"Look, I'm sorry if I…"

"Hey, no problem. I'm new here too," Darryl sighs, "Looked to me like you had some kind of battle with Frank."

"Yeah. He's the guy that had me thrown out of Greece. I guess I just kicked his butt on some cosmic level."

For months now I've wanted to kick his butt on *this* level. He's a true S.O.B. I wish he were the last of his kind—but he isn't."

For a moment, Andre does not compute. Then he is acutely flummoxed.

"You…know…Frank? How…"

"Okay. I'm not allowed to divulge any of this, but after what went down in there…"

"You mean that moment? That infinite moment?" says Andre.

"All of it. Your lament, your gut-wrenching honesty, the room, Vincent's face changing its characteris…"

"I didn't see that…But Frank, what's he got to do with this?" says Andre, still puzzled.

"Nothing with Vincent's people, that's certain. Frank's a Foreign Service Officer—Athens Intelligence—except in his case, possibly stupidity. He ordered me to shadow you…Listen, this is kind of classified. Care to get in where it's a bit more private?"

Andre reels from the revelation as he lands in Darryl's passenger seat. *A minute ago I was on cloud ten.* "It's not enough the slime ball wrecked my love life? Now he wants to pin something heavy on me?"

"He claims you were using the girl."

"That's outrageous! I…"

"I know that now." The tremor is gone. There is a sudden deadly calm in Darryl's voice. "I also know he's up to something. He's not as stupid as he presents. This evening has caused me to look through a different lens than the one I have been. I've got a bad feeling in my gut about this whole affair…But tell me this. What were you doing in *Arabian Antiquities* for forty-five minutes last Tuesday?"

"Following a hunch." Andre watches a slight feeling of guilt pass through him like a shadow—amazed he even caught something so subtle.

"About what?" says Darryl.

"I have a professional interest in antiquities. Has to do with my architectural clients. I did a bit of research. A few of the pieces in there are from the same period and general locale—Tunisia—as the exquisite sculpture which guarded the entrance to the submarine cave in the villa on Solagros. I was feigning buying one of them, trying to get the owner's source."

"And who's that? Did he tell you?"

"All he would say is, they were imported through Greece by a Madam Dupree. Showed me some papers—probably forgeries. I really don't know where to go next with this."

"Let me look into it," says Darryl breaking into a grin. "I'll trust we both know this conversation never happened. This is especially true if you should speak with Sheryl. Knowing Frank, her phone is most certainly bugged. Here's my card. My personal cell number's on the back. Call me through a pay phone only. Keep in touch if anything significant develops. See you here next Thursday, unless Frank pulls the plug. I'll be keeping track of you from a distance."

Andre exits the black Buick shaking. Ten seconds later Darryl and his parting grin lose themselves onto the freeway entrance in the Marin night.

52

Stefanos' Curse

Stefanos knows two things about the bust. One, Kostas escaped successfully through the quick-exit, side tunnel—where the zodiac was stashed—because of a coded postcard he sent to Stefanos' aunt. Two, the postcard—depicting one of the small outer islands—said, "The locals here all act kind of lifeless." This told Stefanos there were probably no captives, hence no follow-up interrogation. He assumes everyone connected with the sub were shot, popped cyanide tablets, or shot themselves in the head, succumbing instantly.

He's combed the papers and found no shred of the event leaked to the press, so neither his nor Kostas' identities are known to the population at large. He reasons that, because radical Islamist elements are involved, the anti-terrorist network wishes to remain below the waterline so as to catch much bigger fish. *I am a small fish. I have better than a fifty-fifty chance of living out my days undetected.*

Stefanos has ample time to reflect upon this sudden turn of events. Like Kostas, his father looms large, even in his day-to-day activities. But allegiance to his murdered father trumps his own drive for personal gain. Blocks him from honestly questioning his involvement with those who would employ such extreme tactics as suicide—rather than capture. Shields him from recognizing the eerie irony that these tactics are the chosen drug of those lunatics out to destroy the very civilization he hopes to be comfortable living and hiding in.

He cannot see that he is another in the long line of Judas Iscariots, Marcus Brutuses, and Benedict Arnolds who would sell their souls, loved ones, or causes to achieve some transitory—usually monetary—compensation. But with a father who reveled in smuggling contraband, how could Stefanos have turned out otherwise?

His soul's journey is marked with a desperateness which is constantly prodding him to awaken from his toxic dream. If asked, Vincent would likely say he set it up exactly this way prior to this particular lifetime. Set up an extreme scenario to jar himself awake because he missed milder signals during other lifetimes.

Thus far, he seems to have missed all the signals again. And this time they are huge. If the theory holds, his next lifetime will be a study in anguish until and unless he wakes up. For now, "My current predicament is all Kostas' fault," is his mantra.

Stefanos and Kostas have no registered business in common. However, since Kostas is implicated, Stefanos supposes he will be investigated once Kostas' bank statements are analyzed. They are listed as co-beneficiaries through a roundabout sequence of documents.

An analysis of either of their books will certainly result in the authorities probing deeper. *In eight years, neither the produce company nor the export business has shown a verifiable profit, yet we've purchased and outfitted the villa on Solagros, not to mention my comfortable penthouse and Kostas' Athens pad off Avisynia Square.* So he goes with the probabilities, stuffs his cache of Euros in a duffel bag, and runs.

Yet with all his optimistic—for him—analyses, he stands on the shore of the Ionian Sea, three miles from the Albanian border and curses. Curses loud enough to be heard on Kostas' island hideaway, two hundred miles south.

Kostas, you are lower than the lowest dog. If I were smart I would abandon you. Cross the border. But the chance to smash in your pretty face! Ah! I must. Perhaps I will even strangle you. You deserve what your father got!

Stefanos' base anger overrules his fickle paranoia. So much for waking up this time around. Perhaps if he had the benefit of a Vincent or a Kapetan Yanni, he'd be able to discharge the anger without having to act it out on someone. He'd likely learn that he in fact has the object wrong.

It is no longer Kostas' father Demitrios he wishes to get at through Kostas. He already dispatched him. It is his own father whom he hates for shoving him down this path from which rescue is all but impossible, and redemption is out of the question.

53

The Soccer Factor

Nazneem Hafiz feels such pride for her daughter Kallie, her feet seem to barely touch the ground. Kallie has finally gotten the chance to play meaningful minutes because the normal starter is ill today. She's just scored her first-ever goal for her private soccer club. And it happens just as her father, Salim, hurries up to the sideline late from a meeting.

When her teammates surround Kallie in a team squeeze after her goal, Salim has to choke back his tears. Out of pride, certainly, but also out of guilt that one day soon she will never see her mates again—at least as it now stands. If his increasingly repulsive plot is successful, she will be confined to a secret family compound in rural Pakistan and forbidden to go outside without a bourka and an escort. To see her now, her long, girlish legs exposed, her dark hair chasing after her as she runs—the embodiment of effervescence—makes Salim feel faint. *How could I have ever thought that constrictive, fundamental Islam is superior to Western freedom? This is worth killing tens of thousands for?*

"Great job Kallie!" both parents scream, pumping their fists. The other parents congratulate them and return to cheering as their team goes on defense. From all outward appearances, Salim and Nazneem—Sal and Nazzy—are just another soccer mom and dad.

Only a very small handful of business people in Atlanta know this is the same man who amassed a fortune in Silicon Valley by being the first software engineer to write the program that enables email attachments to be formatted and sent. And fewer know that M.I.T. graduate Nazneem was his co-author.

Only four people on the planet know that Salim is the funding source and point man in a plot five thousand times more deadly than anything Osama Bin Laden and his lieutenants have thus far conceived. And his wife, Nazneem, is not one of these four.

Right now as he reacts when Kallie steals the ball, blows past a defender, and makes a perfect pass to her best friend Courtney—a girl-next-door blonde—for a goal, Salim makes a decision that will likely seal his fate. When the game ends, he hugs Kallie more tightly, more desperately really, than ever before, and perhaps ever again. *No arranged marriage for you, my dearest daughter.*

54

Off the Rock

Kostas sets out at sunset for the three-hour run to Oia on Santorini. He's had a lot of time to perch on his rock and think. But his thinking has been one-dimensional, or if truth be told, Sheryl-dimensional.

He has not considered how she and Landi know each other. How they might have a professional connection. That is to say, a governmental one. *They are both beautiful Americans—of course they would meet.* Stefanos' paranoia would be of value to him now, but it is absent, its source secluded somewhere near the Albanian border in northern Greece.

This romantic, hot-blooded Greek can't contain himself he is so excited to see Sheryl. He's rehearsed his lines. One line really. "I'm sorry." Yes he's jealous of Andre. The Kapetan did volunteer his name and city of residence and nothing more. Except that he and Sheryl acted as if they had some form of friendship. He quickly added that he was sure they'd never met before. They paid him handsomely to get them safely to Santorini, and as a cunning old seafarer, he'd done just that. Even if it meant pulling some wool over Kostas' eyes.

The Kapetan never mentioned the raid on the villa. And Kostas did not wish to risk bringing it up. *The authorities either totally kept the lid on it, or this is another of Kapetan Yanni's poker-face stunts. I don't know what to think. Yanni did question in his roundabout way that he'd not seen any activity over at the villa. 'Just a watchman. Some new hire? Were you away on business as you so often are. Gone a long time. Looks like you have been darkening in the sun. Is this your new toy? A zodiac with a big outboard to really feel the salty spray rush by you.'*

A little voice inside Kostas keeps chirping to itself. *Yes you're happy to see Sheryl...But you also miss Landi and here you are doing to her what you did to Sheryl...Snap out of it! The last thing you need now is to go soft on me. But you did call Landi didn't you? You just happened to get Sheryl. This is not a crime.*

This interior dialogue does not let up until nearly ten o'clock when Kostas docks his craft in the shadow of the small pier at the base of the 300-step staircase leading up to the town of Oia. He weighs his options. He could dock elsewhere and take a cab to the top then walk down to the water. But this leaves him no escape. He thinks it best to keep the zodiac handy in case he needs a quick exit. Then he could send it out to sea and jump off, buying some time. He is so intent on seeing Sheryl he overrules any last-minute cautions as mental jabber.

If only you had time to think it through when Sheryl came on the phone, you would have arranged a much different, more remote rendezvous. But this place is quite secluded. The stairway stops all but the fit.

Kostas slinks to a vantage at the corner of the small open-air café and peers in, just in time to see Sheryl carry two steaming cups over to an empty table. His whole body smiles at this simple action. They often finished off an evening in the Plaka with lattes in intimate places like this one. They'd use the buzz to stay up into the small hours making love.

His heart racing, he eases onto the stone walkway, and casually approaches the entry. Sheryl doesn't recognize him at first, owing to the full beard, sunburn, and rugged clothing. He shrugs at her look of surprise, then slips into the chair across from her, oblivious to the other couples and foursomes at tables nearby, Sheryl is so naturally present—and strangely calm—with the waves lapping against the concrete dock, she covertly and repeatedly pinches herself to avoid slipping into blue-Sheryl. That will not work for this encounter.

"Sheryl, I wish to thank you for indulging this meeting. I am sorry for the grief I have caused you. Sorry for the deception, the lies." He takes a sip of the latte. "Thank you for ordering these."

With not so much as a nod, Sheryl launches at him. "I'm sorry it has ended this way. I can't believe I misjudged you so badly. This has happened to me before. I thought I had learned from the last time. All those trips away on business were nothing more than excuses to see Landi. Though I must say, you have impeccable taste in women."

Kostas shows a pained smile at the compliment. "I hope against hope you can forgive me for my addiction. I have come to know it as a sickness—a basic dissatisfaction with life as it has been dealt to me. Everything changed when my father was killed. My heart glazed over. Everything I did after that was false."

Sheryl senses ice water flowing in her veins. "I appreciate the sentiment, but it's way too late for therapy. Or confession. Or whatever you care to call it."

Kostas has to get it out before she runs away. "I have so much anger. I met with Kapetan Yanni nearly a week ago and have spent most of the time since screaming at everything I could think of: my business partner, my father, God, even you for being so innocent. I have beat the only tree on my hideout until the poor thing is unrecognizable."

"You have a hideout? What for? You have a plush villa. Are you going native? Oops. I forgot you are a native."

They both laugh.

Kostas goes light-headed from his slip-up. "I have a retreat place I've set up just to get away from the pressures of my business life."

"Really? I can't imagine any pressures in an export business. Just fun."

Kostas was getting uncomfortable. "It's kind of close in here. Could we stroll out on the dock for some air."

"We could but there's someone who may object."

"Who would poss…"

Kostas stops in mid sentence as a disguised Landi turns around from an adjacent table, stands, and tosses off her red wig.

"Hello Darling. I have an apology for *you*. I'm so sorry you are under arrest. If you try to escape, you will be shot. Everyone in this place is CIA, Interpol, or Greek Intelligence. Put your hands above your head and do not make any quick moves."

147

55

Artifact Tracking

"Darryl. This is Andre Bell. We spoke after Vincent's group."

"G'mornin'. What's up?"

"I'm calling from a common work phone in my office. Can we talk?"

"Go ahead. The line is secure. I'm in the parking garage, by the way."

"Uh…Okay. The dealer over at *Arabian Antiquities* called me at work just now. He says that a new shipment of smaller, affordable articles will be arriving at his cousin's store in Coral Gables, Florida on the seventeenth. The cousin will be shooting them with a digital camera. He asked if I would be interested. Invited me over for an internet viewing. I told him that coincidentally I would be in Miami on unrelated business during that time. He agreed to give me the name of the shop if I ID'd myself so he'd get a share of the commission. That's the day after tomorrow. So I'm off to Florida. Had to book a red eye tonight."

"What do you mean?"

"I mean I'm going."

"What do you hope to find there? Could be a long shot."

"I hope to find out who Madam Dupree is."

"I already know who she is. At least I'm 90% certain."

"What? Who is she?"

"Dupree is her maiden name."

"So? What's her married name?"

"Jansen."

"Jansen! As in Sheryl Jansen?" The phone receiver seems to shrink from Andre's ear even though he's still holding it there.

"Actually as in Jesse Jansen, former debutante, as in wife of our Ambassador to Panama, Sam Jansen, as in mother of Sheryl Jansen."

"How the hell did you come up with that?" Andre feels faint like he's just caught a glimpse of watching himself in a movie he didn't know was being filmed.

Darryl shrugs. "It's what I do. Oh and guess what I can tell you about this conversation?"

"It never happened."

"Right. And I can also tell you I can't stop you from going to Miami, because I'm not supposed to let you know that I know that you're going."

Andre chuckles. "Somehow I get the feeling we'll be sitting outside the same shop. *Atlantis Artifacts*. Your car or mine?

Darryl knows he could get demoted for colluding with a suspect. But like Sam Jansen, he has no choice but to follow his gut instinct.

"See you down south Sunday morning. I'll bring the biscotti—and the car. You bring the orange juice. Ciao."

Andre hangs up the phone and admits out loud to no one in particular, how much brotherhood and appreciation he feels for Darryl—dense federal agent or not.

56

Unrequited Call

It's well after midnight at Oia on Santorini. *The Fish Lady Grill* is back to normal. Kostas has been led away, weeping like a baby. The betrayer has become the betrayed. The café has re-filled with its normal summer night tourist crowd, many just crawling out for dinner near midnight. Many eateries in the islands don't even open until after 10 PM. Summer in Greece is one grand spree for the pleasure-seeking night owl. The place is populated with suave, athletic-looking men. Bronzed and exotic women. Two of the latter variety sit at an outside table under the stars, nearest the water.

"Here, use my phone, it's secure. Call your man. You know you want to!" Landi teases Sheryl by plunking down her phone in front of Sheryl like a chess piece. "It's about 2 PM there. Trust me. My line is magic. And secure. Call him at work."

"Aren't you the Cupid."

"Hey, You just passed the Kostas litmus test. Besides, I've run every check imaginable on sweet Andre. He's so clean it's scary."

"You're not interested in him I hope?"

"I'm just trying to protect my girlfriend—and my country. But I admit, I am attracted to his package. Hard working, talented, athletic. And if you're attracted to him-sexy. Did you know he's been going to seminars run by a spiritual teacher? The guy's multi-dimensional. You better grab him before I do."

They both laugh. Sheryl because she's sure Landi is teasing. Landi because she, in that moment, for the first time, briefly entertains the idea of being with Andre, finding it terribly—almost incestuously—amusing.

"What about Frank's intelligence?" Sheryl asks, breaking the awkward spell.

"Frank's "intelligence"? That's an oxymoron to end all oxymorons."

They laugh again and take sips on their champagnes.

"But really, Frank has a whole case built up. I've seen the reports."

Landi's face contracts. "Let's just say Frank is a complicated person. And the things complicated people do, take time to understand. How about we leave it there?"

"But I work for the guy," Sheryl protests. "I need some guidelines to know how to deal with him."

"Fair enough. Stay out of his way, but keep your eyes and ears open. Report anything—even the smallest odd detail—to me, person-to-person. And don't think I've not noticed the phone still sitting there."

Sheryl clears her mind, recalls and dials Andre's office number.

"Thatcher and Huff, Andre Bell's office."

"Could I speak with Andre, please? This is Sheryl Jansen calling."

"I'm sorry Miss Jansen. Andre just left this morning on business. He'll not be returning for at least a week. May I have your contact information?"

"Do you know where he's going?"

"I'm sorry, I'm not at liberty to say."

"I see."

"Shall I tell him you called, if he checks in?"

"Sure. He has my contact numbers. Tell him it's important. Tell him I'm granting an extension to the twenty days—effective retroactively."

"An extension. To the twenty days. I'll tell him."

"Thank you." Sheryl hangs up and tries Andre's home. She gets the message machine, half enjoying, half dreading the sound of his voice. She panics at the beep.

"Hi, we need to talk, call me…No wait…I'll call you. Leave me…no never mind. I'm sorry…I don't…" Sheryl can't believe she's coming apart in front of Landi. Her face turns red. "Uh…I don't…I guess I lost your cell number."

Now her mind starts spitting back a summary of Landi's past comments. *God, any phone could be bugged. Who's listening? Frank? Maybe. Landi's handlers? Maybe? Both? Al Qaeda? Can't rule anybody out.*

Realizing she's left ten seconds and counting of dead air on her message, Sheryl quietly terminates the call.

"That went well," deadpans Landi. "Now the poor guy's totally bewildered."

Andre, at home packing, bends his ear to his answering machine and listens to Sheryl's voice with a huge dose of melancholy—and, he admits, suspicion. He's not one to talk to himself but since returning from Greece he's got a whole conversation going. And often it's audible.

"What is up with that woman? Whatever you do, don't be an idiot. Don't pick up. You'll lie and say she's your true love. You'll start asking about her mother. You'll put your foot in your mouth. You'll betray Darryl…"

Oddly, Andre has more allegiance to Darryl in the moment than he does to Sheryl.

"What if Darryl is taken off the case? What if the guy's plane crashes? What if he's eliminated? Then you're on your own with no allies. Stay focused. You're no good to a lover serving time. First, clear yourself with Frank. Frank! What a jerk. An intelligence agent. Hah! More like a conspiracy buff. What an amateur."

If it comes down to a choice of protecting him or her mother, who would Sheryl choose? "Is blood thicker than a twenty-eight-hour romance? Don't answer that! Idiot! You don't want to know."

152

57

Immunity

"Here's the deal darling. We have overwhelming evidence that you have aided and abetted Al Qaeda. Under our current bilateral counterterrorism agreement with Greece, you will be extradited to Miami. You will be tried in a U.S. court under the Patriot Act. In other words, you don't have a prayer of beating this. The good news is, our agreement does not allow us to execute you. The bad news is, you will be so old by the time you get out—if you don't die of TB or pneumonia, or kill yourself from the psychological fallout of repeated sexual assaults—that your life for all practical purposes is over."

"This is not fair! I'm a Greek citizen! I will die over there. I know it." Kostas is screaming. "I just found out who those guys really are. I can't believe they committed suicide right in front of me. If I had known, I…"

"In today's world, ignorance is no longer an excuse!" Landi is practically yelling. "Do you have any idea how many deaths Al Qaeda is responsible for? You should have checked out these people before you got involved with them. Because they are moral Neanderthals, they take the cash that people like you give them, for items whose significance they have no appreciation of, and build training camps for suicide bombers. They buy weapons and bomb-making materials with it. They even pay off the families of the bombers for Christ's sake!"

Landi's argument is more passionate, more genuine, and Kostas knows it. *I want to beat my head into that block wall…No! This is what cowards do. You must not torture yourself…What would you do father? Is this the fate you wanted me to avoid? I'm afraid I have failed you.*

Kostas is only able to muster a weak moan.

Landi sees that her point has sunk in.

"Our interrogators were thorough with you. And—this is significant—they all agree you didn't know the true identities of these creeps. You were at the bottom of the communication ladder. We believe Stefanos set up the contact and knows who they are. No matter. In the climate of today's courts, your life—as you knew it—is over...So I'm prepared to offer your lucky ass something of a way out."

"You...you could do that? What do I have to do, make a deal with the devil?"

"Actually, you're not far off. I want you to lead us to Stefanos."

"Stefanos! It would be my pleasure. Believe me. But I will not give him up without being set free," says Kostas who for a moment forgot he's no longer in control.

"I know you are smarter than to ask for that. Your emotions are outrunning your cool. But in your case, *any* relief from the fate that awaits your sorry behind, is relative freedom."

"So tell me, what does this so-called freedom look like?"

"It depends. First, we have to catch Stefanos. If we fail for any reason, all bets are off. Second, you will agree to go peaceably to Miami. You will be given immunity. There will be a trial in federal court. You will receive a mostly suspended sentence. Except for the certainty that you will have to serve some time in a white-collar prison. Believe me, even if it's a year, it beats one day in Guantanamo."

"What happens after that year?"

"You will be on a very long, probably permanent, parole. This will be served out in the Miami area. You will be given a green card. You will have to actually work for a living. Pay taxes to your merciful Uncle Sam. A man with your talents should have no trouble. If you should participate in anything illegal, your sentence will be automatically, irrevocably reinstated. And then you're gonna need armor-plated underwear."

"I'll think about this. Are any more, as you say, 'strings' hooked onto this?" It comes out half whiny, half sarcastic. Kostas can't stomach that his fate rests in the hands of his former mistress. Can't stomach that *she* was the one playing *him*. *I hate myself. When she leaves I will beat my head on the bars until…No! There is no redemption in that stupidity. Only more pain.*

Landi sighs. "There is one more requirement. You must report once a week to a parole officer."

"On top of everything else, I don't see this as a problem."

"You might. I've pulled a few strings. And it's a lot of responsibility. And I'd have to relocate there and settle down a bit…What I'm saying is, I've arranged to be your parole officer. At least at first."

"Why would you do this? Do they give you something for this 'privilege'?"

"No, only a desk to ride. Believe me, I'd just as soon see you rot. But in the end that won't do the most good."

"Good for whom? Maybe for you."

"I thought your child should have the opportunity to see you regularly. Growing up completely fatherless is a can of worms from what I've seen."

"What…?"

"Apparently my birth control failed. I'm pregnant. And you are the only possible father. I've decided to have the baby. I know it will be a beautiful child."

All Kostas can do—to his utter shock and through his watering eyes—is nod his head and smile a pained smile.

The image of Demitri, Kostas' father playing soccer with him around age four floods into his inner vision. He brings his hands to his face and imperceptibly rubs the spot on his forehead recently healed from hitting walls when events weren't going his way.

58
Sheryl the Spy

It's 6 PM Friday and Sheryl is still at work. She's been given no significant assignments, which is perfect, because she has become obsessed with
watching Frank. From a great distance of course, so as not to interfere if
Landi's also watching him, which seems all but certain.

Saying she needs some space to concentrate on a report, she arranges
to meet Landi's stand-in at 6:30 by the main and only entrance. Elsie
reluctantly agrees and camps out there.

Sheryl took note that Frank left just before 4 PM and thought she'd
overheard his secretary order a car to the airport. Sheryl decides to have
a look around his office.

Access is no problem. The offices are locked at quitting time each day. Since
she's still lowest person on the totem pole with a security clearance—and
they would never trust it to an intern—this mundane task falls to her
most of the time. She feigns working late, says goodnight to the last of her
co-workers, then sets about locking the offices, stopping last at Frank's door.

Heart racing, she slips into his office.

All hard copies of classified data are stored in a secure vault to which few
have access. Everyone's computer is linked and protected by a sequence
of passwords. Any log on or attempted log on is recorded. Sheryl knows
Frank's computer is hands off. She also knows he's never learned to type.
And, like her, he doodles. Compulsively. Especially when he's on the phone.
He keeps a very large, old-fashioned paper pad on his desk, which takes
up a good deal of its surface.

Her heart sinks. *Damn! His desk pad is new and perfectly blank. The old one
is not in the waste basket. That's odd. I'm pretty sure the janitors don't arrive
until around 9 PM.*

The file drawers in the desk are locked. There are no pictures of family. Just one of himself, spear gun in hand, about to enter the water. *Probably in the islands, judging by the color of the water.* There's a cup from Florida Atlantic University that holds his pens. And a road map of Greece.

She checks the secretary's basket. Nothing. On a hunch, she slips into the men's room and empties the large can under the paper-towel dispenser. This yields the crumpled desk paper overlain with a pile of mildly repulsive scraps inside.

She reasons that Frank left so quickly he didn't have time to throw it in the classified waste for shredding. Or perhaps, if anything classified was in fact present by his hand, he'd have been reprimanded for a security breach. In any event, Sheryl jams the slightly moist paper into her pants, locks Frank's door, and escapes with her treasure to Elsie at the front exit, then on to the sanctuary of her flat.

Unfortunately, in her excitement, she forgets to account for the always-on-duty security cameras, which capture her entering the men's rest room—and Frank's office.

59

Comparing Notes II

Sheryl analyzes her mined, blow-dried treasure awaiting her girlfriend's return. Landi has spent the past day and a half handling her personal life and placed Elsie on Sheryl duty. Landi picks her up at 1:30 PM.

Sheryl and Landi go out for a late lunch to an outdoor café in the Plaka, not far from where Sheryl made the phone call to the Embassy when she and Andre were dodging Stefanos' dragnet. After they order, Sheryl unfolds her treasure.

"I dug this out of the trash can in the men's room early yesterday evening. I waited until you were back on to show you. It's Frank's desk pad—or was. It's the last one he used. Wrote his flight info down. See right here.

Landi examines the block printing.

"What? He's going to Miami and returning almost immediately?"

"Almost. Actually five hours later—probably on the same plane. More like two in Miami with Customs then security re-entry. And check this out. 'Meet J @ 5:15 PM UPG $$.'"

The longer she stares at the shorthand, the more intensely quiet Landi grows.

"You got this from the men's room trash?" Landi has an air of scutiny. Really more of accusation.

"Ya...Yes," stammers Sheryl.

"Are you aware of the security camera. I know there's one at the entrance. I've seen it."

"Oh God," says Sheryl panicking. "There may even be one inside the damn room! And I tried to rifle Frank's desk as well—but it was locked."

"What time was this?"

"About 5:45 PM."

Landi pulls out her cell and hits a speed dial key. "Orchid Op. Hey. I've got an Alpha-priority situation. I need some tapes pulled and massaged. Affirmative. From the Intel Chief's office, Athens Embassy. And all cameras outside it and possibly inside the 2nd-floor east wing Embassy rest room. No, the men's. Yes Athens. Brilliant. Check thirty minutes either side of 1800. Local time, Friday. If you catch a hot-looking brunette on any of that footage, purge it. Yes a female—in the men's room. I know. Yes, even you will think she's hot. If you don't I'm having you checked. Do it now. Orchid out."

"I'm really sorry," offers Sheryl, embarrassed.

"Fer chrissakes girl. You *are* hot. Don't apologize!"

"I mean for causing all this trouble. I'm such a novice."

"Damn girl! Your instincts may have split this case open. Don't worry about the tapes. Gives Rodney something to do. Gives the taxpayers their money's worth. It's a win/win. And I suspect we caught it in time. Frank's the only likely person to review that footage, and he's on a plane over the Atlantic—until tomorrow night. This is a brutal business."

"I'm learning that. You can fix those tapes—from the States? Never mind. I'm sure you can. It's hard for me to know what's real right now. And I wonder who 'J' is?"

Landi doesn't even hear Sheryl. She's been counting on her fingers. Intent and one-pointed, she re-dials her phone like lighting a fuse.

"Yo. Orchid again. Give me Big Dog...Yo Dog! Orchid. Possible dirty player. What do you mean you're already looking? Who? No way. His daughter dug it up on this end. Same instinct. Yeah, genetics. Inbound on Iberia 6123 Miami. Maybe one hour fifteen. Plus Customs. Meeting a connection. A bogie. Send me hard image and a name whenever you get it. Yeah. Red hair. That's him. Probably white suit. I think he sleeps in it. No. I don't sleep, you know that. Love you too."

"Sounds like my dad weighed in," grins Sheryl. "Good work, Super Girl. Our Slimeboy's not even there yet!"

"That's why I get the big migraines. Ah, but relaxation. That's the antidote. We can just sit here and enjoy the afternoon while our boys do their thing. I predict pictures on my phone screen in two hours. How about an appetizer before dinner? I could dig some pickles. Uncle Sam's buying. We've earned it."

"Pickles? Before dinner?"

"Yeah pickles. And frozen yogurt. Coffee frozen yogurt. It's a long story."

60

Jesse "Dupree" Jansen

Jesse Jansen has never really stopped being a southern belle. One doesn't stop such things. One doesn't care to stop perfection. One sometimes lets it be swallowed by something larger, but that which was swallowed never truly digests, coming up to air itself every now and then.

Born and bred on a six-thousand-acre estate in the northern Florida panhandle, land of pine forests, clear rivers, cypress bayous, and snow-white beaches, Jesse only saw the idyllic side of life. She was educated in private academies and the University of Florida, her parents' alma mater, where she met Sam, a well-connected fraternity man with a winning smile and the build of a track star. They met at a banquet where he gave his incoming address as president of Blue Key, the campus equivalent of the Florida Legislature. He held the audience alternately in stitches and tears at what was supposed to be a dry event. She was smitten and made it her obsession to win him. He didn't have a prayer of resisting.

She is the creation of Ellen and Manson Dupree, both themselves products of families who were major players in the pulp mill industry. These were people who can play a mean game of tennis in the morning, hobnob with a good ol' boy senator over lunch, and storm through the mill in the afternoon, outcussing the foreman over the latest OSHA directive. At sunset, they'd slam down a pitcher of daiquiris, followed by so much cholesterol it would make a lobster have a heart attack.

When Jesse brought Sam home, the parents thought it a disaster. He was just too different. They didn't like his dangerous idealism, his semi-polish, his average fraternity. And especially his Yankee rearing. Yes he was in law school, but specializing in International Relations. The only relations the parents thought Uncle Sam required were big guns and a pulpit to tell the rest of the world to kiss off. Of course when young Sam got his first Ambassadorship, he was hailed as the son they'd always wanted. As if the past had never happened.

About this time, without fanfare, they released Jesse's considerable trust fund. But the grand parent apology never actually happened. Southern aristocracy almost never does its own dirty laundry—even within the shielded walls of its compounds. In their view, those types of emotional catharses are relegated to the sentiment-laden living rooms of the working class.

As if the gods of altruism were writing the script, about that time, Jesse stumbled onto philanthropy as a lifestyle. To her credit, this interest—which grew like a blaze into an all-consuming passion—was far and away outside the box of her upbringing. In an unconventional yet valid way, this gave her the identity she'd always needed, having rejected her parents' world view when they rejected her husband.

When Sheryl came along, Jesse found it challenging to fit her into an already full life. Between micro-managing her philanthropic projects, looking after her demanding and deteriorating parents, dancing with the protocols of playing ambassador's wife, keeping her relationship with said ambassador on an even keel, and keeping her treasured connection with a pair of sorority sisters, Sheryl got her mother's leftovers.

Barely warm and marginally nutritious to continue the metaphor. And the most recurring of these was a dispassionate ration of tersely-worded edicts designed to streamline Jesse's mothering time. Eventually the system failed the daughter. Thus Sheryl's primary recourse became seeking the seemingly natural yet unstable solace of blue-Sheryl below the surface of Indigo Lake.

Jesse will never compute that her awkwardly-social, cult-vulnerable, hostility-repressed daughter is primarily the logical result of the sheer force of her own narcissism.

Her best hope—and current obsession—is to entice Sheryl to join her on one of her projects. If asked, she would not be able to say why she has this obsession. Perhaps it's because, on the soul level, she senses that the camaraderie will catalyze a makeover of their family dynamic.

On this already sultry morning, she pulls her cherry-colored Cadillac convertible into the welcome shade of the short term parking garage at the Miami airport, puts on some Aretha Franklin and stretches out in the front seat.

She worries about the upcoming week. It's make-it-or–break-it time for saving the last large parcel on Key Largo from turning into some developer's luxury- home-private-golf-course wet dream.

The place is technically its own key. Back in the 1960's, the then developer built a bridge over to it from Key Largo proper. The place is called Heron Island and it is a jewel, although quite tarnished. A swarm of volunteers are poised to undo years of alien species invasion, hardwood poaching, and illegal land filling. She desperately needs the proceeds from this next round of antiquities sales to be able to complete the required eighty-percent down payment. She's grateful for her bighearted collaborator and business partner, whose involvement and generosity allows her to fund her passion.

She's also disturbed by her husband Sam's phone call earlier this morning. He's taken a sudden interest in the private life of her charity's business. Wants to know all about the artifacts. How the documentation is generated. How the records are kept. The tax angle. The duty fees. Questions she doesn't know the answers to. All these details are handled by her partner and his accountant. Her job is to learn the product, make the sales, and split the proceeds in half. Period.

She's watched her husband get to the bottom of many scandals in his two-plus decades of government service. One could even argue that it's made his career. *He doesn't just possess cogent analytical skills, he's got instinct. Like a bloodhound obsessed with a scent. He would not be asking these kinds of questions if he'd not gotten wind of something.*

When approached by people who care about worthy causes, she recognized that this avocation would be so very good for her, and for her and Sam's relationship. It would give her a purpose apart from playing the Ambassador's wife. Something that would add to his stature. More importantly, something that would set her apart from him, keep her occupied, no, preserve her vivacity—hence her magnetism—into and through middle age. The sound of suitcase wheels on the concrete floor pulls Jesse out of her reflecting.

"Hey Jess! How's things?" calls a familiar voice from behind her.

"Hey Darlin'. Goin' swell. Real swell. Comfortable flight?"

"Yep. An' I have to turn right around and head back. Soon as we make our trade."

"Well I swan. You must be busy back there. So how's my girl doin'?"

"Ducky as kin be. Got herself a big promotion."

"I heard. I trust she's earned it?"

"O yes ma'am. She's a hard worker—and smart—just like her folks." Frank grins. "Now here's ten items, all numbered. Here's their papers, describing each item. The numbers all correspond. The appraised retail is the first figure after the number. Once you distribute these, you'll have a pretty fair sum toward tying up that property. If you need all this to make your deal go down, you can square up on the next round."

"That's truly generous. Are you sure?"

"Absolutely. Would be my honor to help a good cause…Do you have the split from the last round?"

"Right here. Cashiers check for two hundred seventy-six thousand and change. Along with the sales receipts." Jesse hands over a sealed brown envelope "This is all on the up and up, right? I mean with taxes and duties and all that kind of thing?"

"Of course. Why do you ask?"

"Just covering my bases. The sales, especially after turning over this round, are really adding up. Sam says they're starting to look harder at non-profits.

I want to make sure I can survive an audit."

"Just pass the year-end statement you get from my accountant to your accountant, like always. *(Oh shit. Sam's sniffing around.)* We're so honest we squeak—like a baby chick."

"I knew you'd have good news. Okay Frankie. Have a safe flight back."

"Thanks Jess. And you have fun pedaling those treasures. You must feel like Santa Claus. Oops my cell's going off. And I gotta run."

Frank jogs off, and parks himself behind a pillar ten spaces away. "Mankowski here. Yes sir. I'm aware of the manhunt. They captured Kostas! When? Wonder why I wasn't told. That's uh, probably a good thing...Yes, that needs to be checked out...His partner? Uh huh. Stefanos Souvlakis...I'll do it. No problem...I'll brief you Monday morning then. Yes sir. You too sir."

Frank Mankowski slaps at the envelope in his suit jacket pocket and moves briskly back toward the Miami air terminal. It's pushing eighty-five degrees and humid. He starts jogging. His mind goes into a controlled race, not unlike the turbines of the jet engines taxiing outside on the tarmac.

61

Airport Happenstance

Andre steps out of Miami International into the sticky subtropical morning.

He actually welcomes the intense warmth after leaving the frigid Bay Area summer fog. He boards a rental car shuttle outside the American Domestic Concourse.

While his shuttle idles near a down-queue concourse, Andre's eye rests on some unique, Aztec-flavored detailing integral to the canopy support columns. In the next instant, his heart begins racing as he catches a glimpse of a thin, red-haired, forty-something man in a wrinkled white suit passing—running actually—in front of his shuttle.

My God! This is the same man, wearing the same suit, who grilled me in Greece and kept me from Sheryl. The bastard who I virtually killed in front of Vincent's people two nights ago.

Even from this anonymous vantage, Andre senses the man's discord. *This can only be Frank Mankowski! Mankowski, in the flesh. Whoa…nearly clipped by a taxi while crossing through traffic, on the dead run.*

The red-headed figure disappears through a bank of doors, into Concourse G and its slew of international air carriers. *Am I hallucinating?*

Andre's eyes burn. His throat feels dead. He goes momentarily mad. He imagines his psyche just boarded a train bound for a siding where it will be grilled by the three-judge panel of Alfred Hitchcock, Timothy Leary, and Earl Warren. While the sane part of him watches as if it were bound and gagged.

62

Nazzy and Naib

Nazzy Hafiz insisted she be given a small space for a kitchen garden in her and Salim's Atlanta complex. Just enough room to grow some bibb lettuce, parsley, Persian cucumbers, cherry tomatoes, and a few herbs. An antidote to her computer-oriented world. A private respite where she can get purposefully dirty, relaxed, and not be observed.

Lost in the sweet mindlessness of turning soil and pulling weeds, she is startled by Naib, her husband's computer lab caretaker.

"Assalamu alaikum!" he intones, peering through the gate opening which she's left accidentally ajar.

"Walaikum as salaam," she replies automatically. Then she blushes, suddenly feeling naked in her cutoff shorts and tee shirt.

"Would you like some assistance?" deadpans Naib.

"No. No thank you. This is my private garden and I like working in it alone," she retorts, emphasizing "alone."

"Of course. Are you not afraid of the neighbors' spying?"

"Spying?" says Nazzy, her heart racing.

"Yes. Of what they might think to see a Muslim woman working outside dressed as a western teenager."

"How I dress in my compound is my business." *I'm tired of repressing my hatred of Naib—and Khazin the other fundamentalist lab rat. They give me the creeps. Why Sal hired them is beyond my comprehension.*

"A woman must keep chaste in all ways," Naib lectures. "But I suppose you are useful for the image we wish to portray."

"And what image is this?" *Having this guy around here is awful. We might as well be living among the Pashtun.*

Naib realizes he is about to cross a line which Salim had warned him not to cross. "Leave my family and their habits alone," he had said. "These will make us appear to be normal people in the community."

"Forgive me. I have overstepped my position. Salaam and good day."

63

Phone Session

Andre secures his rental car and makes the easy drive to Key Biscayne. There's a beach he'd once discovered on winter break from college, out at the south end that is usually not crowded and has nice lighting at sunset. *After that glimpse of Frank—or his double—I need some form of cleansing even if it's hurried.*

He does a quick change into his trunks and hits the warm bay for a well-timed exertion. He's learned enough from Vincent to let each stoke be an event unto itself and to feel the water glide past his body moment to moment. He notices the movement of his legs and brings his focus there. Through his goggles he appreciates even this murky blue, now made decreasingly vibrant, yet more mystical, under the slanting sun. The in-suck and out-blow of his breathing almost trances him into a very long swim until an internal alarm is activated and he races back to his start point where his towel and cell phone await.

"Vincent's office," intones a friendly voice, attached to Maggie, Vincent's angelic assistant.

"Hello," he says panting. "This is Andre Bell. I have a phone session with Vincent."

"Hi, Andre. Great to hear from you. Vincent is expecting your call. One moment."

I can't believe I'm paying to expose my most imbedded problem. Where did the idiocy come from to book this session. And over the phone? Are you nuts? What can this spiritual madman possibly offer you?

"Hello, this is Vincent speaking. How may I be of service?"

The sonorous certainty in Vincent's voice shocks Andre out of his doubt. Out of his rational mind telling him he's lost it. Out of his naiveté at trusting a crazy, self-proclaimed spiritual teacher. A moment ago he was going to back out. Now some other part of him takes over like he's doing the most normal thing in the world.

"Thank you for accommodating me. My name is Andre, The guy with the Grecian drama. You had me maim my interrogator last Thursday night."

"Oh yes. That was a splendid piece of work. You're new to my groups correct?"

"Yes. Two Thursday nights so far."

"Right then. I trust the Gendarmes have not hauled you in as yet?" quips Vincent. "You're not calling from jail are you?"

"Oh no. Actually, I'm in Miami, trying to get to the bottom of the case against me. Taking matters into my own hands you could say."

"Miami! That's something. So how might I assist you? Sounds like you're moving forward quite well on your own."

"I've got this thing with women." Andre can't believe his own directness. His "plan" was to skate around his issue. *You've stepped fully into it now.*

"What sort of thing?"

"I'm afraid to pursue them."

"Do you have one in mind, or is this general?"

"Well, both I guess. It's rare for me to even have one remotely in my life. I freeze up around them. Can't really engage. But there's this woman, Sheryl—she works at the American Embassy in Athens."

"How long have you known her?"

"Over three weeks now. But we only spent a little over a day together in person."

"One day?"

"Yes but it was like an eternity. And now it's fallen apart."

"Why?"

"It's possible she or her mother is mixed up in the smuggling."

"Smuggling?"

"Pirated artifacts."

"Andre, I don't see how I can help you. Sounds like you need a private eye. Not a spiritual advisor."

"I really do need help. Because if she's innocent—and they verify me as innocent, which I am—then we'll be able to be together. And I don't want to blow it. No matter how good it might be initially, I know this deficiency is going to rear its ugly head. I need to get to the bottom of this uneasiness, this haunting shyness."

"Is this happening right now?"

"Is what happening?"

"This feeling of uneasiness."

"It's always with me. It's sown onto my skin."

"Indeed. Then we'll have a run with it. But if I sense the slightest bit of contrivance, we'll reschedule the remainder of your hour for another time. So, bring yourself fully present with your body as it breathes. Become fully aware of the sounds you hear. Gaze out and be with whatever is in your field of vision. Let me know when you're truly here."

Andre follows the instructions precisely. He has the intuitive sense to put the cell phone on speaker. Fortunately, there are a few bikini-clad, attractive women among those people scattered about who've gathered to catch the sunset. Though even the nearest of them are well out of earshot, all Andre has to do is lean forward as if he's about to go talk to one of them and he's in the feeling.

Andre speaks, yet he becomes aware that the words are issuing from some deep center within him. He hears himself say, "I'm very much here. And I'm in the feeling."

"Good. Now I'm speaking directly to the feeling. If this feeling sowed onto Andre's skin could speak, in one sentence, and express itself beautifully, what would it say?" Vincent's gentle yet direct voice catapults Andre to a place where words simply spew out.

Andre's own answer would shock him if he weren't in this current state of trust and openness.

"You'll never penetrate me!"

"Good. You'll never penetrate me!" says Vincent. "Penetrate what? I'm asking the feeling."

"Penetrate my...my armor."

"Armor! Good! What's the armor for? What's it protecting?"

"My heart."

"Your heart. Andre's heart? Whatever for?"

"From getting hurt."

"Has your heart been hurt before?"

"A long time ago." Andre closes his eyes against the glare of the setting sun.

"Yes, a long time ago," echoes Vincent. "Where are you? Close your eyes. Focus you inner vision. What do you see?"

Andre struggles a bit, for an instant becoming self conscious he's on a beach in a process with a man on the other edge of the continent. A man he hardly knows—but with whom he implicitly entrusts the care of his very soul. In this moment, the fellow's voice is more soothing than any music he's ever heard. He puts the phone at the head of his beach towel and lies down face up with his ear next to it. He lets his current concerns drop away. "A long time ago" keeps reverberating through him. Over and over and over.

Vincent's kindly—yet clear—voice breaks in.

"Where are you? Tell me what you see."

Andre gently re-focuses on the particulars in these odd surroundings that he is most definitely viewing from behind his closed eyelids.

"I see a bed. A very lavish bed. It's quite familiar."

"What else is in the room?"

"Statues. Magnificently ornate! A marble floor. A sink. A pitcher of water... stunningly elegant. Vases of flowers. And curtains. Blue velvet. The wind is blowing them."

"Is someone there with you?"

"I can't tell."

"Yes you can. Look about the room. Move around if you have to. Who is there?"

"Someone *was* there. I sense her. Oh no!"

"What's wrong? Tell me what you see."

"I can't!"

"Yes you can."

"I don't want to see."

"You must look. I'm asking you—Andre's soul—to look. And to report what you see."

"It's too awful." Andre begins sobbing.

"Your soul is seeing this. Tell me what you see. I can't help you if you don't tell me."

"Oh God. Oh God." Andre sobs. Yet oddly, there is a part of him witnessing and keeping most of the lid on it. *Don't get your self carted off a public beach and into the psych ward…Shut up Ego! Stay out of this!*

"That's it. Let the feelings come. Breathe. Stay with the feelings."

God I'm fortunate. Feels like Vincent is sitting right next to me. Guiding me.

"I'm speaking to Andre's soul. Tell me, what do you see? Who else is there with you?" Vincent's insistence rings with a neutrality that causes Andre to come clean.

"She's dead. She's beautiful—and she's dead," says Andre, his voice quivering.

"Yes she's dead," echoes Vincent. "Who killed her? Did you kill her?"

"No. But I might as well have."

"Why might you have killed her?"

"She killed herself because I used my power to take her away from her husband. She could no longer bear the pain. To me she was an obsession—and a plaything. I didn't know the hurt I was inflicting. I am so sorry." At this, Andre breaks into a muffled sobbing.

"Just feel it fully. Allow yourself to feel all the pain that you caused her in your unconsciousness. This step is absolutely essential. Take as long as you need," Vincent urges, but ever so gently.

Andre spends the next few minutes in a deep state of remorse.

"Sir! Sir are you all right?" says a voice in the distance—really in another universe. It belongs to one of the women on the beach who, sensing his distress, has come over to see if he needs help.

A startled Andre raises up on his elbows, opens his eyes, and gazes up at her empathic face against the post-sunset light show.

"I'm better than I've ever been in my life. But thanks for your kindness. I'm having a phone session with my teacher and I tapped into some pretty deep emotions." He considers being embarrassed at his intimate answer, but breaks into a genuine smile instead.

She smiles back, turns and strides back toward her towel.

"Hello! Hello, Andre? What's happening?" Vincent thinks they've been disconnected.

Andre turns sideways and whispers into the phone. "Sorry Vincent. Someone here on the beach just came over to check on me. Thought I was losing it."

"Well then, are you?"

"Oh no! I'm on fire with gratitude."

"And what are you doing on a beach? Putting on a show?"

"There's hardly any one here. I thought it would work. I needed a warm-water swim after all I've been through these past few weeks. Sorry."

"What's important is, did you complete your self-confession? Did you fully experience all the pain you caused?"

"Yes. I had just come out of it when she came over."

"Indeed? She…is she interested?"

"Interested? In me?" Andre laughs at what he presumes is a joke. But when he gives a quick glance over across the sand at the woman who tried to rescue him, their eyes meet effortlessly. He smiles. To his surprise she smiles back. "This is really different. Maybe she *is* interested."

"I wouldn't be surprised. Women can sense when a man has cleared himself. The irony is, once you've struck the perfect chord and exorcised your power broker—or your inner victim—women will sense it. They'll seek to bask in your presence without fully understanding why. Unless of course they've also gone through a similar process."

"So tell me something Vincent. Do we ever get second chances with people from our past? From our past lives I mean?"

"Of course. We're often tumbling through time one after another. Maybe it's more like leapfrogging. Anyway, don't go too far into your mind about it. It's of the Mystery. It's best to come from a place of not-knowing."

"Got it. Thank you for your help. And for just being so available."

"I'm happy to be of service. Contact me when you return and we'll complete your clearing around this issue. I suspect your father will show up in here somewhere, if he hasn't already."

"You'll be the first to meet him when he does. Good bye Vincent."

"Goodbye Andre."

Andre sets the phone down and closes his eyes. The picture of the dead woman from his session is right there as if it's been on hold. He looks straight into her face and through newly innocent eyes, verifies what he has already felt. Really what his tears have already told him. *The beautiful woman whose death I caused is Sheryl—or perhaps a version of Sheryl—in a much earlier lifetime.*

64

A Familiar Face

"These fruit coolers are devastating!" declares Sheryl as she and Landi unwind at their garden cafe table in the warm evening. "Sure you don't want one?"

"Nah. I'm good. But I'm glad you're takin' advantage of Uncle Sam. I'll stick to my pickles and yogurt."

"Now really, what's that about?"

"I guess I can't hide it from my friend. You are my friend, ain't you sweets?"

"Of course. We are the Mermaid Sisters," says Sheryl. And she means it.

"To make a long story short, My protection failed with Kostas. I'm pregnant, and I'm having the baby. I told him yesterday."

"Whoa. That's a big change." Sheryl wrestles with a sharp barb of jealousy. *Ouch! Okay Sheryl dear, just let it drop off your brused psyche down into oblivion where it belongs. The guy was bad news.* "Is it what you want?"

"I took some time and—yea, it's okay. More than okay. It's my ticket off this merry-go-round. It's been a good ride. I've grabbed a few brass rings. Although I haven't been able to tell him yet, my therapist would say that for me, moving on is the perfect choice."

"You see a therapist? I had no idea..."

"I'm telling you because I know you've been down that road," replies Landi, *There. I said it. Phew. No more pretending I don't know about Sheryl's past.*

"You really are thorough. I guess at your level, you need to know who you're dealing with," Sheryl tentatively affirms, ever amazed by the secrets people know—and keep.

Landi draws a deep breath. "Hey, I'm coming clean. I want us to be sisters. So I want you to know what I know."

"Thank you," replies Sheryl, a tear forming. "I've never had a girlfriend sister-type person. No true-blue friends that would go to the mat for me—or I for them. The curse of an only child I suppose. Still drives my hyper-social mother crazy. Takes it as an affront to her mothering skills."

"From where I sit, looks like she did one hell of a good job!" Landi affirms. "I mean, you're a person I'd trust with my friggin' life—especially in the water!"

"Don't ask me how I know, but I also trust you…with my life…absolutely. Every day in fact."

At this, the two career sisters take each other's hands across the table. Landi, the older by three years, does not fight the moistening of her eyes. And Sheryl, already misty, is likewise touched beyond words. They hold this connection for a time, drink in its depth and naturally break free as, like the tide, the inevitable ebb occurs.

"Landi—I love saying your name—I must confess I had a brief pang of jealousy when you first told me. A baby ties you to someone for life. That's real stuff. I think it's how God speaks to us. In big statements like that. And keeping the child—that's like your reply to God."

"The thought of terminating the beautiful child this will surely be, just kills *me*. There's no way. And we'll be well taken care of. It's in my contract."

"Well then congratulations are in order. Lets' get a bottle of Champagne." Sheryl signals for the waiter. Landi stops her.

"You'll have to drink the whole thing sweets. Alcohol's bad for the baby."

"Oh. Sorry. I bet Kostas is kind of sad the two of you'll be living so far away."

"I actually think he's genuinely excited. As excited as someone like him can be. He's turned state's evidence, and because of our treaty with Greece, he'll ultimately be paroled in the States. He'll be a parolee for the rest of his life.

"Holy Moses! Kostas living in America. What a concept."

"I pulled some strings. More like collected on some debts. I arranged to be his parole guardian. This means I have control over his visitation privileges. If he blows it, he won't see the kid. If he blows it badly, he grows old in the tank. I don't think he'll go down that road. I'm convinced there *is* someone home in there."

Sheryl decides *she* needs the champagne and orders it for herself.

"All I can say is *wow*! Where do you plan to live?"

"I'm transferring to Miami. I can ride a desk there. Be the voice on the other end of the phone. I've got property in the Bahamas that I've been slowly developing. It's a forty-minute plane ride."

"That's great! My folks have a place a little north and inland of West Palm. Practically in the neighborhood. We'll be able to hang together! Here's to always being close!"

Sheryl raises her glass to Landi's pickle and takes a long pull on her effervescing drink.

"And here's to Auntie Sheryl!" offers Landi, wiping a tear.

They chatter through dinner about the terms and conditions of Kostas' deal. The impending possible capture of Stefanos. The nuances of Frank's possible involvement.

Sheryl is amazed at how much classified information Landi is letting her in on.

Then Landi's phone vibrates.

"Orchid. Yeah send it and get me an ID on her—yesterday. Good work. I'll hang on..." Then she whispers, "Sheryl! They're sending a photo of Frank's contact!"

The image comes through with amazing clarity. She scans it with the trained eye of a criminal anthropologist.

"Looks like your standard Southern Belle. Sweet actually. Too bad the bottom is about to drop out of her world. Check her out."

Landi hands her phone triumphantly to Sheryl. It takes less than two seconds for her to recognize the visage. She nearly showers Landi with the cough-induced spray from the big sip of champagne she's just taken.

"Holy Christ! That's my mother!" utters Sheryl in a whispered yell.

65

Mankowski Aboard

Frank barely makes his return flight to Athens. He laughs privately that he's on the same aircraft, same seat as his flight over. He pulls out the in-flight magazine and returns to his half-finished crossword puzzle. He can't keep his mind on it and begins doodling in the margin.

He draws a caricature of Landi complete with oversized bosom and daggers where the hands should be. Face like a large predatory cat—perhaps a jaguar. He fantasizes about wrestling with—and entering—her. This starts an arousal.

"Excuse me sir, can I get you something? Coffee, tea, juice, soda? Beer, wine, bourbon, scotch? "

She's sexy enough, especially in her uniform. Have I seen her before? Perhaps she's stationed in Greece…Go for the suave, adult reply—the one item not on the list but you know every cart carries.

"Thanks, I'll have a tonic water—on the rocks," he says, smiling at her half genuinely, half as subtle advance.

Frank detects her eyebrows raise ever so slightly. Although he guesses that she must be pushing 35, he glimpses a child in her returned smile. He's elated with himself that he's even interested in impressing her. He revels briefly in this scrap he's thrown himself. But by the time she returns with the bitter beverage, the fantasy has more than cooled. The implications of the call that came at the airport has de-prioritized everything else.

Nursing the bitter beverage, he considers the new facts from his director's phone call. *So Kostas is in custody and about to be used as bait to lure in Stefanos. I had hoped that Kostas' and Stefanos' interconnection would not be acted upon this fast. Of course Kostas would do anything to save his ass. So he squealed.*

But why would Special Ops want my help in closing this trap? My presence at the sting could blow everything. Besides, this is Landi's turf and I was lucky to get away with interrogating Andre and shipping him off. Ha! My one victory over Landi. And to back it up with irrefutable intelligence. What a stroke of luck that Andre actually went into an antiquities shop—and that Darryl got pictures!

But why this sudden shift of policy? I feel like a cat trying to live in a dog's world. Is my cover blown?

Frank is relieved to be in the loop, but terrified at what dragon may crouch behind this sudden seismic shift. He shudders as the axiom every intelligence official knows as gospel, pulsates through his head: *Things are never what they seem.*

I'll request—no! I'll just go down to the cellblock and interview Kostas to see how much he knows. It'll be recorded for sure. Does Kostas know who I am? How should I behave when the trap is sprung on Stefanos? Should I try to position myself to be an invisible part of the bust? Landi must have requested that I help out. Are they short-staffed? This doesn't smell right.

"Goddamn Landi. She's too hot to be this good," he whispers, scribbling over her caricature, obliterating it. It's common knowledge that the better looking women in Special Ops are expected—trained actually—to use their charms to obtain information. Even to gain intimate access for assassinations. *I would give a small fortune to gain the favors of someone that exciting. Even for one night.* He smirks at his mature—for him—desire.

I've got to stop flying so much. I'd rather work every waking hour—on the ground. There's simply too much idle time on a plane. The world below is too far away.

And there's too much time to overhear that little voice inside, questioning what he's doing. Mostly he hates that voice. The voice on this flight is no exception. He's never excited about what the voice is trying to say. Except for the part that's been droning on for weeks now: *You have to get out of Greece. Get your butt to D.C. where you might meet some new women, exciting women, appropriate women. Damn it to hell! I love—and hate—that part of the little voice that just said "appropriate".*

He summons the flight attendant and orders a double scotch to chase his tonic. He plans to get soused and pass out, surmising she would never be interested in the warped and neurotic likes of him. He is so wrapped up in his familiar blanket of self scorn, he misses her frequent glances. Her own radar reaching out for eye contact. For a way—any way—out of this prison of lonely skies.

66

Dinner Date

"I'll have the grilled scallops and wild rice with asparagus...Oh! And a house salad, vinegrette on the side," says Bretta, smiling at the waitress as if they were co-conspirators in pleasure.

"I can't argue with that," says Andre. "Make it two."

Andre studies Bretta's face, not caring if he's staring. *I'm astounded at my attraction to this sweet woman. How is it that she invited me out? She's a bit on the thin side. I hope she's not anorexic. She does seem authentic. One of those girl-next-door blonde types that I've always considered unapproachable. Yet there's no denying, here she is, beaming back at me.*

"So, who were you talking to on the beach? How could what they were saying cause such a powerful reaction?" Bretta inquires, truly wanting to know.

"It's a *he*, though he does come across as a *they*. He's so multi-dimensional. His name is Vincent. He's a mystic and spiritual teacher. Lives out on the California Coast. He was raised in Assisi Italy—where Saint Francis is from."

"I've met a few Italians here. Dated one briefly. Charming people but so European. Hard to understand sometimes. And their egos are pretty, uh, *developed* I guess you might say."

"Vincent came to Santa Barbara in his twenties and had some kind of spontaneous awakening there. Claims it was triggered by the quality of the light. He's pretty Americanized. Has only the remnants of an accent. Still has that cosmopolitan flare though. Just an amazing person to hang with."

"Is he like a...guru?"

"If anything, he's the anti-guru. No robes, no headgear. Dresses normally. But the stuff that comes across in his teaching...it's so profoundly intense.

184

A cosmic fusion of light beams and heavy water."

"What's he saying—in a nutshell?"

Andre laughs. "I've only had three encounters, so I just have nutshell knowledge. But I'll try. The main thing he says is, 'There is no life outside this moment'. In fact, he basically says that if you want to know God, just look out consciously from wherever you are. From Now. God is not some pompous being on a throne. For all practical purposes, God *is* the present moment—or more precisely, the present moment is God revealed."

Bretta takes several seconds and looks around the restaurant patio. Takes in the collective hum of the conversation. Takes in the background jazz. The march of the busboys. The elegance of the water pourers. The ambrosia of the eighty-degree evening. The imported Italian floor tile.

"Wow. I can kind of sense that. When I look at the other people, the décor, even the drinks and the condiments, it's almost pulsating."

Andre is pleasurably shocked at the depth of Bretta's perception.

"That's it! And Vincent says when you're truly present, you move naturally and gracefully into silence. You want to be there. Crave it, actually."

They look at one another in total gratitude to be having this ecstatic feeling at the same time. Their hands naturally meet across the tabletop. There is literally nothing to say. The moment lasts—goes eternal. Goes magical. Having surrendered their personalities, they simply feel it. Bask in its warmth. Revel in its depth. And celebrate it. Together.

But what they don't know—and really don't want to know—is the downside of the ecstasy. Unless a reveler is very careful, he or she will come to associate the *magic* with the person in their field at the time the magic is present. Bretta, having never before consciously experienced cosmic love to this degree, is ardently projecting onto Andre that he is its source.

For his part, Andre should have been on guard against the trap of this dynamic. He's read all the books. Gone to some lectures. Even got it from Vincent. But unfortunately, he's not yet acknowledged—let alone internalized—the potential downside of such universal bliss and magic. And he is yet to realize the same drama is playing itself out with him and Sheryl.

The problem with awakening is that you start to love everything in your path. And from the moment Andre had his insight and opening on Cape Florida Beach during tonight's glorious sunset, Bretta was squarely in Andre's path. And—for lack of better terminology—her *soul* recognized that his *soul* was experiencing the divine on earth. And thus, with two souls in proximity desiring to be drowned together in their natural realm—the ocean of the divine—inevitably, a relationship is born.

Bretta and Andre effortlessly break free when the waitress returns with their salads. They instantly fall in love with her to such a degree that she too is drawn to them. After her fourth—and totally unnecessary—visit, she has no qualms about asking them somewhat intimate questions.

"Are you two Jesus freaks?"

Andre and Bretta nearly go into hysterics.

"Not really. But I hear he did have some cool things to say. Why do you ask?" Andre replies after calming a bit.

"To tell the truth, at first I thought you were on something."

"Like XTC?" whispers Bretta.

"Yeah. But I can see that you're not. You seem naturally high. Both of you. What's your secret?"

"We seem to have gotten ourselves hooked on the moment."

"The moment?"

Andre looks her straight in the eye. He feels a twinge of how Vincent must feel all the time.

"They say the physical universe constantly breaks down and re-creates itself moment to moment. If you slow yourself down, and feel into the silence between re-creations, you can pick up on it. There's even a profound silence between each word. It exists even in the space between you and I. Right now. In fact, only right now," Andre offers. "Just be with the dishes, the music, everything in the space, even your toughest clientele—without judgment. There is no past, no future. Just let it all be exactly what it is. Tune into it. Let it fill you. Don't think about it. Don't think at all."

It doesn't take long for the poor girl—a working coed attending nearby Florida International University—to have several sweet, pulsating, moments of the same direct experience. She beams at both of them and it's obvious to them that, for the rest of their time in the Blue Coral, she is tangoing among the tables with her trays of food, completely in love with her customers.

Andre and Bretta share a thin slice of made-on-the-premises key lime pie. A house delicacy that has put the Blue Coral on the elite dining map. They feed each other micro bites to make the culinary rapture last as long as possible.

"Wow!" exclaims Bretta. "If I'm in such an intense state of joy from this little bit of pie, I can't imagine what would happen to me if I were making love right now."

"The truth is, you are making love right now."

"Yes I am. More ravishingly than I ever have. And I have a premonition that I'm going to discover a lot more ways to make it before the night is over."

"And I'd love to be part of your discovery."

Andre can't believe he's just floated an obvious innuendo.

"Why be a part, when you can be the entire discovery?" Bretta purrs, steering Andre out the door toward her bright yellow convertible.

67

Naib's Mission

Like any successful organization, Al Qaeda has checks and balances built into its structure. Naib, the technician is more than a technician. Born in Iran to secular parents he was recognized at age sixteen as being technically gifted. He was selected to be trained as a chemical engineer in Russia and, after a fateful conversion to Wahabi Islam, eventually found his way to a position in Pakistan's top-secret nuclear weapons program.

This employment became a tutelage under a brilliant western-educated physicist lasting three years—until Naib became disillusioned by Pakistan's flirtation with the West. At this vulnerable juncture, he was easily recruited by one of Al Qaeda's top lieutenants. And when prompted and pointed, Naib Al-Bukhari developed into a virtual one-man doomsday machine bent on eradicating as many infidels in one fell swoop as possible.

At his cell leader Salim's request, he has spent several days measuring the waves emanating from his creation then checking and graphing those results against statistical probabilities related to the expected yield of a nuclear blast.

He's checked and cross-checked and is now convinced beyond a doubt that he's assembled a weapon at least two point five times more powerful than anything ever previously exploded above ground on the planet. And it fits neatly into two large normal-looking suitcases. Even more frightening, because of its inherent stability, it can be deployed from travel mode to detonation-ready mode in as short a time span as twenty-five minutes.

Within Al Qaeda, Naib is the check in relation to Salim, his cell leader. And he has had an unsettling feeling for weeks now that Salim is stalling. Keeping him from carrying out his momentous jihad.

68

Mother and Daughter

"Hi Momma," says Sheryl, mustering her best false-cheer greeting.

"Sheryl! Sweetie! So good to hear you. Sam said you'd called. How's things?"

"Okay Mom, okay. How's the land-saving project going?"

"Pretty good darlin'. But that dad-gum developer's nippin' at my heels. I gotta turn this deal in seven days or it's all lost. You simply must see this Key. A friendly reporter came out and called it an emerald against the sea's blue skin. It's like going back in time. So beautiful. We got an army of volunteers ready to restore it on its way back to one hundred per cent natural. A rare chance in today's world. When you come back, I'd love for you to manage the work. I'm so close I can smell the juleps."

Sheryl nearly goes ballistic at her mother's assumptions: *"Of course you're coming back. Of course you'll manage my project."* Instead of reacting, she stuffs her anger and stays on-purpose like a genuine intelligence operative. "What's keeping you from closing the deal?"

Jesse exhales heavily across the two oceans that separate them.

"Same thing that makes the world go around—or so they tell me. Cold cash. A few hundred thousand dollars of it is all I need to cook up."

"Sounds expensive Mom. How are you raising it? Concerts? Dinners?"

"I wish. There's so many competing causes. And they're mostly all valid. This came up fast. Too fast. We're way beyond bake sales. Lucked out a month back. Reeled in a couple of large donors. And the newspaper write up really helped. But, truth be told, I've had to set up a business that donates all its profits to the Trust."

"Wow. The profits must be enormous. What are you up to?"

"I'm surprised your boss hasn't let it slip. But then he would keep it silent. He's such a modest young man. We're in the antiquities business. And that is absolutely not for publication."

"Frank? You're in business with Frank? I had no idea on earth!" *Sheryl, you can be a Class A liar. Maybe intelligence is for you after all.* "What is it you're selling Mom?"

"Antiquities. You know, vases, statues, even a few ingots. Frank has this direct line to a private dig some friends of his are bankrolling. Exclusive rights. Amazing stuff, really. Extremely well preserved. It's been ducky. He's very generous with the profit sharing. He covers his overhead out of his half."

"Oh. So it's a fifty-fifty split. That *is* generous."

"Well darlin', he was whelped right down here in Everglades City, you know. He wants to see this special place saved near as bad as I do. But listen to me ramblin' on. How's your new position treatin' you?"

"The work gets more interesting every day Momma. But I'm kind of ready to come stateside. Even if it's for a short visit. Daddy said he'd think on it."

"Let me tell you sweetheart, if my child wants to come home, that's more than fine by me. You just come anytime your heart says it's time. Lord knows your father is a wonderful man but he will not dictate your comings and goings. How long's it been? Eight months?"

"Nine and a half."

"That's terrible enough time spent in that bucolic backwater. When you come back, I can bet you'll be ready to stare your demons down."

"I don't like to put labels on them." Sheryl's defenses are fully triggered. It's her childhood all over again. The assumptions. The condescension. The subtle judgments.

190

"You know what I mean darlin'."

"They're just poor choices. Nobody's perfect. Not even you." *I can't believe I said that.* "Momma, I'm sorry. It's 1AM here and I'm..."

"These are busy times. Seems as if the whole world's under a cloud of stress."

"You're right Momma, I have to get to sleep. You take care."

"Okay darlin'. Hugs and kisses. And I will see you soon. And don't bother to ask your father's permission again. I'm telling him you're coming home soon."

"Okay Momma, good night."

Sheryl gets the sign from Landi that the call was successfully recorded. She can't tell if the tear she's fighting is because she and her mother can't simply say "I love you" and mean it, or because her Mom's dreams are in line for a big fall.

"My God Landi, what the hell's going to happen to her? She obviously has no clue where these pieces originate from." Sheryl holds back what she knows will be a torrent of tears.

"I don't know," sighs Landi. "This is really a first-class mess. You're right about her innocence. But at some point we'll have to recover the antiquities. All that money will have to be paid back to boot."

"But that'll mean she'll lose the Key. It'll be thrown to the developers! Her blood pressure is already off the chart. This will kill her." Sheryl is sobbing now for her mother but more so for her own realization of the surprising depth of feeling she has for her.

"I'm sorry girlfriend. I'm so, so sorry," murmurs Landi. Simply holding Sheryl. Just being there.

69

Gone with the Wind

"Yes I told her she could come home. She's my daughter too," declares Jesse as she pulls back the covers and flops onto the bed.

Sam Jansen stares blankly out the window of his hotel suite in Coral Gables. Part of his three-nights-a-month package for high-level civil servants who must fly abroad frequently.

"And what's wrong with my business? Frank assures me it's totally above board."

"I never said anything was wrong with it. I just wanted to know the tax angle. You know how complicated our returns are." Sam tries to convince himself it isn't a total lie.

"You think for one minute I don't know when Sam Jansen is on one of his famous witch hunts? I've been watching his highness from the viewing stand for almost three decades!"

"You know what I love about you?" says Sam sliding into bed.

"This better be good Mister."

"The way you make me feel like Rhett Butler."

"Wrong answer. Rhett told Scarlet he didn't give a damn. Is that what you're telling me?"

"No I'm not! I'm talking about the ninety-eight percent of their relationship where he worshipped the clay she walked on. That's how you make me feel. Always have. Even though I'm a damn Yankee, you are my Scarlet."

"Your silver tongue wiggled your hide out of that one. But I hope we don't end up in some ill-timed tragedy like them."

"That won't happen because my dear, I do give a damn," says a smiling Sam, breathing easier.

"Good. Then it's settled. Sheryl comes home. The Key is saved. We're not indicted for tax fraud," Jesse chirps, like she's reciting lines in a grade-school play. She cuddles up to Sam.

"And after these final six months in Panama, we're gone with the wind to the South Pacific for as long as we care to stay." Sam kisses the side of her face.

And after having found out what Frank Mankowski is really up to, Sam Jansen hopes to God he has just spoken a true prophecy. And he hopes that when he does return from Panama, South Florida, as he knows it, is still here.

70

In Bretta's Bed

The setting of Bretta's condo—on the west side of Key Biscayne, looking back across the water at Miami—is rather exquisite. Upon entering, at first Andre is amused. Even in wild California, he's never seen anything like this. The inside is like an herb store, a health clinic, and a crystal store combined.

"Whoa," says Andre, taking in the spectacle. "What have I gotten myself into? You're not going to cast a spell on me, are you?"

"You're the spell-caster. I wish I'd run into you five years ago."

"Oh? So I'm a little late, but I'm here now."

"Yes, and I'm beyond grateful. And I know the past is a can of worms."

"Actually the past isn't totally irrelevant. I just found out today that we can consciously re-enter our past as a vehicle for healing. It's like sending in an emissary from the past's future."

"I'm afraid it's too late for me."

"Really? I don't think it's ever too late."

"Perhaps for some parts of us that's true. Andre, I've not had such a sweet evening in ages. I don't want to compromise that, but there's something I've not told you," says Bretta, her voice cracking.

Bretta faces Andre who braces for the worst.

Here it comes. She's just-divorced or transsexual or…

"I have terminal leukemia. At least that's the way the medical people put it."

"Oh no!" Andre gasps. He falls backward onto a couch, his head spinning.

"Hey, I'm not dead yet. At my last doctor contact, she said I'm still somewhat in Stage One. All I know is I have some hard days. Every once in a while I feel normal. Today was like that. And yesterday. Sometimes it will last a week. Then when we met on the beach, and the dinner, I mean, right now I feel as though I'll live forever." Bretta sits down next to him.

"That's because eternity is revealing itself to you…" Andre holds her hands in his. His eyes are full of tears. "I want to say I'm sorry, but you are so incredibly alive and beautiful, I…" They hold each other crying mixtures of tears. Tears of joy, of grief, of gratitude.

After a time, Bretta speaks first.

"Andre, would you just lie in bed and hold me tonight? I've not had that for so long. I've got a couple girlfriends who've stuck it out. But they're up in Orlando. Most everybody else bowed out along the way. When I gave up on doctors and went for alternative healing, especially the guys, including my fiance, took me for crazy and ran. I mean, look at this place. I must come off as a witch?"

Andre takes a long look around at the jars of herbs, oils, and tinctures. At the collection of healing magazines. At the self-help library. At the intricately arranged quartz crystals. Mesmerized, he stares at one for several seconds, powerless to avert his eyes. It brings him into an exalted state of grace from which he speaks before he can distract himself with commentary.

"This is no witches cave. What I see here is the den of a princess. She's become her own teacher in the fine art of self love. She's filled her tower with the potions and implements she needs for that noble endeavor. And the more she learns, the more she loves herself, thus the more beautiful she becomes. Ultimately, she dissolves in a passing cloud causing the most wondrous rain the earth has ever known."

At that, Andre scoops the speechless Bretta up and carries her dancing to the bedroom loft where they lie embracing tenderly for a few minutes before falling into the soundest sleep either of them has had for weeks.

71

Sunday Evening Briefing

"We know there are two calls from passport-wing Embassy telephones to Meli Productos. That's the front company owned by Stefanos Souvlakis, our target. One call was several months ago. The other was twelve minutes before the bust on the Solagros villa went down. It was after hours. Security cameras place Mankowski in the building at that time. But not unusual for him. The guy has no life. He'd be here twenty-four seven if he didn't need sleep. Most nights he's in his office until midnight, One AM. Back in by seven thirty. Serious workaholic."

"And a moonlighter. We know he's been running antiquities to Miami for fun and profit. Anyway, thanks Charles," says Landi, shuffling some papers. "I want him along tomorrow when we bite down on Stefanos. I've got a burnin' hunch he'll try to take Stefanos out when we close on him. I'm 60/40 they have history. And Frank does not want it divulged. Having him along is a risk but he has to be caught in an act. Mike, your job is to shadow Frank, and if he goes for Stefanos, drop him. But don't do him. We can't interrogate a corpse."

"What if you're over reacting?" says Hector, a veteran agent who's seen it all. "I mean, what if he's a double and we haven't been told? Wouldn't be the first time."

"I have it on authority the guy's a sleaze," says Landi aggressively defending her turf.

"Having a hot rocket doesn't make him a security risk," Hector protests.

"Are you speaking from experience, or wishful thinking?" This is vintage Landi. And why she is the team leader. Even Hector has to laugh along with the others.

"Alright soldiers, tomorrow is a big one. Get rested. See you at 0600 sharp.

72

Visitation

At 9:10 PM Frank Mankowski's taxi deposits him at the American Embassy.

"Evening Frank. Ain't seen you all weekend. Thought you might be on R&R," says Bradley the night security guard.

"That'll happen just after hell freezes over."

"Yes sir. I'll have to trust you on that one," grins Bradley as he lets Frank pass through.

Frank heads straight for the small cluster of jail cells in the basement of the east wing. He presents his badge with its color-coded, top-secret clearance level. The guard scans it and admits him into the cell block. Frank grabs a plastic chair and sits down opposite Kostas with the bars to his cell between them.

"So you are the famous Kostas Terzi. I don't believe I've had the pleasure. I'm Frank Mankowski, Chief of the Intelligence Division."

"Where do you fit in? Do you work for Landi?"

"Let's just say we serve the same master," says Frank keeping his gaze fixed on Kostas' eyes.

"So what do you wish with me? I was about to drift off. Tomorrow's my big day."

"I heard," Frank drones. "Do you know why they want Stefanos?"

"They didn't say. I don't think it's about money. That only leaves one possibility. His contacts."

"Precisely. What did he tell you about them?" Frank still has his stare literally fastened onto Kostas' face.

"He keeps it all to himself. I think it makes him feel important."

"Does that piss you off?"

"Not really. It was his paranoia that got to me. Took all the fun out of the operation," says Kostas, embarrassed that his newfound honestly just exposed that part of him he came to despise when he rejected his father's values.

"So you're telling me it's fun dealing with an organization that would rather kill you—kill your country, your way of life—than give you the time of day? Frank practically has his head through the bars, his eyes burning into Kostas' eyes.

"I thought they were just Arab thugs…until I saw them commit suicide. Landi told me more about them. I'm sick about it. Stefanos probably knew but like I say, he keeps things to himself."

"Did he ever mention any names, any code words, anything that would lead us to these creeps?"

"He only told me when the shipments were coming. And where to transport them. Which pieces to pull out and take to him."

"He wanted some of this brought to him?"

Kostas sighs. "Yes. For something special. He never said what this is."

"And you never asked?"

"No. This is his business. He calls me a partner—but the truth is I am only another employee. I should say favorite—favored—employee. My payment was my villa, my flat, and all the cash I needed."

"And all the women."

"What I did with my time was my business. And now I must rest. If you will pardon me?" There is a pleading quality in Kostas' voice.

"There better be no slip ups tomorrow. No trying to escape—or you are a dead man. Sleep well Mr. Terzi."

Frank stands up quickly and kicks his chair against a wall—a move which rattles Kostas. He decides for no good reason to let Frank know a detail that he's only just remembered this afternoon.

"And you also Mr. Makowst..."

"Man-kow-ski."

"You know, there is one small detail I remember he told me. About the special shipments, the small pieces I would bring him. He said that even before this last submarine came, there would be no more needed. 'They have all they need' is what he said."

"They have all the small pieces they need. That's what he said?"

"Yes. It is."

Frank's eyes are again locked on Kostas' eyes. The transmission of truth between the two men is undeniable.

"Thank you," whispers Frank gravely. "Thank you."

Frank Mankowski vaults up to his office and grabs a small cache of items—mostly mementos. He charges out the gate saluting Bradley the security guard on his way. He staggers out into the summer Athens night, his blood running like gray glacier water, chilling his body, numbing every fiber and cell, all the way into a core he never knew he had.

73

The Stakeout

Andre Bell and Special Agent Darryl Sheets sit in Darryl's modest rental car in the escalating mid-morning Dade County heat. They gnaw on almond biscotti, sip fresh orange juice, and trade notes.

"Let me get this straight Andre. After all this, you've gone off and snagged a new girlfriend. Even I've heard of the legendary Sheryl Jansen, reincarnated warrior queen. This new one better be worth it."

"She's not exactly a girlfriend. She's someone I met. Someone who needs help."

"We all need help. Hell, I need help. Who's there for me? Little Miss Nobody, that's who."

"Maybe someone's about to happen for you."

"I doubt it. Anyway, what's her problem?"

"Her name is Bretta. Her doctors say she has terminal leukemia and almost all her friends have bailed."

Darryl feels kicked in the groin. "I'm sorry man. I had no idea."

"That's okay. I'm the one who has no idea how this happened. One minute I'm having a soul-wrenching phone session with Vincent. The next minute I'm in a deep dialogue with this sweet—and I admit—captivating woman. Right on that beach at the south end of Key Biscayne."

"Hell of a development. What you gonna do? It's not like you live around here."

"I haven't gone that far with it. What am I going to do? I could ask the same question if Sheryl strolled in right now. I don't think there's any answer. Perhaps if that moment comes, it will contain the answer."

"Spoken like a true Vincent's boy… Now would you gaze upon this."

Andre's and Darryl's jaws drop as Jesse's fire-engine-red, late 80's Cadillac convertible eases in two spaces down. A svelte middle-aged woman in a feather-laden floppy hat, silver high heels, white Capri pants, and a modest halter top, covered by a blue see-through silk jacket, emerges from the Caddy.

She practically caresses the meter as she feeds it, then waltzes to the trunk and exhumes a suitcase like it were a prop in an opera. Traffic stops for her of its own accord as she leads the luggage across the street into *Atlantis Artifacts*.

There is no possible commentary for what they have just witnessed. Darryl recovers from his daze enough to jerk his thumb toward the store, signaling Andre to exit the car and start his reconnaissance.

Andre enters the shop and appears to interest himself in browsing the myriad of pieces on display. He keeps an ear tuned to Jesse's conversation with the owner, Hamid, an impeccably dressed and manicured Turkish man in his mid-forties.

"Now Hamid, you know as well as me how rare these statuettes are. And feast your eyes on this bust. We're talking 2nd Century BC. And this scepter. Exquisite. Ancient. They were just learning how to skillfully work metal. Okay. Here's my best number—on the whole package. I don't want to sell individual pieces." Jesse writes it down on a pad and turns it around to show Hamid. He doesn't even wince.

"Let me get my checkbook," he deadpans.

At one point Andre decides to move past the counter where Jesse has her pieces arranged. As he passes behind her, Andre gets one of those rushes like a wind that begins in the groin and blows up through the spine, swirls around the heart, and exits through the top of the head. Not unlike looking over a precipice with no guardrail. In this momentary fleeting space between two beings, Jesse emanates—at least to Andre—an overwhelming physical sense of her daughter Sheryl's essence. Her uniqueness. Her poise. Her breathtaking presence.

He has had no warning. No whispered premonition from his soul that her mother's proximity would trigger this longing. A longing he can't satisfy. Certainly not now. Maybe never.

He fumbles around the display farthest from her, where unobserved, he is able to fasten his gaze—not really to her per se—but to that ethereal part of her which is in resonance with Sheryl. To put it simply, he is hopelessly re-smitten.

"How may I help you?" says Hamid.

To his alarm, Andre realizes he's been completely off in his mind, holed up in a bed-and-breakfast on a remote Greek Island with Sheryl. He missed Jesse's exit he was so far gone.

"Oh...Uh yes. I'm interested in early Tunisian artifacts. Forgive me for noticing but those pieces that just came—are they Tunisian?

"Yes they are—mostly. But I'm afraid they're spoken for. One of our wealthiest patrons has given us a standing order for anything that arrives from there. On occasion, he'll reject an isolated piece. From past experience, it's quite possible more than one of the items in this shipment will be returned. I could take your information and contact you if this is to happen."

"That's not necessary. Even though I'm from San Francisco and rarely get down this way, I will…"

"San Francisco! I have a cousin who owns a shop near there."

"Would that be *Arabian Antiquities*?"

"It is! Do you know it?"

"Yes," replies Andre, "I go in there frequently. "Aslan told me about your shop.

Said it was very beautiful and well stocked. I have to agree."

"Thank you Mr...."

"Bell. Andre Bell."

"I am Hamid Adivar. Would you have time for tea? "

No time. Not now. "Tea" to a Turkish shop owner means at least an hour discussing philosophy. This is followed by intricate lectures on his most prized antiquities. Answering questions. Then the bargaining. Total time: Three hours plus. I've already gained more than I imagined possible.

"I would like that very much. I confess I was passing by on my way to Key West. At the moment, I have a friend waiting for me outside who's not interested in anything old. He only allotted me fifteen minutes. We Americans are a strange bunch. Some of us hunger for the enduring beauty that ancient objects provide us, while most others worship only in the Temple of the New. I'm afraid my friend is one of those. I may be able to return on my own in the next few days and would enjoy tea and conversation at that time."

"I understand," says Hamid, "and will look forward to that day."

Andre rejoins Darryl in the car and urges him to speed away. Darryl complies willingly.

"What happened in there? Why the drama?"

"A lot."

"C'mon then spill it. Or do you need to call Vincent to process it first," says Darryl seemingly about to pounce on Andre.

"Besides the fact that five minutes in the vicinity of Sheryl's mom brought me crashing back to heartache, something is very wrong in that place."

"Like how?" says Darryl pulling off the travel lanes and guiding the rental car to rest under a line of palm trees so he can concentrate.

"Well, Hamid, the owner was polite enough but he wouldn't let me get near Jesse's shipment. Claimed it was all Tunisian stuff and he has a standing buyer for anything Tunisian."

"Sounds plausible. So what's the problem?"

"There were some very pricey, very desirable pieces in there…"

"That would be normal in such an establishment in that district," says Darryl, rather annoyed.

"True. And I'm no in-depth expert but it was obvious to me that most of the prize pieces in there *were* Tunisian. If this deep pockets client is for real, he'd grab them. I mean, there was a Carthaginian statue of Queen Dido in there that any serious Tunisian collector would give a limb for."

"Damn! That makes something about Jesse's shipment incongruous."

"Exactly. And that's not all. Again, I'm no authority—and I only got a glance at those pieces—but if I had to bet, I'd have to say they were fakes."

"How the hell would you know that?" The hairs on the back of Darryl's neck are standing up. This always happens to him when some relevant truth is emerging. He's learned to trust it implicitly.

"Well, I've personally seen and touched a lot of stuff from the Carthaginian Era—Modern Tunisia used to be ancient Carthage—and it has a certain look. I'd have to say, it emits a unique vibration, different from, say the pieces from ancient Athens or Rhodes. Anyway, at first glance, it didn't have the vibration. In fact, it didn't have any vibration. Yet this guy Hamid wrote Jesse a fat check without even bargaining. Turks always bargain. It's a cultural betrayal not to. Something doesn't add up."

"Jesus I'm glad you went in there and not me."

204

This is as far as Darryl is willing to go with his outward praise. But his inner brakeman stops him from deputizing Andre and putting him on the payroll right then and there. He was high up enough to wield that level of power—especially on an international case.

"I guess I'm glad I went in there. But now my world's exploded once again."

"Because of the like-mother, like-daughter thing?"

"I'm so screwed up, I already know when I see Bretta again, I'll fall under her spell."

"I don't mean to get Vincent-esque on you but isn't that what being in the moment is all about? Really. I mean, I'm under your spell right now. You're as good as any agent I've worked with. And I already love you like a brother."

"I feel that too. But…"

"Wait!" Darryl protests. "So now you grok Jesse—in all her southern belle wildness—and you feel waves of Sheryl. You meet Bretta, your compassion goes into hyper drive. Hell, if you're lucky enough to have it, compassion is just love expanded. Now you're feeling everybody. And just when you think you're saturated, it's Thursday again. You stumble under Vincent's spell. You're automatically high—or at least deep into the moment. As he says, 'Awakened life is always here. In this moment and nowhere else.' It never leaves. We leave it."

"Christ Darryl. I had you pegged for a goon.

"Now wait a minute! Am I that…"

"Alright." Says Andre realizing his faux pas. "Sorry. A *sweet* goon for sure. And an aware one. Where did you get that kind of insight?" Andre looks up into the coconut palms arching over the car and feels as though he's floating.

"I always kind of knew all this. I remember it from when I was a little guy. I suspect everyone can with the right stimulus. So when I had to shadow you into Vincent's meetings, it started to line up for me and it hasn't stopped. Maybe it's timing. Maybe it's fate. Have you read any of his books? I bought them all. If they tried to bottle his message, my organization would have to take it off the shelves. It's a good thing he's still treading water in relative obscurity. His teaching is too dangerous for the average citizen."

"You're probably right…Okay. So we're comrades in moment-hood. And I have to say, right here, right now, I'm majorly bummed."

"What the hell for?" says Darryl, feeling like the air's gone out of him—again.

"My idea all along was to tail Jesse to her digs. While you had me playing sleuth, she got away. It sounds stupid but the way I feel now, for a nickel and a song, I'd go get Bretta and rent a place near Jesse—if I could find her. I'd wait there until Sheryl comes to visit—or hell freezes over."

"I can't sing, but here's a nickel," says Darryl, handing his business card to Andre. "Here's Jesse's address—on the back. Her and Sam's compound is up on Indigo Lake, northwest of Palm Beach. Way inland. Pretty exclusive. I'm not up on the local rental market. But this is Florida, and almost everything's for rent here. Call me when you're settled. I may need the couch."

74

Veiled Threat

Kallie lounges poolside sunning herself on a chaise. She lies motionless letting the summer heat burn onto her bare arms and legs. Though they are on the other side of a stucco wall, she can't help overhearing a conversation between Salim, her father, and Naib, the strange-looking employee whom she rarely sees. His pasty skin and withdrawn demeanor give her the creeps. She goes out of her way to stay away from him as well as Khazin his surly co-worker. It seems as if they frown every time they see her. She's glad their quarters are near the rear property line behind the lab.

"Effendi, do you mean to tell me you have not yet spoken to Sarfaraz! How can this be?" I gave you the calculations and projection over a week ago. We are ready. We have no reason to delay. The western world must pay for its arrogance, its shallowness," fumes Naib with open indignation.

Salim laughs inwardly. *Ha! I have finally prodded Naib to jettison his prized stoicism. At last an undignified reaction from this appalling man, this human virus.*

Born into a family endowed with wealth, Salim had all the good fortune life could offer. Educated at The American University of Paris near his parents' flat in a cosmopolitan neighborhood, he was exposed to Western thought and culture from day one.

Like so many upper and middle-class modern Muslims, along with his drive to achieve technical prowess, came the nagging feeling that he was somehow betraying his heritage. Unconsciously, this group—Salim included—has realized en mass that strong, ideology-based institutions have been the matrix within which Western technological superiority has come to flower, leaving Islam in the dust.

In response, certain of these brightest individuals have struck out and created a hybrid of traditional and modern Islam. This crossbred creature has merged politics with the spiritual for the first time in Islam's history.

Twelve years ago, when Salim began his involvement with radical Islamists, he felt differently about the West. He swallowed the hook that by joining them he would restore the dignity of all Muslims. "We will never again be looked upon as a second-rate culture with quaint customs. We must restore our status in the world. If this means by violent actions, then so be it." He would affirm this constantly to his co-conspirators.

Living in America, I have come to enjoy my American friends more than the Islamic allies I am bound to. The same allies who will think nothing of eliminating me and my family should I abandon the mission. Working and playing among my enemy, I have come to see their humanness. Their love of family. Their humor. The validity of their values. Of course they have shortcomings. But to kill them because of their brand of personal freedom—this is true insanity. Now that Kallie and Nazzy are immersed in their culture—and thriving—I appreciate them more each day.

Honest logic has led me to conclude that just because a few powerful of the Western elite are terrorists in their own right, this does not give me the license for mass murder. In fact, most of the Americans I associate with want to change the policies of their government. At this point, I can concoct no rationale for the wholesale slaughter of innocents.

I will kill myself before I will allow any of them to be killed.

Naib takes Salim's silence as an insult. "What more must I do before your blessing is given? You have seen my verification and my prediction. This will be the greatest achievement ever against the enemies of Allah whom we now live among. And to insure this, I shall be the human detonator."

"This is a generous gesture," replies Salim, secretly excited at the idea of Naib's annihilation. "I have been informed that Sarfaraz and I will speak this evening about *the weather*. I will inform you of the outcome."

"Allah be praised," intones Naib as he bows and leaves Salim's presence.

On the other side of the wall, Kallie's sweet lifeblood feels like it's been injected with some terrible, organ-eating venom. She does not understand everything that is said, but she knows her father to be a powerful man and Naib a creepy, and likely dangerous man.

With the uncluttered innocence of a sheltered child, she absorbs the evil feeling of their plot like a toxic plume from a chemical explosion. She senses that what they are hatching means the end of her happiness. Her friendships. Her very life. She buries her head in a large towel sobbing violently into it long after she's certain the men have dispersed.

75

Sting Morning

Getting Kostas, his zodiac, and all the support people in place for Stefanos' capture is a logistical nightmare. At 6 AM, Landi's team—plus Frank—are assembled in the situation room in the Embassy basement for a briefing. The plan is rehashed and refined. Final positionings and responsibilities are assigned. At 7:35 AM there is a rush to get everything on the road to the Heliport adjacent to Athens International.

Frank learns there are to be three choppers. He casually approaches the logistics agent in charge of each one telling him he's been asked to ride with one of the others. None of them cares to fuss about such a small detail because they are overwhelmed with equipment checklists. The operation involves twenty-five ego-driven, half awake agents and a lot of gear. They are more than happy to cross him off their inventory. It affords them more cargo space.

As the transport vans fill up and space gets tight, he deftly offers to the frazzled chief logistics coordinator that he'll take a couple of passengers in his personal embassy car to the heliport. The man, who, as Frank's luck would have it, was not at last night's briefing, thinks it a great idea. Frank slips off to his car alone.

Landi is frantically making calls to her stateside support team as well as to the U.S. base at Araxos on the Ionian Sea northwest of Athens where they will land to load the zodiac, some weaponry and a sniper team. She becomes distracted by a problem with clearance to land the choppers at Corfu. It had all been pre-arranged. But certain factions in Greek security are beyond tired of catering to the Americans.

Caught up in details and diplomacy (and in doing it all perfectly), she assumes the agent she had assigned at last night's briefing is watching Frank. But he understood his watchman role to be in effect only at and after their arrival on the beach. He, along with everybody else, is keeping an eye on Kostas instead. He has celebrity status at this point because a few spicy details have been passed around about his and Landi's liaisons.

The vans pull out and Frank falls in at the rear of the convoy. He lags a bit behind and at the intersection where the last turnoff to the airport is possible, he swerves onto that road accelerating toward the International Terminal as fast as the sparse traffic allows. It will not be until shortly after the transport choppers land at Araxos Air Base that he is missed. By that time, he will have boarded a flight to Tel Aviv using a passport with his picture, but engraved with the name of Herman Heitman. He is no longer trackable.

76

In Sheryl's Blue Silence

Sheryl couldn't be happier that she was not required to go along on the sting. Leave that to the heavyweights. She busies herself with some routine paperwork. She picks at her bag lunch. She can't figure herself out.

Why aren't you calling Andre? Landi's people gave you his cell number. He's innocent. Landi says so. My gut says so. Only sleazy Frank is pointing fingers at him.

Sheryl's rationalizing self comes to her defense. *So what if Frank has Andre's line tapped and overhears them planning an illegal rendezvous? Damn him. He's got to be dirty. And he's hell-bent on putting Andre away. All he needs is some small excuse to add to his circumstantial pile of crap. And I am unwilling to give him a shred of a reason. I'm not calling.*

At the thought of Frank, Sheryl feels sullied. Dirty. *I need water.*

"Hey Elsie," she calls to her stand-in body guard, "I'm slipping down to the gym for a bit. Don't worry, the guards know to detain me if I try to leave the building on my own."

"Okay. Just don't make me look bad again." Elsie half scolds, half teases.

The gym is empty owing to the fact that most people who would use it are either on the Stefanos operation or supporting it. Sheryl runs through an abbreviated karate routine, aiming her kicks at Frank's imagined face and genitals. *God. Now I feel even dirtier…'God'? Why did I use that word? God. God. God…*

Sheryl enters the shower and turns on both hot and cold full blast. The walls are cobalt blue tile. The floor is a creamy natural stone. With a little self deception, she can imagine she's walking on the sea bottom. *Maybe blue-Sheryl is here.*

She gets very still. And she shudders. Shudders because she seldom uses the word "God" anymore. Yet the word rings in her ears. She intentionally brings her hands up to cover them and stands motionless letting the water drum the top of her head. A voice speaks which she thinks is simply one part of her.

"The true reason you are not calling Andre is because that would make the fantasy too real. Make the uncertainty less uncertain. Yes you can be without the uncertainty, but this is not natural to you and not your first choice."

Okay. So I'm addicted to uncertainty, The uncertainties in my life are what drive me. Even with Kostas, I was never sure where things were going. Some part of me said, 'Is he a fling—or something more profound?' Wait a minute...

Like a thunder clap, Sheryl recognizes that when the relationship crashed, the uncertainty was gone. And that is the harder, more obscure pill to swallow.

I see that now. No wonder I was so angry. These uncertainties, in a perverse way, give me the illusion of life. So I unconsciously hold onto them. Without them, my world would be flat—and dull.

Instantly, this revelation leads her to question whether or not she possesses the stability that enables real love to bloom. *Perhaps my immaturity is who I am. All I am. Do I love Andre? Or is he just the latest flavor in a string of addictive uncertainties?*

If she could answer *yes* to loving him, right now, she'd rush upstairs, pick up her phone and call him. Frank's shadow be damned. Instead, she stares at one specific tile and feels so immensely, so numbingly sad, she can't even cry.

77

Kostas and Freedom

The only Greek Islands not in the Aegean arm of the Mediterranean are the Ionian Islands off the northwest coast—of which Corfu is the most visited. From much of its north coast, Albania is visible. And to Stefanos, Albania is freedom. From there, a few easy steps and he lands in Turkey where he can rot in relative comfort until he becomes a forgotten footnote in the hierarchy of wanted criminals.

Landi could not risk staging the zodiac anywhere near the coastal hamlet of Roda where Kostas claims he is to meet Stefanos. So they land one chopper in the parking lot at the small harbor on Mathraki, an unspoiled island two hours away by zodiac. Here they disgorge Kostas, his boat, and enough gear to give the appearance that he's come a long way north from the southern Aegean islands.

So it is that Kostas pilots his craft out of Mathraki harbor in the late afternoon. The wind is up and the spray is breaking over the boat. Kostas loves this brief taste of freedom. What he doesn't know is that his clothes & gear have been secretly outfitted with tracking transmitters. Oblivious, he reflects on the escape that might have been.

I could have told them the rendezvous was on Mathraki and I needed to depart from Corfu. I'd have passed by the beach where Stefanos is hiding, and jumped off with a snorkel just after locking the zodiac on course toward the other island. How easy it would have been!

But the thought of having to endure being a fugitive with Stefanos—even briefly—turns his stomach. *How could I cooperate with my father's murderer? This way I, Kostas Terzi, still have a life which is to include my child. And a new start in America. And what will Stefanos have? Probably an open-ended stay at Guantanamo prison, complete with daily torture sessions. Ironically, we'll end up only a hundred miles apart, but it may as well be a hundred worlds.*

A scant two weeks ago, if Kostas could have looked into a mirror and seen the wounds riddling his soul, he would likely have reacted by smashing the mirror. Would likely have continued his flirtation with the familiar shadow, retreating into some bastardized version of arrogance and missing another rare chance to walk toward a more whole version of himself.

Now he is pleased with his choice to go straight for Stefanos' jugular. And just as pleased because he was able to extract one important concession from Landi. *Not only did she agree to drop any and all charges they might concoct against Kapetan Yanni, but she also agreed to afford him protection against the inevitable Al Qaeda reprisals, effective the day I agreed to cooperate. I thank my stars Yanni hasn't been and won't be eradicated simply because his usefulness has ceased. Now he's safe.*

It hits Kostas that this is the first time in years he has genuinely cared for someone else's welfare. He's sure his heart is, this moment, expanding outward to bump up against the underside of his skin. He can't tell if the water on his face is from the zodiac spray or his joy-laden tears.

Landi acted immediately and got more than she bargained for. It turns out the Kapetan kept a detailed log of the goings and comings of the couriers, complete with their descriptions thinking it might prove useful someday. He even went so far as to inquire of his neighbors—under the guise of island gossip—as to how the operatives arrived and departed Solagros—including the names of private launches. This was not difficult since Solagros is so small and everyone's business is everyone else's business. The ripple effect of this intelligence is already proving to be enormously fruitful.

At about 6:30 in the early evening Kostas nears the north shore of Corfu. He slows the zodiac to a crawl so as to prevent a stir among the local authorities.

He puts up a pole and a line and trolls for fish, which is the universal archetype to men of all stripes for an unthreatening individual minding his own business, and one who does not want his solitude interrupted.

A chill passes through Kostas. *What if Stefanos doesn't show? What if he's ill? What if Al Qaeda tracked and popped him? Would Landi even know? You dolt! You have been so focused on the travel and capture plans for today you've not considered the obvious. If you don't deliver Stefanos for any reason, there will be no Miami, no parole, no visitations. You'll be the one living the Guantanamo nightmare, cursing Stefanos even more fiercely than you do now.*

78

Code Black

After a long swim trying to keep up with Andre at Hollywood Beach and a very late lunch, Darryl drops Andre back at Bretta's condo down on Key Biscayne. He pulls off under a palm in the Crandon Park parking lot and slumps down out of mental fatigue.

All day he's been wrestling with his next move. *Thankfully there was the beach-and-lunch diversion with Andre. Now I gotta face the posibilities. Just sit tight. Or go over Frank's head and risk career suicide. Yet, if Frank is dirty, should he be divulging this information about the fake antiquities? And what the hell was Frank doing in Miami the day before Jesse's sale? Coincidence? Was Andre hallucinating at the airport?*

Darryl has friends in Homeland Security but no one with enough authority-enough overview capability—to sort through all the players: Foreign Service Intel Chief, Ambassador's wife, Ambassador's daughter, Turkish National.

As if attuned to a coincident clock, Darryl's cell chimes go off. He grimaces when Frank's icon comes up on the display. Then he remembers. *Take the same medicine you gave Andre. If it's of the moment and you find yourself in the same moment with it, you must trust it completely.*

"Hello Chief."

"Listen Darryl, get your ass to Dobbins Air Reserve Base outside Atlanta. I'm leaving Tel Aviv right now on a rocket. Meet me near the strip. Look for agent Mackenzie. Code Black."

"Copy that Chief. Piece of cake. I'm in Miami."

"Miami? What's there?"

"I followed Andre Bell here. He's clean."

"I know. 2100 at Dobbins. Ten-four."

Darryl barrels for the Miami airport, his heart racing, his mind reduced to a stream of staccato potpourri. *With my badge and credential, I can bump anyone on the next flight to Atlanta—any airline. I'll be there early. That's a done deal. So what the hell's going on? I've heard of Mackenzie. Reports only to the Secretary of Defense. And why didn't the chief even argue about Andre?*

"Jesus Christ," he utters out loud, "Code Black has never been activated. Code Black is nuclear terrorist threat—imminent."

79

Moving In

Landi Riquelme is not having a good day. Besides directing the logistics of the operation, she's had to personally handle a hostile Greek Police bureaucracy and an uncooperative Greek Intelligence higher-up. Then report to her superior that Frank is missing—all in between dealing with snafus in landing clearances for the choppers.

Right now, she tells herself she knows only one thing: *Girl if you botch the capture of Stefanos, your ass will be carted out on a demotion-mobile. If you lose one agent, your larger ass will be terminated with a drastic cut in its pension. And you will go bankrupt from paying for years of therapy for perfection gone south—not to mention your tropical paradise lost.*

Her advance team, two faux couples, has already taken up positions on beach towels in Roda, the quintessential, affordable Greek beach town. It's fraught with an overabundance of tavernas and makeshift restaurants on and near the main beach, itself a nearly mile-long sandy spit, flanked at either end by natural rock jetties. The rendezvous between Stefanos and Kostas is to take place near the westernmost end.

The second wave of agents arrives looking like a bunch of typical forty-something, American-male carousers, just let out of a cage by their wives for a week in the sun. They commandeer an outside table attached to a bar across the main drag from—and in full view of—the west end of the beach. They order several rounds of ginger ale—in glasses, behaving as if it were some potent Australian ale.

Twenty minutes later, enter Landi complete with red wig, white beach jacket, and string bikini. She's accompanied by blonde, tough-girl Soleil, her complement in the CIA's web of female operatives. Another team couple is halfway into the mile-long stroll from the east jetty toward the western end carrying a hand-held cooler full of communications gear and a pair of loaded hand guns.

It's nearly August and the swimming is most comfortable in the early evening after the scorching heat of the day has passed, so the beach is busy. Not good for potential collateral damage but perfect for the agents to blend in.

The shadows are beginning to grow long when Kostas' zodiac appears rounding the western jetty at a slow crawl. As he closes to within 20 yards of the beach, a catlike stick figure in a long-sleeve peasant shirt and straw hat emerges from behind some large boulders at the waterline and waves him in. Stefanos Souvlakis surfaces from his burrow in full view of his disguised pursuers.

80

Swine Galore

"Looks like you've had time to get ugly like the rest of the dogs," mocks Stefanos as the two men pull the zodiac ashore. "Bet your American beauty wouldn't want you now!"

This macho provocation is all it takes for Kostas to explode into near insanity. He hates everything about Stefanos, especially his sense of humor. He throttles Stefanos violently by the shirt sleeves, pushes him to the sand and screams into his face.

"I know you killed my father. I also know my father tried to save your father from drowning, despite being cheated by him. May you rot in living hell *bromoskilo!*" This epithet means "you stink like a dog", and is considered a great insult—the near equivalent of challenging the recipient to a duel.

From her vantage on a bench near the street, Landi has seen and heard enough. Her red wig is also a high-tech audio transmitter/receiver. "Move in now! If they run, shoot only to disable!" *God I'm actually glad that Frank is not here to complicate the scene.*

"Wait! Hold one!" Just as her people are about to take their first steps toward the pair, Landi spots three men in dress clothes and street shoes exiting a van across the street. They begin to take long strides toward Kostas and Stefanos. Each has a paper bag over one hand.

"Three bogies my eleven o'clock. Armed. Team Two hit their knees now! Team One, secure the blue sedan. Teams Three and Four, secure primary targets."

The tranquil sunset tableau erupts in gunfire with bodies running and bodies falling. The bogies collapse in a writhing heap of bloody limbs. Landi's agents are on top of them just before two of the three can take their own lives. It's become evident from this tactic that these are Al Qaeda. And it will turn out that they are the cream of the Greek terrorist arm of that cell.

"Drivers bring the vans in now!" yells Landi as she sprints toward her primary targets, both of whom are on the ground struggling.

"Let me go you ugly wart!" shrieks Stefanos. "I have all the money we need. Don't throw your life away!"

By sheer force of adrenaline-driven will, Kostas has the meaner man face down in a hammerlock and is about to break his arm as Landi and Soleil arrive. Because Kostas has always bent to his orders, Stefanos assumed he possessed the superior strength. His inflated ego is shaken to learn otherwise.

"I know it's not in my agreement—but let me break his arm," says Kostas in dead seriousness. "This swine killed my father and made it look like suicide. It has robbed my life."

"Don't worry. Where he's going, he'll wish his arm was broken so he could be tucked safely in an infirmary bed away from the predators," laughs Landi. "You can release him now. And I'll note in your record you assisted critically in his capture."

"Bastard! You're all bastards. I'm Greek. You have no power over me," Stefanos croaks.

"Check the latest treaty," replies Landi. "The only string is—we can't execute your traitorous ass. But where terrorists are involved, it's practically an automatic deportation to Guantanamo. As far as I'm concerned, that place is too good for your kind. Even the death we just saved you from at the hands of your 'friends' is too good for you. It may take you five years, it may take twenty-five, but when you finally come to terms with the pig you've become, the horror that you've financed, the remorse will eat you alive. And that's if you're lucky."

"But I can finger people. People in your own organization!"

"Too late. We already have the red-haired prick," she lies.

Stefanos visibly recoils like he has just been kicked in the ribs.

"Hey look here," Soleil chirps, lifting a leather duffel from behind the rocks. Not only a massive wad of cash, but a list of all kinds of juicy-looking account numbers in a little red book. All of a sudden, I think it's Christmas in July."

81

Father and Daughter

All Salim Hafiz knows is that right now his daughter cannot be in the same room with him. He infers that she's become aware of the plans that are afoot. He makes sure he picks her up alone from soccer practice. After dropping off a couple of her teammates, Kallie falls silent. Salim pulls the car to a stop near a small lake in a neighborhood adjoining theirs.

"Kallie, we must talk."

"I know what you're planning. Who are you? And who are those monsters on our property?" Kallie says in an outburst, fighting back tears.

"I cannot disagree. I too have come to view them as monsters. The problem is, a number of years ago, I started out as one of them. And now I can't just wave my arm and have them disappear."

"Why not? Why does Naib hold any power over you? You are his boss."

"You don't know how dangerous he is," Salim replies.

"Is he going to blow us up?"

"No. Not us."

"He's a suicide bomber isn't he? The kids at school talk about them. It makes me hate myself. To think that I had the same religion as…"

"What do you mean *had*?"

"I denounce the religion that says we should kill non-believers. This makes us no better than the Crusaders!"

"Kallie, you best not think you are like..."

"Daddy, if someone I know that lives on our property does that, my life is over. My friends—everyone—will hate me. Forever."

"I promise I will never let that happen. But you must listen to me and do exactly as I say."

82

No One Will Ever Know

"Agent Sheets?"

"Yes sir," answers Darryl.

"I'm Agent Mackenzie. Call me Mac. Meet Agent Unger."

Darryl shakes hands with Mac and a muscular hulk of a man who could be a tailback in the NFL. Darryl, at six-one, broad-shouldered, and rock solid, feels like a mouse next to Agent Unger.

"Agent Mankowski will arrive in twenty-two minutes. Consider yourself on loan to Homeland Security. You're here for two big reasons. One, your record indicates superior intelligence and an abnormal percentage of successful missions. Two, you know too much about Mankowski's seeming inconsistencies. Are we clear so far?"

"Yes sir…uh Mac."

"Good. Now what I'm about to tell you is known only by the four of us, the President, the Secretary of Defense, and a five-man, stake-out team planted sixty miles north of here in an Atlanta suburb. Oh, and a handful of scientists. Are we clear so far?"

"Perfectly," utters Darryl, his mouth going dry.

"The subjects under surveillance are in an outbuilding—really a laboratory— on the grounds of an estate owned by Salim Hafiz, a Pakistani software mogul who is also a collector of Mediterranean artifacts. Over the last fourteen months, he's purchased a quantity of small antiquities through a shop in South Florida.

Arabian Antiquities in Coral Gables?" asks Darryl.

"Precisely. I know that you were staking them out two days ago. With Andre Bell."

"Yes Mac, that's true but…"

"Let me spare you some trouble. Frank pulled this whole charade with Mr. Bell to throw off any Al Qaeda agents that may have infiltrated our Athens Embassy. Make it look to them like he was a bloodhound following a scent. All to take suspicion away from himself. We were quite sure Stefanos did not divulge Frank's identity to Al Qaeda. Just not his tight-ass style. Made it easy for Frank to look like he's just another dumb agent following a false trail. You know of the bust of that villa in the Greek Islands?"

Darryl nods.

"Well, for us, that was unfortunate timing, but we had to let it go down or we'd have totally tipped our hand that we knew something more was going on than money laundering."

"You had me fooled. I was trying to figure out who to call to put Frank away," confesses Darryl. "And I imagine the Code Black Frank gave me has to do with this *something more?*"

"Right. Frank was responsible for bringing the antiquities into the country through an arrangement with a smuggler who approached him in Greece. At first we assumed this was just an Al Qaeda money-laundering scheme— until we tested one of the pieces. Turns out—and we discovered it by sheer luck—that they imbedded micro amounts of weapons-grade plutonium throughout each piece. Disguised it through some ingenious chemistry to make it play like background radiation. One of our lab rats dropped the damn thing and shattered it—and the radiation readings went off the scale. Took days to mop it up. We had a hellish time duplicating what they had done. The rat is still in quarantine."

"So let me guess," says Darryl grimly. "They're harvesting the plutonium from these trinkets and putting it together to make a nuclear device."

"Not just a device. A mega-bomb with enough yield to flatten all the Burroughs in New York City. And kill millions in the surrounding region."

"Good Christ!" exclaims Darryl. "Why don't we have every special operations unit staged to storm the place?"

"It may come to that," says Mac. "But right now, the President has directed us to keep this entirely under the radar. The reasoning being that if word leaks, the region will go lawless from people fleeing. Total chaos. Hundreds of panic-related deaths. In the confusion we may not get all the players involved. And we don't want any of them dead. If we get just one to talk, we can chop a big section out of their heart. We miss one in a big chaotic operation, they can regroup quicker, because that one loner still knows all the ropes. And don't forget, Pakistan is a major ally.

"That brings us to the international relations angle. We make a spectacle out of one of their fiscal heroes—a folk hero really, they take it personally, the opposition blows it up into a campaign, and their president—hell their government—looses the rest of his public support. There falls a huge domino in the Middle East—the wrong way."

"But the creep bankrolling this. How does he get what's coming to him?"

"We put him away for tax evasion in a white-collar prison. Very dignified. After nine or ten months, he's so distraught from his fall from opulence, he's found hanged in his cell. We shower public condolences on his family. Nice quiet end to a potentially noisy story...Hey, here's Frank's screamer. I'll brief all of you enroute about the assault plan. Let's go de-fuse a very hot burrito!"

Darryl enters a waiting white van. *Suppose we do stop this madness. Amazing how easy it is to justify staging the killing of a high-profile terrorist to make it look like he fell apart. It's playing God. Pure and simple. Helluva planet.*

83

Homeward Bound

"Girlfriend, I was lucky to get through yesterday with my career in one piece," replies Landi in response to Sheryl's congratulations. "But that goddamn Frank slithered through a crack. Made me look like a raw newbie. And when I went to my section chief to put a dragnet out for his sorry ass, they called me back an hour later to say he's on a White-op! Damn!"

"What's a *White-op*?" Sheryl inquires.

"That's slang for 'Presidential Mission'. Something's not what it seems. But that's always the friggin' case in this business. You hate it, but you gotta love it at the same time."

"That sleazeball is working for the president?" says Sheryl grimacing and falling into the nearest chair, jettisoning her recent fantasy of wrecking his career. If the truth be told and given the chance, she'd wreck his reproductive system too.

"Yeah. And the word is, Mr. Slime's not coming back here to Greece either. His office is cleaned out. All but the aquarium."

"Wow. That's huge…But what about his smuggling that crap to Florida? And where does that leave my Mom?" Sheryl visibly shudders. She shudders again when it fully hits her that Frank is not returning. *He must be doing something serious. And for the President no less.*

"At this point, I have no clue—let alone a theory. But if his side business is part of this White-op…who knows? Maybe it's not as bad as I thought. All I know is, I'm blowing this pop stand. All my mop-up is Stateside. I'm hitching a ride tomorrow on a super-fast military transport out of Israel. They have space. Why don't you bail with me—before your new boss shows up?"

"This is so sudden I…"

"Look girlfriend, your Mom needs you, hell, I need you—and you'll at least be on the same continent as your man."

"He's not my man!" Sheryl protests.

"That may be true—but you are his woman. It's tattooed all over you. You just can't see it."

"I don't know why I'm resisting. I want to go home. I want to find out if Andre and I are as magical as I once thought. Why am I resisting? What's wrong with me?"

"That's so simple to answer it's funny," says Landi breaking into a huge smile.

"Enlighten me then. Please!"

"When our spirit—our soul—who knows what the hell we really are?— when it gets a glimpse of its true destiny it does the damnedest thing. It actually starts to resist, preferring to stay suspended in a state of not accepting. Happened with me and Kostas. Until I actually experienced the child I'm carrying. Then I embraced what I had to do."

"Whoa! I never pegged you for a wise woman. Now you're blowing me away. Just yesterday I came to realize that I'm addicted to uncertainty. I'm stuck in it. Paralyzed really. You're saying the way out is through some stimulus. But I don't have anything like the obvious signal of a pregnancy. I just go into my head about it. And into the replay of a thirty-hour period of ecstasy that once was." Sheryl sighs and hangs her head.

"This is good. Last time you said it was twenty-eight hours. That means it's growing." Landi gets one of her wily Harlem grins going.

"Okay girlfriend. I'm busted. But where's my stimulus?" Sheryl pouts.

"What I'm trying to say is, in your case, the fact that this resistance is so alive in you *is* the signal, *is* the stimulus. When you were in the cult, did you have resistance to the head honcho? Gabriel? Was that his handle?"

"Yes, Gabriel. And no. No resistance."

"How about our friendly sperm donor, Kostas? Any resistance?" Landi asks.

"Not really,"

"Exactly my point. You have a thirty-hour window into the nature of something that knocks your socks off—a gift really—and what do you do? You resist of course. Because something in you knows if you go for this—if you leave the state of uncertainty, you are operating in new territory. You're no longer the cult-leader's doll, no longer the eccentric Greek's goddess, you're simply—and probably ultimately—Andre Bell's wife. And for a girl like you, that's so ordinary, it scares the crap out of you." Landi ends up in a crouch, delivering her closing argument right into Sheryl's face.

"My God, you're totally on. I will do anything to avoid ordinary."

"Let me tell *you* something girlfriend, I don't care if you end up with a pretty architect house, two cars, and two point three kids. I don't care if you have a nine-to-five job until you're sixty-two and a half. It's what's inside that counts. And inside, you have not one shred of ordinary. You are your own cult leader! Now, are we packing—or what?"

84

The Morning Of

Nazneem Hafiz is an extremely intelligent woman. Intelligent enough to deduce that her husband's work is riddled with defects. His technical output is confusing and confused. Yesterday she read his latest design abstract and discovered it was hopelessly stagnated in circular reasoning. More like the crude cartoons of a mental adolescent than the exploits of an elegant mind. And looking closer, she shudders at her own intuition that this outcome was intentional.

She has noticed that over the past several years Salim's enthusiasm for writing innovative programs has evaporated. So gradual it is hard to identify a turning point. The joy seems to have gone out of him.

She first began to notice his deep melancholy a few months after they moved east from Silicon Valley. And now her daughter has caught it as well. Nazneem recalls painfully that the move was his idea. "A change of scene. Good for a new round of creativity," he had said. She loved mixing and fencing with the brilliant minds orbiting around Stanford. Their life here is fine enough and Kallie seems well adjusted—but that edge of optimism, of delight really, is absent.

During breakfast this very morning, Nazneem is horrified to glimpse Salim's hands shaking. She decides that she must get Salim alone, away from the technicians, and get to the bottom of his behavior.

While taking Kallie to her friend's house for the day, at a long stoplight, Kallie hands her mother a note from Salim.

My dear Wife,

During the night Kallie has packed the car with enough essentials for an extended trip. You must..."

"What is Salim doing? He wishes me to drive to Brooklyn, take an apartment, and send a letter to him at his sister's neighbor's house in Menlo Park when we are settled. Has he lost his mind? I know he hasn't been himself but…how can we leave? Our life is here."

"He wrote the note because if we stay there Naib and Khazin will kill us." Kallie 's voice nearly breaks into a whimper. But she checks it. She knows her family will never be together again if she's not strong. "They are not who we think they are. They intend to blow New York City off the face of the earth," she says with a calmness that far exceeds her years.

She's had all night to work it through. Time to build her resolve. Time to help put her father's plan in play. Gather a suitcase. Stuff it with cash from her father's unlocked desk. Load several sheaves of crucial papers. Photos. Sneak it all to the garage. Personal effects. Clothes, food, essentials. Lift the trunk lid. Silently. By a dim light. Concentrate. For a chance at some shred of continuity in their lives. After tonight.

Nazneem cringes more from the tone in Kallie's voice than from the actual words. She starts to pull the car over but Kallie tells her she must act normal—in case they are being watched.

"How can this be? These men are our employees. We break bread with them on holy days. Treat them well."

"Mother, have you not noticed their strangeness?"

"Yes but I attributed this to their tragic upbringings. None of this makes sense. If what you say is true, why is Salim sending us to the very place they intend to blow up?"

"Because father has a perfect plan to stop them. Stop their bomb. But if they escape, they will never think to look for us there to kill us—as they have threatened to do."

"I can't believe this."

"I overheard them discussing it. I swear by the Prophet."

Nazneem takes a hard glance at her daughter and senses pure truth emanating from her. She continues to drive north toward New York on the Interstate, taking *her* turn at fighting back a bursting reservoir of tears.

Four cars back, two men in a late-model delivery van take note that the car with the two women inside began to swerve, slow and pull over, then righted itself and returned to highway speed.

85

Salim's Intervention

A gifted computer wizard can't help but view the world as a maze of funnels and switches superimposed upon a matrix of possibilities with the capability of input at any stage. Any action at a designated funnel or switch will achieve an inevitable, controllable response. Locally. Perfectly. Until the next input at the next switch.

So this morning, as head of the Atlanta sleeper cell, Salim gives his blessing to the activation of the final assembly of Naib's mega bomb and its transport to New York for detonation. But along with his blessing Salim insists that Naib and his henchman Khazin share a sacred evening meal with him. For sustenance. For the invocation of Allah's grace on their mission.

He explains that Kallie is staying overnight with a girlfriend. And he'd sent his wife Nazneem over to Birmingham to negotiate with a supplier to mass produce the software for his latest invention. And he would be honored to personally provide the feast.

At 6 PM, the three conspirators unroll their prayer rugs on the veranda and pray for success. Salim then presents a simple yet stimulating meal of lavash and Moroccan chorba—a spicy tomato-and-lamb-stock-based chickpea soup.

The talk is of specifics relating to the easiest placement of the bomb for non-detection and maximum deaths. They agree on a room in an upscale hotel at the southern end of Central Park. There is a sense of camaraderie and elation in the air. Salim almost has himself convinced.

"We must leave promptly in three hours," Naib announces. "Khazin and I must finish preparing the device for safe transport. I beg of you a good evening Master."

"I release you to your task. Though I have something more to share which I trust you will find significant," replies Salim with a twinkle in his eye.

"You have aroused my curiosity," says Naib.

"And mine," echoes Khazin. "After our prayers—and such a fine meal and sendoff, I imagine nothing more is possible for our satisfaction."

"That's where you are wrong my friend. Wait one moment."

Salim scurries to the kitchen and returns with a plate of what he knows to be Naib's great weakness: stuffed figs. Upon seeing the bounty of delights, Naib and Khazin break into schoolboy laughter.

"Master," says Naib, "you have outdone yourself once again." He plucks one of the treats from the tray and brings it to his nose. The subtle aromatic blend of cloves, cocoa, and orange peel combined with the succulence of the expertly dried fruit transports Naib back to his grandmother's Ramadan kitchen in his native Iran. Probably the only happy memory he has left. "I will save this as a reward for getting everything packed," he says, reaching for a napkin to wrap it.

Salim had counted on Naib and Khazin to begin stuffing themselves with the figs. He has laced them with strychnine. *The poison begins acting in 15 minutes. They will be racked with violent muscular contractions to the point where the extremities flail and the bones inside them snap—which means that if Khazin eats one and Naib doesn't, my plan is foiled. Naib will tear me apart to get his bomb on the road to Manhattan.*

I could shoot him but I don't have access to a gun. Truth be told, I'm afraid of them. I could stab Naib but I am not expert. And I can't overpower them both. This action might backfire and my love ones would ultimately perish in the fireball. I can live with the fact that this intervention may cost me my life. As long as it doesn't kill millions, it's more than a fair trade off. My wife and daughter are resilient. They will miss me for a time, but they will recover.

Just before Khazin snatches up a fig, Salim pulls the tray back.

"What a perfect plea to Allah! To withhold one's own pleasure until the task is completed. I will assist you in the preparations. We will feast on the fruit together to complete both our meal—and our time together. And of course the launching of the final phase of our long-awaited jihad."

86

Counterforce

Devin "Mac" Mackenzie, through his technical team's advanced listening apparatus, has heard enough. He briefs his agents one last time.

"The mother and daughter are being tracked on their way north and will be detained simultaneously. There is the possibility they are carrying the bomb and that all the dinner talk is a calculated diversion because they are aware that they are being observed."

"Agents Chet Unger and Darryl Sheets, you are Blue Team. You will provide the main assault over the side fence and into the lab. Frank Mankowski and I are Red Team. We will prevent the targets from exiting through the house and poolside yard respectively. The stakeout agents are Yellow Team. They will secure the larger perimeter. All side arms are to employ silencers."

"Securing the bomb itself is our primary mission. We must neutralize this Naib character in case he has some quick detonation sequence. Though I doubt it. I want him alive because like Mr. Hafiz, he can finger other people in Al Qaeda. All right teams. Let's take positions. Move on my signal," Mac finishes.

The idea behind sleeper cells is that they do nothing unusual until they are activated. But Naib and Khazin are abnormal characters to begin with, so the plan has been to pass Khazin off as a caretaker with Naib hidden from the view of the neighbors completely.

He stays underground in the lab nearly around the clock, coming out occasionally for a bit of sun. Since he and Khazin are roughly the same height and build, they always wear identical clothes so that a chance viewing by a neighbor would give the impression of only one live-in caretaker on the property. Besides, in this upscale neighborhood, many homes have domestic servants, gardeners and caretakers, a few of whom live on the premises. One will attract almost no attention. No jealous effects. Two, and the neighbors start noticing, start envying.

The lab was designed as Khazin's quarters and, to outward appearance, is simply a classy outbuilding. What doesn't show is its oversize basement which serves as the lab proper. Naib, the austere lab rat, has a cot down there in an oversize closet. He keeps the bomb in there with him. Sleeps with it like a lover.

There are two ways of entering the basement laboratory: the stairs—which at the bottom are secured by an electronically-controlled steel door—and the elevator. Mac's reassuring voice breaks the silence on the closed-circuit audio channel.

"All three are in the outbuilding. We're not going in after them because it's too defensible. They've got to get the hardware into a vehicle. We'll get them then. Blue Team, ambush them between the lab building and the garage. Get in position. Move! Go, go, go!"

What Mac doesn't know is that tech-rat Naib, in his paranoia and thoroughness has built a scanner which picks up amplified sound waves. This device sits on one of the lab tables and emits a squawk for the duration of any audio broadcast within a 150-foot radius. It can't decipher the words. But it can certainly squawk. Even though the nature of Mac's signal is digital, the thing picks it up and squawks faintly because the nearest transmitter is on the periphery of the device's range.

"What is that?" says Salim unaware of the device's existence.

"This tells me if someone is broadcasting near us," whispers Naib gravely. "Either we have uninvited company or someone in the house has turned on a radio or TV. Or a car with a radio drove in and shut off. The signal is faint."

"I suppose it's possible Kallie has returned and is in her room," replies Salim, about to break a sweat. *Oh Allah! Does Naib have other spy boxes? Were they trained on me. Did he watch me as the figs were poisoned?*

"This is very unlikely. The nature of the signal is different." Naib appears to be listening with his whole being.

"Perhaps I should check." Salim worries that something has gone wrong with the plan. *Did Nazneem not believe his note? Have she and Kallie returned?* He starts toward the elevator. Naib grabs his arm.

"I doubt it's Kallie. She packed the car last night like she was leaving for years," Naib says with a cold scowl.

Salim's blood turns to glacier water. *The bastard must have a closed circuit video feed in the garage.*

At that moment, in the near dark, Darryl and Chet vault the wall like accomplished gymnasts and conceal themselves behind shrubbery. They barely settle in before they hear a mechanical noise. The whirring of a motor. A clank. A door rolling open. A lone figure emerges, clad in polyester workout pants and a dark t-shirt.

One second after he passes Darryl's position, Darryl sets upon him, simultaneously covering his mouth and dealing a knockout blow to the back of his head. The limp figure's knife drops to the gravel path. A surgical strike. By a highly-trained human weapon. Seconds later Khazim is dragged behind the shrubs and bound and gagged by Chet Unger.

"Status: Blue Team," says Mac, hearing what he thought happened.

"One bandit secured. Permission to enter chamber. Elevator entrance. Surprise viable. Over."

"Granted. We're right behind. Godspeed. Out."

Darryl was focused until Mac said *Godspeed. What an odd expression. In the buildup, I've temporarily forgotten God. Is God on my side? If, as Vincent says, the moment is God, what is this evil doing here? Is this some kind of biblical charade playing out? Are good and evil cyclical? Interchangable? Irreversibly linked? In the next moment, am I going up in a holocaust of nuclear fire at the hands of a deranged fanatic? How could God sanction something so random?*

Then like a gentle slap, he gets it. Gets his advice to Andre not eight hours earlier. *Darryl my lad, you're just future-tripping. As long as you stay in this moment, you're fine. If the great blast comes, go with it. Surrender. Because it is of the moment. If bullets come, return fire—in that moment. Otherwise, slow it down. It's all sacred. Kill only if your own death—or a team member's—is imminent. Be aware.*

Naib hears the squawks. Louder now. Hears the elevator returning. His training in an elite Afghani camp takes full control. He touches the point of his assault rifle to Salim's head. He calculates. *I can rig something of a nuclear blast in five perhaps six minutes. Perhaps enough to take out part of Atlanta. Better than nothing. I just need a little time alone to concentrate on how to integrate the trigger more quickly than I have ever done.*

Salim, who has been made to lie face down on the floor, knows Naib well enough to deduce his plan. *It's all logic. Funnels and switches. If Naib shoots me, the people in the elevator will hear the shot and be alerted. They will come out firing. If it's Khazin returning with a report of intruders, I'll be sent up alone in the elevator. Dead. By the time the intruders process that diversion, Naib will have rigged the explosion, blowing half of Atlanta into the sky.*

Naib weighs all the factors and makes his decision. *If my intent is righteous, Allah will allow.*

"Master Salim. I must trust you. Stand at the elevator door. For the sake of Allah's will, if someone other than Khazin, your wife or daughter exits the elevator—delay them."

"Of course I will," Salim lies. *I would rip your eyes out if I thought I could wound you before you shot me.* "May I get up now?"

"Yes. I am not sorry. I must trust no one. Only myself. You understand."

"Of course. The mission must not be stopped," says Salim with all the sincerity he can muster. "If need be, I'll slice my neck in front of them. Do you have a knife?"

"By my bed…Too late! The door is about to open. I need but five minutes," says Naib eerily calm. "Hold them," he entreats.

Naib feigns leaving, whirls around and smacks Salim in the face with the butt of his weapon then hastens to his closet.

Six seconds later the elevator door opens.

"Take me to Naib or you'll never see your wife and child again!" whispers Chet Unger into Salim's ear while thrusting his pistol into the man's ribcage.

Salim's forehead is gushing blood. He forces himself not to black out.

"I don't know what you're talking about! This is a computer lab!" Salim tries to yell. Then he leans over and whispers back toward Chet's ear, "He's arming a nuclear bomb. In the closet at the far end. He's completely deranged. Hurry!"

Chet motions for Darryl to act while he keeps Salim covered, in case it's a ploy. They can hear Mac struggling to open the steel door at the base of the stairway.

"Of course I will open the door. Do you think I want my lab damaged. Give me a moment," asserts Salim again trying to yell. Then, "The code is 6666," he says softly. "Enter it and the door will open."

While Mac and Frank gain entry to the lab, Darryl steals up to the closet at the far end. He can hear muffled activity inside. Because Naib has a small task light on, Darryl can make out the outline of a bolt between the double doors, locking them from the inside. A cheap-looking setup he surmises. Weak metal, possibly even brass. No match for his Beretta. Without hesitation, in one fluid motion, he shoots the bolt, grabs one of the handles, rips open the door, and hits the back of Naib's neck a glancing blow with the barrel of his still smoking gun.

The human skeleton of a man falls backward past Darryl and onto the floor like a Halloween display. The groggy Naib manages to continue clutching an electrode in each hand. He's convinced that crossing them will trigger some magnitude of explosion. By sheer force of will, he begins to bring them together.

In response, Darryl steps on each of Naib's wrists with his full weight, grinding them into the concrete floor until Frank Mankowski carefully separates the electrodes from the man's hands. He keeps the copper tubes as far away from each other as their wires will allow.

Darryl finally stands the babbling bomb-maker up, deftly grabbing his arms and locking them behind the man's back so he can't kill himself.

"Unger! Check his hands, check his pockets. Check every crevice he's got for cyanide—or a detonator," Mac commands. Then he barks into his radio, "Two targets secured in the basement. Yellow team, sweep the property. I mean every nook, every closet, behind every friggin' plant. Do it, then do it again. White Team stay on the perimeter in case a stray tries to slip through. We're gonna go slow and pack this up quietly. We've got all night. And it looks like our way of life has got a lot longer to live. Mac out."

"What the hell?" says Unger. "The guy's got a half-eaten fig in his shirt pocket. Smells pretty damn good."

"Don't touch it!" screams Salim from the other side of the room.

87

Holy Land Sendoff

Sheryl Jansen and Landi Riquelme catch a dazzling sunset as their military transport lumbers off a top-secret runway in central Israel, bound for south Florida. The sunset lighting combined with an especially dramatic, salmon-colored cloudbank and its reflection off the Mediterranean, sends the two friends into a state of awe.

Just as Sheryl predictably starts to slip into blue-Sheryl, Landi unknowingly intervenes.

"So girlfriend, when do I get to meet the remarkable Mr. Bell?

"Not before I get my second chance!" Sheryl retorts, shocked at her burst of defensiveness. And now that her distrust is rolling, she can't stop it. "If he gets one look at you before I can find out if he and I are on the same train, we're done for—crashed, cancelled, caput. Especially if you look back at him—which I know you will."

"Sheryl!" Landi, psychically stabbed from the attack, gives a quiet shout. "Sweetie. Look at me. I didn't mean I was going to go after h…"

"I have no idea where that came from. I'm so sorry," says Sheryl taking Landi's hand and pressing it to the side of her face—for a long minute. "I'm so weird. I think I know myself and then I have an outburst like that. Like I'm possessed."

"You've been through a lot. Kostas' lies. Your escape. Andre's ejection. Frank. Your mother… Maybe it's just leftover gunk from Kostas and you and I—or…"

"Or maybe I'm just a possessive bitch and it's finally coming out. If I don't want sweet Andre, nobody gets him. Especially not someone close. He's mine alone to love—or banish from any part of my world."

"You are jealous—more of Andre than Landi. The source of this is centuries old and remains masked from you."

"What did you say?" asks Sheryl, taking Landi's hand and squeezing.

"Nothing. I was lost in my thoughts," Landi replies.

"Great! Now I'm hearing voices." Sheryl says. "I must be losing it." But deep in her heart Sheryl is pretty sure she overheard truth speaking.

"C'mon girlfriend, we should settle in. Let the stress drop away. We're goin' home."

"Landi, you have such calm built into your voice. I'll never forget our first meeting in the gym. I was out of control. You gave me such comfort. And you're doing it again."

"No worries sweets. I would do anything for you."

"And I for you. I'm sorry I blew up back there. I'm not myself sometimes. I love you—really."

Landi just smiles and points out the window.

As their plane levels off, leaving Israel and Greece behind, the drowsy friends gape as the salmon sky blooms into a blood-red specter that fills them with a primal form of awe. Because they are flying toward it, the color lingers on for an unnaturally long interlude before the onset of pure darkness, ushered in with the unseen presence of a new moon.

88

From the Mouths of Babes

"We are Homeland Security. Keep your hands in front of you where we can see them. We are going to open your car doors. We need you to exit slowly. No quick moves. Is that clear?"

"Yes officer. Do you know my husband? He is Salim Hafiz. Is he alright?" Nazneem Hafiz`is on the verge of breaking down. It's all she can do to breathe, let alone move out of the car.

"We have orders to bring you and your daughter to Dobbins Air Force Base. That is all we know. Hold out your hands. Both of you." The agent starts to cuff them.

"We are not criminals!" Nazzneem cries. "We are American!"

"Mom!" Kallie exclaims. "Cool it! I think everything is okay. If something bad has happened, they would be throwing us in the van like animals."

"If anything has befallen Salim I couldn't bear it! Would you find out if my husband is unharmed? He is a good man. You will see."

On their way to New York City, Nazneem and Kallie had gotten as far north as the southern outskirts of Washington D.C. They are driven a short distance to Andrews Air Force Base and shuttled back to Dobbins. A mere hour and one-half after being stopped, they have exited a chopper and sit in an interrogation room.

Two men with grave faces enter, a wiry, red haired fellow in a white suit and a tanned, gym-instructor type. Both have paved over their exhaustion with coffee.

"Good morning. I'm Agent Mackenzie and this is Agent Mankowski. I'll get right to the point…"

"Where is my husband? If you know enough to arrest us, you must know of him. I can't bear not knowing what's become of him. Left alone to handle those two beasts. Please!"

"Ma'am, the good news is, your husband survived. The bad news is, he's in a world of trouble. As are you. That is why you will tell us what you know."

"I will tell you," Kallie interrupts. "It was I whom he told his secrets to. I, who packed our car and urged my mother to drive to New York. To the very place those awful men were going to unleash their bomb!"

"Whoa now young lady. New York! That sounds preposterous."

"I have proof," she says undaunted. *Surely I can convince these creeps my father is not like Khazin and Naib.*

"How old are you, Miss?"

"What is the meaning of your question? To discredit me because I am a crazy teenager? You seem smarter than that."

At this, Mac and Frank have to restrain themselves from laughter. Perhaps it's their lack of sleep. Their giddiness over foiling the plot. But mostly, they have to admire Kallie's unexpected, fresh-air moxie.

"Okay Miss. Let's have your *proof.*"

Kallie has seen enough Law and Order and CSI's to know how to formulate her response.

"I know you are playing dumb. I know that if the bomb had gone off anywhere on the Eastern seaboard, we would not be here talking like normal people. This tells me that you have stopped the madness that was about to happen. And I have a feeling my father helped you. Because he did not wish this to happen either. There was a time when he did. But he changed some time ago. His plan was to stop the bombers—even if he had to pay with his life to do it."

"This is a nice story," says Mac.

This is your proof?" says Frank.

"As I said, my father sent us into the heart New York. He did this because he knew it was the last place these terrible men would look for us. Because New York was their target. There they would get the greatest amount of deaths…But is this my proof? No. This is."

Kallie pulls Salim's detailed note to her mother from the neck of her sweatshirt—out of her bra. She hands it to Mac.

"Here is your proof. My father left it to me to convince my mother to leave Atlanta. He provided these words to help me. Because if he tried to do it in person, she would have lost it around the house and it would have tipped off the bombers. My father is very logical. He told me he had to take responsibility for starting this whole mess—and if it meant he would die killing the fanatics he had invited into our home, that would be God's will. He believes in a fair and logical God. So he was willing to accept that. Now if you have a shred of decency and humanness in you, you will at least tell my mother what has befallen him."

Upon hearing this young girl defend her father so eloquently, Mac can only look straight ahead. He focuses on a stain on the wall, blinks a few times, and silently passes the note to Frank who is fighting his own battle at being smitten by her. Mac makes an odd gesture with his hand at a smoky internal glass wall. Half a minute later a head-bandaged Salim enters the room where he is leapt upon by his daughter and has to hold up his wife from fainting.

89

Darryl's Denouement

It's now seven hours after the White-op has gone down. Darryl stares out at the tree-studded hills. He's not moved from his hotel balcony for the last three of those hours. He stirs and re-stirs this huge stew of images and what-ifs until he is mentally, emotionally, and spiritually exhausted. Yet he doesn't even try to silence his thoughts or shut off his turbulent inner movie. He knows he can't.

He replays Mac's debriefing: "Our response to an attack on our largest populated area would have swiftly—and predictably—unleashed our own arsenal against whole blocks of the Islamic world. Collateral *damage* would have to have been re-named collateral *genocide.*"

And then the remarks of Navy Intelligence's Chief Medical Officer: "In the United States, the fallout alone would have rendered the environment permanently uninhabitable from New Hampshire to Washington DC to Pittsburgh. Twelve million immediate deaths plus the resulting cancers would far outstrip our ability to cope. Those who survived on the periphery of the blast would die horribly in the ensuing days. Such is the nature of the Genie that would have been let out of his bottle."

And back to Mac's closing statement: "Thank God that we were able to subdue all the participants. Practically without a sound. Even the neighbors on the adjoining ranchettes weren't roused. And we got them all. From the scientist in charge, to the owner of *Arabian Antiquities*, down to the mules who delivered the last shipment to the suburban Atlanta property. And the biggest prize of all, Naib Al-Bukhari, the anti-Christ genius who would have made Bin Laden look like a child playing with matches. Great job men. Your country owes you everything!"

Then Darryl tears up. *Salim Hafiz, the point man. What an unexpected break. The fact that he cooperated may have saved everything. What if Naib had four minutes more in that closet? Tomorrow I'm writing as strong a recommendation as I know how—for leniency. It's on tape that he offered the strychnine figs to the other two. Before the bomb was to be loaded. Too bad Naib didn't make it. Took too long getting him out of there. Mac couldn't risk an ambulance. Salim really laced those figs. He must have come to detest those monsters.*

Darryl swallows hard, wondering what will happen to the man's innocent-looking and thoroughly shocked wife and kids, who knew their husband and father as a brilliant innovator.

If I were pulling the strings, I'd put Salim on display as an example that humans can change their programming. Can feel their kinship with other beings. Can alter their inevitable course. Christ! Anyone having to go through eternity knowing they were responsible for that level of horror would make them permanently insane. Make their soul insane.

Now I finally believe my friends in the Mossad who have told me many times that a surprising percentage of Palestinian suicide bombers have actually turned themselves in—unable to carry out their horrible mission, despite the brainwashing. I thought they were spouting propaganda. Where did I acquire that cynicism? Even in their adrenalin-induced state, these bomber fanatics got in touch with that raw-truth place inside their own beings that told them what they were about to do was inherently evil and wrong. Either everyone's infused with love—or they're not. What happened last night tells me it has to be so. And yet more than a few are so burdened with acquired hatred, they have forgotten their true nature.

How many close calls are we as a species going to have? I just wish the larger game of civilization had different rules. It's so brutally primitive.

"It's primitive because, for millennia, as a species, you've let the Ego run the show."

Now I'm starting to hear Vincent say things I've never exactly heard Vincent say.

Darryl is so open at this point—even if he's wading in the muck on the margins of sanity—he honestly doesn't care. He tries but can't stop himself from yelling silently at the sky.

So is the universe totally random or totally shepherded—and on an even bigger scale, does it even matter?

C'mon God, send me more voices. I need something clear. Something strong.

But no voice comes. Instead his pleas are answered in the form of a deep, inner silence that comes over him like a blanket.

Darryl inexplicably looks at his hands. Really becomes present with them. He realizes they are part of the miracle that he is. He appreciates them for what they do. Is ashamed of them for some of what they have done. His face tightens and he spontaneously lets out a solitary sob. He doesn't care that this is not like him. In fact, he's ecstatic.

Darryl looks out again at the trees, lit like angels under a fuchsia sky. And for this moment, his questions dissolve.

90

Indigo Lake

"I'm happy to play house with you…but are you sure you don't want to do this alone? I mean, this woman, Sheryl, when she shows up, isn't it better if I'm not around to complicate things? Sounds like you two have a lot to work out."

"Sweet Bretta," says Andre, the last thing I will allow is for you to be alone in your crystal cave in your time of need. Besides, perhaps a change of scene will startle your cells into an unexpected healing mode."

"That's just plain bizarre."

"Why?" protests Andre. "I've read about…"

"Because it's the kind of proclamation I usually make. The kind that sent most of my supposed friends running for the exit. It's bizarre being on the receiving end."

"Perhaps you've met your match," says Andre breaking into a grin.

"I know I have. And I also know I'm second in line—and that's really okay. I plan to enjoy you while I have you. And in this moment I have you forever."

"You're a seriously fast learner," declares Andre. "And in this moment, you are not second to anyone. I have no idea what will happen. I only know we're having this gentle and beautiful collision, and it's giving each of us something fulfilling. How is that not cause for celebration?"

"That's the biggest lesson I'm learning right now," Bretta declares. "Life is meant to be celebrated, no matter what…Wow! Speaking of celebrations, I can't believe we're here already. Feast your eyes on that lake!"

Andre pulls Bretta's convertible onto a pullout next to the edge of a finger of Indigo Lake. They sit transfixed in the mid-morning warmth, taking in the stillness of a fresh-water paradise, adorned with vibrant grasses and scores of snowy egrets, terns, and warblers. They take in a pair of hawks banking overhead and catch a blue heron in a picture-perfect landing.

Bretta slides over and nestles against Andre. To the occasional passersby, they look like a married couple on holiday from the city, in love, and without a care.

And they would almost be right.

91

Sweet Heat

Even in August, there's something welcoming about landing in South Florida. The symphony of tropical flowers and palm fronds. The jigsaw spectacle of cerulean-bordered shorelines. The freedom inherent in island mentality. And the heat. That sweat inducing, liquor-like presence pervading every facet of existence in sultry ocean climates. That blast of feverish, coral-scented breeze which drives a person to instinctively and repeatedly seek the renewal of immersion in liquid. That surrender to let the heat re-embrace the body. Into the deep of night. To laugh at the cold, dark vastness of space. Once a body embraces this version of heaven on earth, it can never return to the misnamed, temperate-climate life style.

Sheryl and Landi rent a silver convertible and head up the coast for a glorious noon-time, jet-lag-antidote swim and wave-play next to the Juno Beach Pier. They are fully in tune with the water and heat having been justly seasoned in the Mediterranean under the Grecian summer sun. Playful sets of three-foot waves provide just the right variety to the intermittent calm. The two friends dive and duck, or ride the white soup laughing like teens. Sheryl eases in and out of blue-Sheryl almost at will. *This is wild! I'm more comfortable—no, more inviting—of blue-Sheryl than I've ever been.*

Several surf gods on the beach try their best pick-up lines but the ladies aren't biting. A light seafood lunch at Jupiter Inlet and they're off to the Jansen compound at Indigo Lake.

Landi didn't want to alter the mood of their swim and luncheon. So she compartmentalized what she had learned upon her and Sheryl's earlier arrival at Elgin Air Force Base. She was privy to the gossip that a highly secretive, highly successful, anti-terrorist, White-op had gone down. Her superior called and ordered her to desist from any criminal implication of Frank Mankowski as a result of events both in and around the Embassy and concerning Jesse Jansen.

She was also ordered not to pursue anything further concerning the intel gained from her Corfu *incident* which certain factions in the Greek government were trying to label as U.S. interference with their sovereignty. And she was commended for gracefully getting Sheryl out of Greece before these factions could question her about Kostas and Stefanos. And commended further for directing the capture of the bogies on the Roda, Corfu beach who were, she was told, safely renditioned to secure interrogation sites in Poland.

She was also told that the yield of information from these prisoners was already proving fertile and that she was to be rewarded with a quantum increase in pay grade. And further told never to speak about the incident again unless authorized by her commanding officer.

The implication was that the White-op, the Corfu incident, and Mrs. Jansen were connected. Basically, "Thank you very much, here's some more money. Now go ride a desk, raise your love child, keep quiet, and have a nice life."

As she and Sheryl turn west off A1A and over the causeway, inland toward Indigo Lake, she decides this is the moment to selectively break the rules and confide in her girlfriend.

"Back at Elgin, I heard that some kind of major bust just went down. Everybody's talking around it but nobody really knows anything resembling a real detail. I suspect our boy Frank is in on it. If that's true, he's not who we think he is. At least not anymore." says Landi for openers.

"Damn! Frank not dirty. That's real news...Wait! Then where does that leave my Mom? Knowing this finicky government of ours, they could concoct anything," snorts Sheryl.

"More than true if you're an ordinary citizen. But she has a huge ace in the hole," replies Landi.

"My Dad," Sheryl chuckles and relaxes a bit. "Yeah. I forget about the Sam factor. If I know him at all, I suspect he's already three steps ahead of the dealer. And I'll bet a dollar to a sea shell he's already talked to Frank."

"Why's that?" asks Landi, caught a bit off guard.

"My Dad's his mentor. God, I hope I never have to see that creep again."

"That makes two of us."

92

Messages

Andre carries Bretta across the threshold of their Indigo Lake cottage. *I have no idea what I'm doing with her. Allowing, no, encouraging her to camp out with me while I wait for Sheryl—who may take weeks to show up—if at all. It's crazy. It's indulgent. But hell, it just feels right.*

From almost square one of my Florida adventure, Bretta's been part of my moment. Adding to its richness. Imparting an unconditional transmittal of affection. I'm addicted to this rare chance to be at ease with an inwardly and outwardly beautiful woman. She's so accepting of my process. She seems to be having a lot more fun hanging with me than facing the four walls in her crystal cave. Besides, she's brought half of it with her.

Having a taste of what feels like a real home—rather than his hotel room and Bretta's lair—Andre feels a wave of responsibility overtake him. Not unlike returning to his trailside home after a trip and handling the mail, the downed branches, the messages.

He calls his office voicemail. He listens as the secretary drones through a couple of standard communications about his projects. *Seems everyone, including the clients and crews are vacationing as well.* Then he gets the jewel. "A Miss Jansen called Thursday the 26th to say that she's granting an extension to the twenty-one days, effective retroactively. Said it was important." And on the 31st: "For some reason a notice was sent here about your passport. Looks official. I'm sending it to your hotel in Miami."

Andre's heart skips a couple beats…*Effective retroactively. Said it was important. And she handled my passport. Like she promised.*

"Good news?" asks Bretta noting Andre's body language.

"I think so. Looks like I can use my passport again."

"Going somewhere?"

As Andre pauses to form his complicated, hopefully honest answer, a cheerful-sounding knock caroms off the front door. Bretta goes to the opening and encounters a ruggedly handsome, luminously smiling man in board shorts, a tank top, sandals and sunglasses, toting a large duffel bag.

Hi. I'm Darryl. You must be Bretta."

93

Mixed Blessings

"Frankie! Well I swan!" exclaims Jesse Jansen as she greets Frank Mankowski at the door to her lake house. "Twice in one week. I thought you went back to tend to things in Greece. C'mon in! I'll take your briefcase."

"Thanks Jess. I got it. Hey, I can only stay a short time. Had some pressing business in Atlanta and shared a ride down here with an associate. Thought the drive would do me good. Get me to unwind a trifle. Been workin' way too hard. Is Sam here?"

"Oh I wish. He left for Panama yesterday. He did say he hoped to hear from you soon. Seemed a bit nervous. Kind of unlike him. In the same breath, he tried to get me to go down there with him. I love the heat. But Panama City in the summer—with no lake? Why would I do that to myself? Besides—and I'm sure you know—Sheryl's coming home. Be here any minute. Fact is I thought you were her."

"Sheryl's coming…here?"

"Why yes…Didn't you know? Guess you were in the skies last week. And she's bringing a girlfriend she worked with over there. Landi something-or-other. Say, let me get you a drink. What's your poison? We're totally stocked."

"Dr. Pepper on ice would hit the spot. If it's not too much trouble," says Frank, trying to put a mask over his racing heartbeat. *Shit! Last thing I need is to face the wrath of those two.*

"Some things never change. You must have that stuff runnin' in your veins," Jesse laughs, motioning Frank into the kitchen.

"I 'spect there's a pinch o' truth in that," replies Frank at first managing, then cracking an honest smile.

"So Frankie, I know you well enough to know you dropped by for a reason," says Jesse popping the soda open. "Was it just to see Sam? Or do we have more business?"

"Thanks kindly," says Frank as Jesse hands him the beverage. "Uh, yes we have a couple loose ends. First off, how's the Save-the-Key Project doing?"

"Typical I suppose. Three hundred K short. 'Nother reason I'm not perspirin' in Panama. Three days to go. Lots of feelers out. I'll mortgage this place if I have to. Papers are ready to sign. Something will happen. I'm in too deep for it not to. I decided to let it go for a day and devote the time to Sheryl."

"Tell you what. I'm being transferred to Washington—a promotion of sorts. So we'll have to shut down our business, but…"

"Oh. Well, congratulations are in order then," toasts Jesse raising her strawberry dacquiri. "Here's to the end of an era."

Frank clicks his glass against hers. "Thanks. But what I need to say is… we've done really well. And I know this is awkward-like and sudden. So here's a contribution from me to Save-the-Key."

Frank lifts his briefcase onto the counter and pops it open.

"Mother of God. Frankie, what is this?"

"There's 4000 one-hundred dollar bills in there. Like I said—it's a contribution. Tax free. And you can keep the last check from Atlantis Artifacts."

Jesse all but collapses onto the nearest couch.

"How?...Why?...I don't even need this much."

"Hey, I know you have significant restoration ahead of you. That extra will go a long way—especially with volunteer bodies. You just relax and let the nature of money take its course. I do have one request though."

"Name it. Anything."

"I want a front-row invite to the Dedication."

"Consider it done."

"Say, do you still have a direct line to Sam?" Frank inquires quietly.

"Yes. I'll ring him for you," Jesse replies, intuiting that this call has something do with Sam's recent nervousness. "You can pick up in his study."

"Thanks," sighs Frank, draining his soda. "I won't be long."

Jesse hits the speed dial and Sam answers after one ring.

"What's up Scarlet?"

"Hey Rhett. I've got a mystery caller on the line. Go ahead caller. We'll talk later,"

Jesse croons, hanging up.

"Sam, it's Frank."

"Whoa. This is a surprise. Good to hear your live voice. Everything alright?

From Sam's loaded, *live voice* comment, Frank knows that Sam knows—certainly not all, but probably a lot.

"Let's just say the Yankees came through in the bottom of the ninth with a walk-off grand slam. It will take the Red Sox faithful decades to recover if they do all all."

"Ha! That's as good as it gets," chirps Sam, instantly relieved. "So what's your next move?"

"I've been asked to join Mac's inside group at Homeland Security. Lots of analysis. You know. Saving the Republic. Long hours. Definitely keep me out of trouble."

"Speaking of trouble, isn't it time to take on a girlfriend? Plenty of lonesome career women in DC from what I've seen."

"If I have a strategy about that, you've certainly just exposed it. I'm optimistic I'll meet somebody."

"My advice would be to steer clear of the young interns."

Despite the ninety-five degree day, Frank actually gets a chill. He wonders if there's anything Sam doesn't know about anyone.

"Yessir. That's good advice. I hope to find a mature gal who'd be up for starting a family," Frank hears himself say.

"Glad to hear that Frank. You know, in my personal life, I've yet to meet a Beltway bachelor who didn't self destruct. That town has eyes and ears in every nook and crevice. If you know what I mean," says Sam making sure he drives his spike through all the layers. This is more than mentoring. This is a warning. And probably the burning of a long-standing bridge— between the two men.

"Very clearly."

"Did Sheryl arrive yet?"

"Not yet."

"So I guess you'll be on your way."

"Yes sir."

"And Frank. Thanks for saving the Republic. Thanks for the millions who will never know."

"You're welcome Sam. Goodbye sir."

Frank hangs up, exchanges pleasantries with Jesse, and lets himself out into the August oven. *I hoped this skeleton would never rear its head. But here it is, thrown smack in my face. By the person dearest to me on the planet. As much a father to me as my own father. No more contact? It's already unbearable.*

Have all my years of fighting this demon, this adolescent fetish for young girls, gone for naught? Because of one lousy slip-up. I've worked like a dog for twenty-five years, day and night. Exhaustion has become my ally. Has kept me occupied. Out of places I shouldn't be.

At last I swear something in my chemistry has changed. Women closer to my own age have become appealing. I can see the young child in them. An eternal quality really. If one simply, yet perseveringly, by some dose of grace, trains himself to look for it.

94

Confrontation

Frank pilots the rental car up the long driveway toward the opening automatic gate. His heart starts racing at the sight of the silver convertible bearing Landi and Sheryl which enters the property ahead of his exit. *Oh no! You're trapped. This is worse than the damn raid...Just stay calm...Shit. You're a friggin' train wreck. Don't fool yourself you idiot.*

As they pull beside each other the cars stop with the door handles less than a foot apart.

"Goddamn it Frank! You almost got my ass demoted!" shouts Landi straight into his face.

"And you cost me the love of my life. And a lot more. You sleaze." Sheryl is totally ballistic, out-shouting Landi. She has perched herself up on the passenger door to look past Landi squarely at him. Like she's going to pounce.

"Okay. Okay. I surrender. Let's take it one at a time," says Frank with the appearance of calm masking the depth of his terror at facing these infuriated creatures. "I know it looks like I'm the archetypal asshole. In your eyes I'm not worth a rotting road kill..."

"I'm in shock! That's the first time I've heard the truth come out of your ugly mug," retorts Landi practically spitting the words.

"I'll give you that. But you and I both know when we are deep cover we do and say whatever we have to for the sake of the mission. And when you blew in, if I had spoken up, it could have wrecked everything."

"You saying I've got a loose mouth?"

"Not at all. But my mission was so precarious and so certainly jeopardized by yours that you'd have had to get your handler in the loop. Then it's Homeland versus CIA and the whole thing would've blown up."

"That's bullshit!" snaps Landi trying to overrule her intuition in light of the day's gossip. "Unless you got the perfect-story explanation."

Think Frank, do you risk classified talk in front of Sheryl?...Ha! Technically, she still works for you...

"You know I can't go into it. But I will say I was part of a micro White-op that foiled a major Code Black. Night before last. And if that's ever repeated, both our careers are as good as over. There can be no leak."

"Jesus H. Christ! How major?...I guess you can't answer that," says Landi censoring herself. She adjusts her vision, lets down her guard, and for a moment tries to see Frank as a dedicated public servant. Then she remembers Sheryl. And Jesse for that matter.

Seeing her pause as a positive, Frank takes a chance.

"I can offer a riddle. Add Hiroshima to itself enough times until all you see is red. Forever," says Frank.

"Christ."

"Pretty much," whispers Frank.

"What about my Mom? Is she in any danger? We know about the antiquities." says Sheryl from her perch.

Frank sighs heavily. *To hell with it. I'm divulging too much but this facet must be cleaned up.*

"The decision was made not to let your Mom in on anything. As far as she knows, she ran a legitimate business. I cut a deal with the bigs early on where she was to keep the proceeds. Convinced them it would make her act completely innocent, thus genuine. Not bad. Uncle Sam in bed with Save-the-Key. We're still going to watch her for at least ten years. Just to be ridiculously safe. I have an agent working his way into place as we speak. She's done her country a great service."

"This is nuts," declares Sheryl. "I suppose your treatment of Andre was *protocol?*"

"Absolutely. A baboon could tell he was innocent. But if he hung around Greece, he'd have been an easy target. And if he's spending time with you, you're an easy target also. Before the Solagros bust, Stefanos would have traded him to Al Qaeda. Even after, once they knew who he was, they'd have tried to take him out, thinking he was CIA. I sent an agent to California to shadow him in case they had infiltrated the Embassy and knew who he was. He was gone so fast I don't think they got any clues about him. Even the agent was not told he was clean. But he's good. Figured it out. So I pulled him into the White-op. Jesus. I'm saying way too much." Frank feels like he has to pee.

"I guess I should thank you for saving his life. But Goddamn it Frank. Did you molest me when I was little. I had a vivid memory…"

"I never touched you. Please believe that. I indulged myself once in a stupid fetish I had. Not even a fetish. More of a fantasy. I was experimenting. I didn't know what I was doing. I…I exposed myself to you. I am so sorry. I have hated myself. But I found out that's a dead end. I'm transferring to DC so I can re…God Sheryl, I am so sorry."

Frank is finally unable to hold down the pain that has been caught in his throat for all those twenty-two years. He buries his head in his hands and his cries issue unchecked from some previously inaccessible cavern. Sobbing openly, the roof of his mouth cracking in the heat. he puts the rental in drive and inches out through the gate into the blazing South Florida afternoon, his inflamed eyes blurring his way.

95

Sharing a Drug

"So Darryl, how long have you known Andre?" asks Bretta, carrying in a pitcher of herbal ice tea she'd made earlier. "Wait. Let me guess. It's got to be either college fraternity brothers or professional associates."

"Professional associates hits it pretty close," replies Darryl.

"Tell her as much as you want. We have no secrets," says Andre.

"No secrets? Wow. I wouldn't know what that felt like. My life revolves around secrets," offers Darryl. "That's probably as much as I should say."

"Oh come on now Darryl. When somebody says that much, it means they want to say a lot more," teases Bretta.

"I want to say more but I've taken an oath not to," replies Darryl with a touch of sadness.

"You poor thing. A professional secret keeper. I can relate," says Bretta wistfully. "I've kept way too many secrets in my short life. And if the truth be told, it hasn't been good for me—for my health."

"Really. What agency? Wait! I knew it. From the moment you answered the door, I had you pegged for an NSA type."

Darryl's earnest sincerity, coupled with the oddness of the setting, multiplied by the unlikely array of characters, sends Bretta and Andre into hysterics.

"Let me in on the joke!" says Darryl on the edge of out-and-out begging.

"I'm not sure…that's even possible," gasps Andre, coming up for air. "Bretta is just your typical wholesome girl—no covert identity, no cloak-and-dagger stuff, no agency. There are people out there like that. Can you imagine it?"

"You mean she's not…I mean…she says she has secrets…"

"My secrets are not your kind of secrets," Bretta has to jump in. "Oh my God…I love the simplicity of your lens on the world."

"What's wrong with my lens? I lead a complicated existence."

"Of course you do. But way too over-focused—in an endearing way," offers Bretta realizing that Darryl's feelings are probably getting bruised.

"So you're really not NSA?"

This sets Bretta & Andre off again.

"The only thing I've spied on lately is a guy on a cell phone at the beach," says Bretta. "And maybe my image in the mirror. Oh, and a very kooky secret agent that just happened to show up on my doorstep."

"Where's he now?…Oh boy. That's me…I guess I am…kind of over-focused." This feminine and foreign view of him strikes Darryl as quite funny and he joins the others again in stitches, laughing to a depth he's not penetrated since early adolescence.

Amused by the oddity of Darryl's employ—and Andre's mysterious yet light-hearted involvement with him—Bretta too loses it, tapping into her pre-cancer lightness of being. A release for all of them, induced by a legal, free, and common drug called laughter.

96

Small Talk

"Y'all must have passed Frank on the road," says Jesse Jansen after the customary hugs. "He left out not five minutes before you arrived."

"We did pass a guy in a hurry driving a small car. We had no idea on earth it was Frank," says Landi trying to derail an uncomfortable conversation between Sheryl and her mother before it could get rolling.

"I forget how beautiful it is here until I come back," says Sheryl, desperate to change the subject. She stares out toward the lake from the glass-walled Florida room and shudders a soul-deep shudder.

"Well I have to say that lake is lonely without you in it," says Jesse handing each young woman a frosty glass of coconut-pineapple juice with a protruding skewer of strawberries. "I often thought you loved that water as much as you loved Sam and I."

Before Sheryl can unscramble the barb from the sentiment, Landi skews the conversation.

"You should see your daughter get on in the Mediterranean. She acts like it's her private lake," teases Landi. "Though I must say, this is pretty special. I can see why you'd not want to leave. It feels like you're on an island on a small ocean. And it's not been messed up. The birdlife here is out of a fairy tale. You must have good karma."

"I thank my stars everyday the State put a moratorium on any further building near the lake. And these eight houses are all well-built and tasteful. Not like the jetsam they pass off as housing these days," lectures Jesse.

"Any new people move in," queries Sheryl, sipping her drink.

"Nah. 'Cept for the Townsend's place. They rent it out by the month. And not every month. Nobody wants it in the summer," Jesse replies.

"Really? I think I see some folks over there getting ready for a swim. Looks like a couple guys and—a girl." Sheryl locks her gaze onto them to the exclusion of all else.

"It's been vacant for weeks. They must have just gotten here. Could be their kids. Hah! Kids. They're all grown adults. Father time ain't playin' any favorites, I can attest to that."

"'Scuse me Mrs. Jansen but you have got to be the best example I've seen of someone locking Father Time in a broom closet! I hope I'm here long enough to learn a secret or two from you."

"Why thank you darlin'. An' please call me Jesse. That's secret number one… Sheryl hon, you okay?"

"Huh? Oh yes Momma," stutters Sheryl, returning jarred from a brief moment in blue-Sheryl. "Say Landi girlfriend, you up for your Indigo Lake inaugural swim?"

Damn! What's this girl up to now? We just got here and she already wants into the damn lake. And we swam our jet dust off in the ocean not two hours ago!

"Uh, if you are my tour guide, I'm ready. Can't have too much exercise before the birth," replies Landi meaning it genuinely.

"Well I swan. I thought I detected a young-un on board. Who's the lucky man that landed such a rare prize as you?" Jesse asks.

"Well, I had this…"

"We'll have to get back to you on that Momma," says Sheryl pulling Landi upstairs to change into their suits. "Right now we have some serious business with the hidden charms of Indigo Lake."

And if it could be seen, the burgeoning iceberg in her midsection would betray that she absolutely isn't kidding.

97

Bretta and Darryl

From the moment Andre steps out onto the lawn and begins walking down the gentle slope toward the lake, he cannot help himself. He glances several times then stares, then glances again across the arm of the lake which separates his temporary digs from the Jansen's.

The H.P. Lovecraft song "Blue Jack of Diamonds" starts up in his mind, like it has so often since Greece. Something about the celebration of sadness it expresses entices him. The instrumentation—thick and mind-syrup-like chimes—yet piercing. Composition years ahead of its time. And those haunting lyrics. *God! I've got to remember to thank Ray for being a 60's psychedelic rock aficionado and injecting me with this song. If Shakespeare were a recording star, he would have penned this masterpiece. This song is me!*

"Andre," snaps Darryl, "It's my job to keep an eye over there. Your job is to keep an eye on sweet Bretta."

"Why And-ray, ain't we more in yer present moment than some house 'cross the water? Y'all just wait'l I tell Vincent on you. Such a sudden an' serious mug. And just a minit ago y'all were so full o' mirth." Bretta sing-songs it like a Yankee trying out for a part as a southern belle.

"If he cain't pay more 'tention to you, that ain't all he's full of," drawls Darryl as they reach the water's edge.

"Y'all 're terr'ble hard on this po' boy," retorts Andre, besting them all at the vernacular. "I'm goin' stick my head in the sand an' pre-tend I'm a Secretive Agent, by gum. Yessir."

Andre's performance was truly not worthy of an Oscar but it was good enough to break the somber ambiance of their march and launch them once more into laughter. With gusto—at Andre's dilemma. His school-boy anxiety. At the pure oddness of their camaraderie. Andre loving his new friend Darryl and, out of respect, Darryl holding himself back from trying to steal Bretta—who had him at hello. And Bretta feeling like she's trapped in a Tarantino movie with the coolest body-and-soul guards on the planet. Laughing more sweetly because seeing Darryl laugh, she finds herself drawn to the boyish openness that is his essence.

And in that moment even as she shrieks and holds onto Andre, lest she topple over from sheer joy, a refined truth hits her. *I love Andre. But his draw is more that of a selfless teacher. A teacher who dispenses his love—not unlike the sun whose rays fall equally on everyone.*

Bretta instinctively—bordering on wantonly—reaches out to Darryl and pulls him into them, completing their coalescence into a triumvirate embrace.

"Alright swim team. Let's wash off the tears and the blessed sweat and let the lake take us to a wetter moment," barks Andre.

They don goggles and ease into the refreshing, spring-fed, clear lake. With the men on either side of Bretta, they swim lazily, marveling at the water clarity and the aquarium-like bottom features.

They enter near one end of the long kidney-shape that defines Indigo Lake. Andre becomes even more animated when the reality of the lake hits him. *Wow! I can get a major workout by swimming the length and back. Must be a mile-plus. A sweet sprint.*

"Bretta! How're you doing?" Andre asks as they near the middle of the narrowest girth.

"Good thanks. Ecstatic if the truth be told. But I don't want to push it. I'm sure we'll be here a while. So I can work up to longer swims. This is perfect for me. I'm sorry, but I best head back."

"Say Darryl, would you be so kind as to escort the princess back to wherever she desires. I've got a date with my breath and it's going to be heavy," Andre half laughs, half shouts. The lake had *him* at hello. He feels like Ponce de Leon.

"Just don't spend yourself on any mermaids. We saw you first," says Darryl, flashing that disarming grin of his.

Andre gives them a thumbs-up and powers off toward the farthest distant shore, craving the ritual of controlled exertion and rhythmic breathing that all swimmers know and share.

Darryl and Bretta ease back toward their small beach. When they arrive, Darryl can no longer restrain himself and scoops the tired and willing Bretta up, circling and weaving all around the yard like some phantom of the ballet.

He lands her on the shaded porch in a wide, thickly-cushioned chaise lounge then reclines in the one next to her.

They watch Andre disappear to a white dot. Synchronously, they turn and smile into one another until their eyes close. They allow their hands to touch, their shoulders to press together, and their exhausted psyches to melt into delicious, renewing, daytime half-sleep.

98

Toward a Blue Rendezvous

"What's the rush girlfriend?" growls Landi, shoveling both legs into her bikini at once. "I don't know how much longer I can wear this thing. Am I starting to show?"

"Are you kidding? No you're not showing," says Sheryl reflexively.

"Don't sandbag me girlfriend…"

"Okay. Maybe just a little bit…But it doesn't matter. With your body, you're going to look luscious right up to the time they tell you to push…I'm sorry I'm acting so strange. I have a strong feeling that Andre—*my man*, as you call him—is here. He's in the lake right now."

"Damn girl!" Landi sighs. "How do you know that? He could be anywhere on the freakin' planet!"

"I can sense these things sometimes," replies Sheryl.

"All right. I'll humor you. But if it turns out to be true, I'm calling my boss and getting you drafted as a profiler."

"A what?"

"A profiler. You know. One of those folks who are handy at paranormal phenomena…Don't look so surprised. We take every advantage we can get," says Landi in response to the jolt in Sheryl's body language.

"But…I couldn't think about using such a gift for…"

"For something besides fun and romance? Look girlfriend, I'd never force you into something like that. Besides, we don't even know if you got the gift. But if you do, well, God and country you know…Hey! C'mon! All mermaids on deck. Yo' Mama's rustlin' some dinner and I ain't keepin' her waiting. I'd race ya, but I know you'd beat me—it's your turf. Thought you couldn't wait to get wet…Ha! Now you're the one who's draggin'."

99

Into a Darker Blue

The two women almost race out a private entrance to the shore, lose their outer garments, and dive in off the end of the dock. The lake is shallower than the Mediterranean. The water is clearer and does not sting. Dissolved minerals impart a natural lubrication not unlike silk. The bottom is mixed patches of white sand and gold-green grass. But the fish are the real show. Dozens of species with enough color variation to make Rembrandt giddy. Add in a pair of luscious, water-loving women and even the lake seems to know its perfection is now more perfect.

In Greece, Sheryl had become accustomed to blue-Sheryl co-existing with Landi's presence. Somehow they mixed delightfully there. They only *seem* to be mixing here in the liquid crystal of Indigo Lake.

While she was still on the dock, Sheryl embraced her blue feeling as it welled up—in fact had started welling up just after the encounter with Frank on the driveway. She intuited that blue-Sheryl would fully overtake her as soon as she got near the water. Even though it is ever familiar, this time the always powerful and beautiful experience is darkened with something primal. Some haunting, heaving force she is fighting to keep at bay. A third force. Not blue-Sheryl, not normal Sheryl. But a vengeful presence, like the pulse unleashed when a forbidden talisman is disturbed.

"Please lake!" she whispers, "dissolve this queasiness."

From the moment she hits the water, Sheryl becomes even more unsettled. Her body swims mechanically with Landi, re-enacting their routine—similar to remembering riding a bicycle.

But this time there are pictures. And a soul-deep trembling to go with them. Pictures projecting onto the blue membrane of the underside of the lake surface. Pictures of her in another time, another life, in a far-distant past.

Sheryl oscillates uncontrollably between what she assumes is her normal self and blue-Sheryl, trying to shut the images off.

Please Lake Spirit...Great Mystery...God...Somebody...Anybody...please! Take the pictures away!

But like an endless set of waves, the images keep coming.

A man she knows to be a centuries-earlier rendition of Andre dominates the scenes. He is holding some position of power. Forcing her to submit to his advances. Forcing her to satisfy him. Ordering her to forsake her husband. Coercing her to enjoy herself. Each image is like a sting on her soul. Each reveals that this travesty has happened scores of times.

This is not even about my husband. I will not allow myself to be so thoroughly dominated. By anyone. Especially by so aggressive a male.

She is obsessed with taking immediate reprisal. So, while he is in another room, she plunges a knife into her heart. She knows this will despoil his political status. And she will finally be free from his overpowering and abusive ego.

From Landi's perspective, the women swim easily in a weave pattern they fashioned in the Grecian coves, staying mostly under water. Moving like fluid within fluid unhurriedly toward the far end of the water body. Landi had gotten used to Sheryl's very occasional trips to the surface for air. But at this moment, it seems to her odd that Sheryl has yet to take a breath—while she has taken several. And they are nearly one-quarter across the expanse.

Meanwhile, having reached the far end of the lake, Andre has turned back. With a vigorous but graceful rhythm he swims unknowingly toward the women. He is mesmerized by the aquarium-like nature of the underwater world before him. After six minutes at his toward-the-finish-line pace, in his peripheral vision, he spots a teal blur knifing fast toward him off the bottom to his left.

My God! Sheryl? This can't be!

Andre is startled at seeing Sheryl in the flesh—a sea nymph at play in this gorgeous water. Suspended in a waking dream, his arms spread out like motionless wings though he still treadles his feet mechanically.

In the next instant when she is three feet away, he sees her angry, pain-laden face and turns his head preparing to comfort her with an embrace. A move that probably saves his life.

Scant seconds before, Sheryl had squatted then pushed hard off the bottom and angled rapidly up a shaft of light toward the white-trunked man swimming toward her. Her hands had assumed the position of the Shaolin Red Eagle Spear—a deadly Kung Fu weapon. A steel weapon she does not have but has learned to simulate with her hands. Hands fused in a prayer-like pose but wielded like a razor whip. Sharpened fingernails aimed like miniature spears. A weapon meant to cause multiple cuts on the skin of an opponent.

Sheryl comes at Andre seeing only the being from ages past. She glances a blow off his face—which would have been lethal but for his turning slightly sideways to embrace her. Her spear-hands whip at the side of his face cutting him deeply on the left cheek and a split second later above his eyes.

It's as if this *revenge-Sheryl* has its own terrifying life.

Landi, stands on the lake bottom and can only look on momentarily frozen in shock as blood billows from the man's face.

Just before the impact, Sheryl's innate consciousness wanted to collide beautifully with Andre. Wanted to wrap around him sensually and pull Indigo Lake around them like a private love blanket. But her current being was overruled by the centuries-old momentum of the revenge. Add in the sporadic yet vibrant pulsing of blue-Sheryl trying to provide a blissful container for the interaction and, in the split-second of choice, mayhem won out.

Disoriented from cycling through her three realities, unsure which century she's in, and terribly troubled at the sight of the blood, Sheryl rockets away from the crime scene, like a fish might do after lunging at bait, then being frightened away by the flash from a bright lure.

100

Dry Land

Landi jolts to alertness, surfaces, and grabs a breath. The water is cloudy with blood. She dog paddles in a circle, half expecting Sheryl to re-attack. But she's nowhere in sight.

"Hey! Don't panic. You'll be okay. I'll help you," she blurts out then immediately chastises herself for her own lack of calm. *His head's submerged. He can't hear you, O brilliant one.* The recent exertions and jet lag are setting in, making her discordant. *These wounds are serious. Damn. Don't know how fast I can get this guy to shore.* She approaches Andre and struggles to keep his head out of the water by pulling up on the waistband of his suit. With her free hand, she peels off his swimming goggles and looks in his eyes. Between dog paddles, her first-aid-survival training kicks in. *Jesus…He's in deep shock. More than I can handle!*

"Help! Anybody! Help!" screams Landi as she struggles to keep both her head and Andre's blood-drenched head above the waterline.

101

The Blue

"It appears that you are trying to obliterate the one being who has pursued you across eternity. The one being whose mission is to love you unconditionally. Yet you have sculpted and fired him into the object of your revenge."

"What!" Sheryl whispers, crouching among the tangled roots in the middle of a large patch of high reeds. *God! I must be nuts. Now I'm hearing voices.*

"Only one voice. Listen closely!"

Sheryl covers her ears but to no avail.

"The cult-time trauma with Gabriel showed you what happens when love gets corrupted with power. You became corrupted. The very thing you judged ancient Andre for that time when you took your own life."

"How do...Who the hell is speaking?" says Sheryl, shaking.

"The affair with Kostas showed you what happens when you love from your ego. Your ego chose him, not your evolved self. Remember how quickly you were willing to abandon your life? Because you were wronged, you swam out into the open sea with no reverence for your precious life."

"Tell me who you are!" Sheryl pleads.

"First you must learn who you have become. Remember how you wanted to kill when you thought it was Kostas who attacked you in the sea off Solagros? This is the ego blinded by revenge. By reaction. Love is not of the ego. Love does not react to being wronged. Love can only love. You have known this but have forgotten. Killing has no role in a being who loves."

"But...I..."

"Notice how blue-Sheryl never became active around Gabriel or Kostas. But around Andre on the boat and in the taxi—and even today, although it was imperfect—the highest part of you wished to share this magic-most part of your being. In fact every time you've been around him you've shared it. This is significant."

"How do you know?" Sheryl whispers, astonished at the apparent wisdom in the voice.

"The revenge you seek against the male Andre is the revenge you wish against yourself. More truly against your past actions which could be called male or aggressive. Hatred of the male is a false projection which all females must ultimately recognize. It is similar for all males."

"But the pictures showed that he dominated me and..."

"You have also been the aggressor. In this lifetime, until now, this has been hidden from you. Agression—which is the parent of revenge—is a clever and hidden form of self-annihilation. Self rejection. Serve this master and ultimately you will self destruct. On the soul level. This means you de-evolve and sentence yourself to many more painful lifetimes before you again reach the awareness you now have. Andre will have moved on and will be elsewhere on his soul's journey when you finally again reach this threshold. And yet, another love object will appear. There is always another love object in every human's future."

"I am not worthy," says Sheryl shaking. "I think I have just done something terrible. Why am I being told this now?"

"Because you are of The Blue. Your body and soul are attuned to The Blue. Your invitation has always been, 'Come into me without fear and be immersed in the inner beauty of God's imagination. Merge with aquamarine. Surge with turquoise to the pinnacle of visual bliss. Empty into Oneness and become full. Be held in the liquid bosom of the Earth Angel. Know freedom. Not by its limits but in its essence. Know that you are an intelligent fraction of Intelligence. Know that your journey at every moment is bathed in splendor. Know that at your core you are identical to that splendor.'"

Before Sheryl's skepticism can fully re-assemble and crystallize, the voice anticipates her.

"We wish to present you with love in its quintessential forms: brightness with its magnetism, color with all its submerged emotion, water with its purity, depth with its enticement. We wish to turn the human race toward its true mission—the promotion and elevation of the planetary environment to a divine art form. Then shall Creation be freed."

"What has this to do with me?" Sheryl asks, desperate and overwhelmed.

"Everything. You have been invited by The Blue. You hold the keys in your hand. Revenge, destruction, regression—or compassion, love, evolution, elevation. Choose wisely. Choose now!"

102

Salvage Operations

From his years of training and living on the edge of danger, even in his state of near-Bretta bliss, Darryl knows to wake up. He is instantly alert and in the water like a shot. Twenty seconds later he reaches Landi and her burden.

Andre's eyes are half closed and glazed over. His breathing is almost inaudible. His face looks like a piece of meat that just escaped from some butcher's cutting board.

"What the hell? What's wrong with Andre? Who are you?" he insists, holding Andre up alongside this female with piercing eyes.

"Landi. From the Jansen place. We gotta stabilize this guy. Jesus. Sheryl *said* Andre was in the lake…"

"Sheryl? She's here?"

"Yea. Somewhere. She slammed into him. On purpose. Cut him with her bare fingertips—like she was praying at him with a shark fin," says Landi putting her hands together like Sheryl had done. "Savage. So fast I barely followed her movement. Never seen anything like it."

"How long's he been down?"

"Not sure if he went down. Instinct kept him afloat. But he's in shock. Shows all the signs. Maybe swallowed a little water too. Can't tell."

"Let me have him!" Darryl slides under Andre's back, replacing Landi. "Hold me up!" He immediately performs the Hiemlich maneuver five times, thrusting his thumb into Andre's abdomen. A little water spurts out of his mouth. Darryl puts an ear to Andre's mouth.

"His air is clear. I think he's good. I'll pull. You push his feet toward shore— and paddle hard," barks Darryl.

You know Sheryl?" Landi gasps between breaths, kicking as hard as she can.

"Know *of* her. We have the same boss," answers Darryl also straining to keep Andre's head above water. "I'm almost never in Athens though."

"You must work for Frank."

"Yea," replies Daryl sheepishly.

"He really messed up Sheryl & Andre's love life."

"So I heard. Helluva place for a lover's quarrel though. There's no way I'm losing him. He's a gem." Darryl says it with a will incapable of knowing defeat.

"So I've heard," she pants.

Abruptly she gives up the idea of small talk about Frank and bends harder to the task at hand. Half a minute later they run aground at the beach, tow Andre onto the shore, and roll him on his back.

Bretta, who has sensed that Andre is in trouble, has hurried over to meet them bringing towels to cover him. His head is still bleeding but a bit less. He seems lost in some other realm.

"I'll bring bandage material," says Bretta scurrying back to the house.

"He's going comatose from the shock and blood loss," says Darryl whispering. "His pulse is weak. But at least it's steady. We need to CPR him. Landi, would you work his air? Real easy…I'll do his chest."

"Andre," Darryl says most gently, "we're going to give you some stimuli to get you going. You will be fine. You are with people who love you." *God. Did I say that? I've never ever said anything close to that.*

After forty-five tense seconds, of chest pumps and several rhythmic mouth-to-mouths from Landi, Andre coughs and tries to sit up, falling backwards after rising only six inches.

"Andre. Andre. Please wake up," cries Bretta throwing gauze and tape to the ground, stroking his hair and covering his bare chest with a towel, blotting up what blood she can. To her relief, Andre recognizes the voice and smiles weakly. He lets out a groan.

"What the hell hit me? Felt like a barracuda."

"Pure mermaid I'm afraid," sighs Landi. "It was Sheryl. She's had so much pent-up emotion about you. I think she just lost it."

"Wait. Who…are you?" By the end of his second word, Andre is struck by Landi's image and instinctively softens his question. *If I'm dead, I'd best relax lest these two angels think I'm some crass human.*

"I'm Landi, Sheryl's friend. From Greece. She had a premonition you were in the lake. But I had no idea she'd…"

Andre trembles involuntarily, fully remembering his pre-swim reality.

"Easy pal," says Darryl eyeing his friend like an ER doctor.

"I thought I was hallucinating that she was in the water. Where's she now?" He tries to sit up again, this time making it to his elbows before falling back.

"Whoa pal. You've lost some blood…She's still out there. Probably hiding in the rushes," Darryl answers.

"She knows every square inch of the bottom," says Landi. "I doubt she's coming in on her own."

"Darryl. Would you go look for her? I think I know what happened. She's not safe to herself right now. I'm good…I'll be good…I'm not moving. Bretta is here. See? She's bandaging me all up. Good as new," says Andre knowing he needs to sell Darryl on his recovery. *But damn I feel weak. Need fluid.*

"Okay. But I need back up," says Darryl, meaning every word.

"Sounds like an inter-agency operation," offers Landi. "How about we back each other up?"

"Agreed. Let's hit it," bids Darryl as he sprints into the lake with Landi on his heels, her second wind kicking in. Amused by the goings on, the miniature baby in her belly kicks an almost imperceptible kick as it adjusts to the sudden, excited motion of the mothership.

103

Andre's Lesson

As soon as Landi and Darryl hit the water, Andre collapses back onto the blankets. "Hey Ms. Brightness, I could use a little water. Cool water."

"Of course sweets. You lost a lot of liquid. And you were swimming. And it's hot. If I had time to think I would ha...I'll run to the house for some. Be back in a flash. You just rest... And relax. Relax. And rest." Bretta unknowingly says this with a penetrating tone, like a hypnotist might.

At the suggestion, it takes Andre less than five seconds to pass out.

"Sheryl was designed into your soul's life to infuse you with the wonders of passion. She is but a doorway to the magic to be found in every member of humanity. In every animal, every plant, every rock. Love her equally as you would love any element in Creation. Know that you are now free to love. Choose your intimates wisely. And keep aware. There is always a risk. Learn to celebrate that truth. This is the nature of love on your planet."

"Andre! Andre!" The panic in Bretta's voice reaches into Andre's reverie.

As if returning from a distant kingdom, Andre opens his eyes to look into the depth of Bretta. He is moved by her tears of concern. And overwhelmed by his gratitude for having this courageous soul sister in his life. *You idiot... Why haven't you just loved her like a true lover? A physical lover.*

"Hey! Bretta! It's okay. I'm here. I swam to the moon and back while you got the water. If you had taken any longer, I would have had to take another lap."

Andre sips, then practically gulps down the water once he's sure it's real.

"Don't tease me mister. You can't rely on your good looks any more. Fact is, you look like you've had a close encounter with a paper shredder."

104

Bronze Deity

Sheryl shudders with the possibility that her hyper-alive treasure of blue-Sheryl is dying. *Has my self-serving violence killed this beautiful force which visits me?*

Can't believe I didn't appreciate it more than I did. What's wrong with me?

"Blue-Sheryl! Come to me now!" Sheryl shouts rising up, palms aloft.

But nothing happens. Except the spawning of a loneliness so empty and vast, so overwhelming in its intensity, it's as if a soul-rooted ache spills from some foreboding cauldron into an absolutely normal Sheryl.

Gone is Sheryl the water nymph. Gone is the fish-and-plant companion. Gone is the merging with sun shafts and blue ethers. *God I'm shaking but can't feel myself shaking. My soul must be shaking…How arrogant to think I can just conjure up blue-Sheryl. As if I own her. As if I deserve her. It obviously doesn't work that way.*

It doesn't take long for Landi and Darryl to find Sheryl frozen like a statue among some high reeds. As they pause before their approach, Darryl struggles to process this sudden influx of women onto the palette of his loner existence.

First Bretta knocks him out with her playful spirit. And then Landi—he's actually kind of scared by her exoticness. He doesn't understand life's not playing fair because the radiance of a newly-pregnant woman makes men weak without them knowing they are under one of the most powerful yet subtle spells humans can transmit.

But upon seeing Sheryl perching in her element like some bronze marine deity, Darryl now understands Andre's weeks of anguish and torch-carrying. After one glance her direction, Darryl already knows Andre's forgiven

Sheryl for almost killing him. Again.

"Alright girlfriend!" Landi yells, knocking Darryl out of his processing. "Can we join you or you gonna attack us too? You're a damn leopard seal. That's what. And a damn berserk one besides." Landi can't help let off some steam at her nut-job sister. And ever the operative, she's also probing for a hint of which reality Sheryl currently inhabits.

Sheryl entertains several clever comebacks but realizes there is a threat in all of them. She can only smile at this self-realization. "I can't believe what just went down. Oh my God. How's Andre? He's not…"

"Andre lives, no thanks to you. Thanks to Agent Darryl here. You owe him your life. Even your daddy couldn't have saved you from this one."

"Hey," says Darryl grinning, "I just squeezed him. Landi here provided the air."

"The air? Oh crap. It was that bad? Well I can't thank you both enough… So Darryl—nice meeting you by the way—is the patient receiving visitors?"

"Yeah. If Bretta hasn't called 9-1-1," retorts Darryl. *God, I feel like the most special person in the world when Sheryl talks to me.*

"Who's Bretta?" Sheryl inquires, acting as if she's the one who's hurt.

105

Requited Conversation

Nobody says a word. Not when Sheryl emerges from the lake. Not when she sits at Andre's feet, looking at the ground. Not when the silence starts to drag.

No one knows whether the moment is sacred or about to explode. Or both. As Andre's and Sheryl's eyes meet, it's like two comets, who've known collision was to be their fate, colliding.

Landi watches Sheryl hoping to God she's stable. Darryl wants to cast a sympathetic gaze upon Bretta but instead yields to his shyness and watches Andre for any signs of trauma. At first Bretta stares at Sheryl the Rival, but instinctively shifts her attention to Darryl instead.

As the silence grows more awkward, Darryl and Bretta follow some inner cue and rise at the same time. Darryl motions to Landi to join them and the trio retreats up the lawn to the house.

"Andre I'm so sorry I…" sighs Sheryl, her eyes locked in his.

"I had it coming," Andre confesses. "This may sound loony but I don't care. I'm afraid I've wronged you in a past life. I'm not worthy of you—of anyone really—until I fully fathom what I did."

"This is all too weird. Just before I struck you I'm sure I was in blue-Sheryl. That state I get into. The one I told you about on the ferry. But this time it was not ecstatic. It was negative. Downright ugly actually. There were these pictures. Ancient pictures. You were dominating me and I hated it. Hated you. I wanted to ruin your name. I took my own life knowing you'd be blamed for causing my suicide…So I struck back. Naked revenge. Plain and simple. I'm not proud of it…Ugh! I don't even know if any of this crap is real."

"I can't be certain either. I've acquired this spiritual teacher since Greece. He would say it's *of the Mystery*. Recently he guided me into what sounds like the same past-life view as you had. It's all so strange. All I can say is the feelings I had about it were real. Are real. I mean they're still part of me—though I've tried to work them through. Mostly. But I'm still in remorse. I was a powerful jerk. Maybe that never gets purged. Maybe I'm fooling myself. Maybe I haven't changed."

"I don't know. And I for sure don't know if I can trust myself around you," says Sheryl, fighting tears. "I'm afraid if I slip into that crazed person, I'd do something terri…"

"I'm willing to risk it," offers Andre. "To be killed by you might even be an honor." Andre begins to crack a smile.

"Relationships shouldn't be a risk," counters Sheryl ignoring the joke. She hears the lie the second it comes out.

"Relationships are always a risk," replies Andre. "Apparently in ours, the risk is much more out in the open. Literally in our face."

Hearing the word *face*, and gazing guiltily at Andre's bandaged cheek and forehead, Sheryl chooses not to prolong the metaphor. "But if we just walk away from this, we'll never know what might have been. Seeing you—alive—here—is…it completes something in me."

Sheryl places her hand on Andre's ankle and is stunned by the electricity in their contact. She basks silently in the rarified air of this simple truth: *Our paths have re-crossed. And in this moment love is. There is utterly nowhere to go.*

Andre notes the electricity and finds it exquisite. But recently he's felt it touching Bretta—or hugging Darryl for that matter. Then he internally whips himself for being so brutally neutral. *This is happening now you jerk.* He places his hand on her tanned forearm.

For their own private reasons, they both linger in this field of human-generated current. Andre could easily pile on more of his own brand of guilt for his ill-timed stoicism. But some innate force won't let him indulge his self loathing.

In the next fleeting instant, it hits him that he has full choice as to how to emote. Indeed whether to emote at all. Relieved, he lets himself tumble fully into the magic eyes, skin, face, body, and spirit of Sheryl Jansen. A hint of tears graces his eyes.

Sheryl is at once re-falling in love yet freaked out about the chance of her entrenched revenge resurfacing. *But didn't the Blue Voice say it was my choice? And didn't Landi coach me that I should surrender to ordinary if that's what it takes to cement a healthy relationship with Andre. Non-blue-Sheryl ordinary… Oh God. I'm just destined to be another normal woman.*

A shiver snakes violently up her spine. Still touching Sheryl, Andre feels her jolt and it pulses naturally through him as well. They can only smile.

In the middle of this pregnant moment, the trio re-emerge from the house. Darryl carries Bretta on his shoulders, with Landi prancing along beside.

"Listen you two," barks Landi, fully back in team leader mode. "We've agreed we need a change of scene. We've worn this lake out. Andre's in no condition to go back to work and scare his clients. He'll call in—no he'll Skype his secretary that he has had a boating accident. Irrefutable visual evidence…He needs salt water to accelerate his healing. Bretta says Jerry, his protégé can handle the current client. So we've decided. We're all going to my place on Grand Bahama. The water there is so blue… anything can happen!" she declares, winking invisibly at Andre whom she thinks is the most enchanting man she's seen in years—bandaged face or no bandaged face.

Sheryl has told her that she and Andre had not been fully intimate. Intuitively, she knows she could—and would love to—unlock the repressed sexual being he undoubtedly harbors. And besides—she chuckles to herself—she needs a skilled architect to design her main house. *What a cool trade!* In an instant, she stuffs that selfish fantasy in the dead-on-arrival file. *How imperfect of your twisted brain to even entertain alienating your sister! Besides your overactive ass is pushing two months pregnant. You have no damn business even thinkin' 'bout the prom.*

Darryl gently lands Bretta. *This is crazy. I actually might have a girlfriend!*

Bretta carries a golf-ball size quartz crystal tightly clenched in one hand. *There's a strength in Darryl I crave basking in. And a precious innocence. I have this rock-bottom knowing I can heal myself with him in my life. I already feel deeply for him…Steady. Just set the crystal down and the others will gravitate to it.*

Darryl helps Andre up while Landi does the same for Sheryl. For reasons which neither could ever attempt to explain, Sheryl and Bretta hug each other as Andre looks on in mild disbelief. And the disbelief spawns a torrent of horrific thought.

What are you doing trusting this whacko woman around your friends? I wonder if Sheryl is faking it and is gonna cut poor Bretta up. Kill her like she almost did me. Twice…Whoa…Stop! Where did that come from? It's not me. Not really… Where did such an ugly thought come from?

"Keep aware. There is always a risk. This is the nature of love on your planet."

Christ! My sanity is unraveling. Voice in my head. Blood on my face.

Even before the two women separate, Andre has started shuffling back toward the house. Something about them hugging is making him physically sick. Re-traumatized to the point where he must remove himself.

Both Bretta and Sheryl sense Andre's withdrawal, move around him, turn and block his way. They just stand there empathic and open. Two pillars of love as it were.

Sensing that Andre is troubled, Darryl and Landi move in close behind him. He stands surrounded in a force field of compassion.

This is odd. I can't not be aware of my uneasy breath. Or the stinging, probably perfect gashes on my face. Or the lawn's tangled precision. Or the inaudible moans of the lake gushing from somewhere behind me. Or that Bretta and Sheryl are living statues wrought by some gentle genius who has never been sober.

I don't have to turn around to know that Sheryl's racy friend and Darryl are right behind me. Their concerns linger inside me like a radio that I just shut off.

I sense the group expectation that I should get with the program. Get excited about the Bahamas. Don't know why I can't. I'm still very stuck. I pine for this woman for weeks and what do I get? A rush of electricity followed by a huge helping of distrust. What a cosmic joke. Vincent would laugh.

"Andre," calls a soft voice. "Are you alright? We love you." Andre appears to the others to be somewhere else. But they are wrong. He is so involved with where he is that they think he is looking through them. In fact, he is looking into them.

"Thank you. I am struggling right now."

"Don't worry buddy. I've got you," says Darryl putting his arms below Andre's elbows.

"I'm stable physically," says Andre wiggling his arms away from Darryl. "Mentally I'm a mess. I'm a phony. The one who can't accept that people are trying to love him. Do probably love him. Probably a lot. Can't accept I'm so identified with my holier-than-thou process that I'm afraid to have a normal human emotion. I'm afraid of you Sheryl. Up until an hour ago, I was secretly hoping you were a criminal or a psycho so I could run away and be done with this entire chapter. And Bretta! You scare me the most. I had to work really hard to find ways not to be intimate with you. You are nothing but pure love in a bikini. There is no way I could come close to matching that purity. So I assumed a teacher role to impose a boundary around me. I am so sorry."

Before Andre can confess his crush on Landi and his sudden jealousy of Darryl cozying up with Bretta, he gets another of many transmissions to come from this voice which he is beginning to suspect is not his. *I must be nuts. Only nuts hear voices.*

"There is no excitement when you actually arrive and you realize it is the striving and the pain and the frustration that is the turn on."

295

"But I have not arrived," Andre says out loud. "I am nowhere."

"Haaaaaaha."

Sheryl, Landi, Bretta, and Darryl are alternately embarrassed, tearful, and concerned. They instinctively move in closer. Bretta presses her crystal into Andre's chest. The five souls linger there suspended in their bodies for what may as well be an eternity.

106

All on Her Own

Back at the Jansen compound, Jesse puts down her binoculars, smiles a wry smile, and dials up Sam.

"Hey Mister. As usual, there's been some strange doings in the lake. But that's normal. Shucks, every time I take a swim I come out not remembering how long I was splashin' around in there. All I take away is that blessed blue color. And the dad-gum fish keep swimmin' in my brain right up until I shower off with fresh water. It's like chug-a-luggin' some kind o' medicine. Like drinkin' a durn kaleidoscope."

"Now Scarlett, we talked about this. You promised to stay out of the lake when you're home alone."

"Now Rhett, we both know a swim does a body good. And you know the lake washes the age right on out o' me. You don't seem to mind that one bitty bit."

"Okay, I don't…but Holy Moses Scarlett, that lake turned Sheryl's world upside down. I swear there's a crazy spirit festering in there. Dangerous crazy. Too much of that lake takes the balance out of a person."

"You're just talkin' like a fraidy cat. I'm tellin' you right now that lake up an' told me to save Heron Island. I didn't even know it existed until the lake spoke up! Now look what's happened. Out of the blue, I got the all the funds I needed."

"That's just a bunch of lucky coincidences. Even if it were true, and the lake did tell you, look what happened to our daughter. She went way off the deep end. We're lucky we got her away from…"

"Hey Mr. Big Britches, our daughter's gonna be okay. Before my very eyes, looks like she's thrown off some sizeable devil. Maybe the very one you're speakin' of. An' maybe it was all meant to be. There's some renters over at the Thompson's. Odd thing is she seems to know them. I'm stayin' way out of it. But even from here I can tell she's finally made some genuine friends—all on her own."

Sam swallows the disorienting pill, recovers, and shifts into his best Rhett-Butler persona, surprising even his deductive self. "Scarlett, it's a great day to be alive."

Epilogue
Everywhere

Either the universe is constructed from love or it's not. Cynics will laugh at the notion saying, "it's not constructed of anything but cold yet active randomness. Or perhaps a series of benign accidents." Awakened beings will verify that this mingling of people and surroundings we call the world is infused with love. Stitched together with love. Bursting at the seams with love.

"Can't you feel it?" they say. "It's everywhere."

He or she may call it gratitude or bliss or grace or peace or even God. Boil away the labels and you're left with plain old love. Buddha embodied it. Jesus lived it. Rumi attained it. Abraham and Moses no doubt earned it. Average people stumble into it and stumble out. It may last a few seconds or a few years. Yet it is the karma of some tragic souls never to become aware it even exists. Theirs—like everyone's—circumstances are designed to wake them up, to get back to the love at their cores. To recognize it in their surroundings. In the eye of the other. But mostly they proceed to miss all the signals designed to ease, prod, or jolt them into love, and so go to their deaths devoid of discovering life's essential experience. Like one of your songs says:

"It's written on the wind, it's everywhere I go."

When loves looks out, it sees only love. In the sky, in the tree, in the other. The being who attains this state of true love has no idea what is operative. No idea that, like the energy in a ray of sun, the power of love is sourcing his whole experience. From the inside. Love must shower the object it gazes upon. No matter what form the object takes. No matter what its politics, its religion, its gender. Totally. Unconditionally. That is love's nature.

What Sheryl and Andre don't fully know is that this love exchange is an earned gift. This could be the closing chapter of their saga. A saga which spans more lifetimes than they will ever recall. Or it could be the beginning of a consensual, conscious, and breathtaking romance. The kind for which legends are recorded. The kind for which masterpieces are commissioned.

The kind which Love had in mind when it dreamed you into existence.

CPSIA information can be obtained at www.ICGtesting.com
Printed in the USA
BVOW07s0506190713

325905BV00002B/7/P